REWRITING DESTINY

Forsaken Sinners MC Series: Book One/Prequel

By Shelly Morgan

REWRITING DESTINY

Limitless Publishing, LLC
Kailua, HI 96734
www.limitlesspublishing.com

Formatting: Limitless Publishing

ISBN-13: 978-1-68058-509-4
ISBN-10: 1-68058-509-6

DEDICATION

To my mother—
You have always stood behind me, no matter what I
did. Thank you for always having faith in me and
being my number one fan.
Love you, Mommy!

CHAPTER 1

Danielle

My mother died when I was three years old.

She had a complicated pregnancy with me and was diagnosed with cervical cancer soon after I was born. The prognosis was terminal. They said she wouldn't make it to see my first birthday, but she was a fighter and made it longer than anyone thought possible. Just not long enough for me to grow up with a mother, or even long enough for me to build one single solid memory of her.

After she died, my dad couldn't handle being a single father with a toddler, or maybe he was a shitty parent to begin with. Either way, he signed his rights over to my grandmother and never looked back. My grandma was one of my aces, though. Even though she was really old and didn't have the energy to take care of a child, she was determined that I have a good childhood and not wind up somewhere in the system. And even though I wasn't able to do all the things that kids my age got to do

1

since she didn't have the energy to do them with me, she loved me fiercely and that's all that matters in the end.

The only good thing you could say my father did was send money every month to my grandmother to help care for me. What money she didn't use was put into a savings account for when I graduated high school. He also set me up with a trust fund that I would have access to when I turned eighteen, to use to go to college or for whatever. How nice of him, right? Yeah…

I don't know much about my father, but my grandmother used to tell me stories about my mom. At first it hurt too much to hear about her, because even though I don't remember her, I missed the idea of having her as my mother. I mean, what child wouldn't miss having a mother, even one they never knew?

My mother's name was Melissa Rose DeChenne, and she was beautiful, with long blonde hair, blue eyes, and a smile that could light up even the darkest of days. She met my father in her freshman year of college and fell hopelessly in love. They were married a year later, and found out they were pregnant with me shortly after. According to Gram, he loved her very much and was good to her. But he became broken when she died, and wanted something better for me. Not sure if that's the truth, or if she was only trying to make it so I wouldn't hate him all my life. Regardless, even if he loved my mother and treated her like a queen, he still left me and I'll never forgive him for that.

I've seen pictures of my mother and father when

they were together, and I can see how happy they were. It makes my heart ache to think about what my life would have been like if she hadn't died. If she was still here, maybe my father wouldn't have left and I wouldn't feel so broken.

Every time I look at those pictures, I try to memorize their faces: my mother's so I never forget her, and my father's so if I ever see him one day, I can turn around and walk away from him like he did to me. But I don't have to try very hard to memorize his face; I see a lot of him whenever I look in the mirror. I have long, thick brown hair and deep green eyes like him. And I had to have gotten my five-foot-six height from him, because in the pictures I've seen, my mother seems tiny. She can't have been taller than five-foot-two. Then there's my strong jawline, high cheekbones, and olive skin, which no doubt came from him. The only things that I can see I got from my mother are her bright smile and her small nose.

When I was thirteen, the Hendrickses moved in next door to me and my grandmother. They were two boys that became my best friends, my only friends, really. Zane was fifteen and his brother Zeke was seventeen. I remember always seeing them in their back yard tossing the football around. You could tell by looking at them that they were close. Zane looked up to his brother, but Zeke looked at his little brother like he was his best friend.

Our friendship began one day when Gram had to go run a couple of errands, so she sent me over to their house. I was a little shy and didn't know what to do at first, but Zane just handed me the football and proceeded to teach me the game and the rest is history. Even though I was younger than both of them, they accepted me. I would go over to their house practically every day. After a while, it almost seemed like I was their little sister since I was there so much. I learned a lot that year from them both; Zane taught me everything there is to know about football, and Zeke taught me a little about motorcycles.

I didn't have much to offer the trio that we were, but I always listened to what they wanted to tell me or what they were trying to teach me. The only thing I shared with them was my love for art. They found me doodling one day and asked me about it. After that, they would always challenge me to draw different things, and they would get harder and harder. I think drawing for them was better than any art class someone my age could have taken. They were very supportive and always honest about what they thought of a drawing. Zeke in particular would always say how amazing my talent was, and encouraged me to be proud of what I drew. He told me that I could make a career out of it, and from that day on, I knew I was going to go to college and major in art. That's pretty impressive, if you ask me. How many thirteen-year-olds know what they want to go to college for?

Zeke graduated the following year and decided he was going to join the Marines. Everyone was very supportive and happy he was going to be doing something so selfless. Well, everyone except for Zane. Of course he was proud of his big brother in most ways, but he was worried Zeke would get hurt and upset because they had plans to go to the same college, University of Texas, to play football together. Then they would spend a couple of years riding cross country on their motorcycles. I think aside from not knowing if he'd be safe, he was upset that Zeke was going off to do something without him. They always did everything together, so when he decided to change those plans and do something for himself first, that would take some getting used to for Zane.

To be honest, I was scared shitless too, but I never showed my fear to either of them. I didn't want to seem like a big baby, plus Zeke had other things to think about. He didn't need to worry about me too. So whenever it was mentioned, I would smile and tell him how proud of him and excited I was. That he'd always be my hero, but now he'd be everyone's hero as well.

I went with them the day Zeke left to start his training. We had breakfast at a family diner close to the bus stop and then waited with him until it was time for him to leave. I remember sitting in one of those hard chairs that are attached to the floor, not looking at him or saying anything. I didn't want him to leave, but I was also afraid I would say something that might make him stay. He wanted to do this, so I wouldn't be the person to make him feel bad about this decision.

Once we saw the bus pull up outside, his parents and Zane got up to tell him goodbye. When he was done, Zeke knelt down in front of me and pulled his old worn football he and Zane always played with out of his bag. "Will you hang on to this while I'm gone?"

I looked down at the football, then back up to him. "You want me to keep it?" I whispered. I wasn't sure why he would give it to me and not his brother.

"Yeah, what do ya say? Only until I get back, though."

I gave him a small smile and reached out to take the football from him. "Okay."

As my tears started to fall, he smiled at us, then turned around and got on the bus, giving one final wave.

Four months later, he informed us that he was getting deployed to Iraq. We drove to Houston for his sending away ceremony to see him off. It was very emotional. There were so many families there saying their goodbyes to their loved ones. Lots of tears were shed.

During the time Zeke was gone, Zane and I made sure to play catch with the football at least a couple times a week. Then I'd tell him about the letters I was writing to his brother and I'd show him the pictures I drew for him. He'd talk about being on the high school football team and how he couldn't wait to go to college to play. Then he'd tell me about the plans he was making for when Zeke got back to the States. That's what they would talk about on the phone when Zeke was able to call home. It helped Zane to know his brother still wanted to carry out all those things they planned on doing before; it would just take a little longer to do them.

REWRITING DESTINY

On a Tuesday, eight months after Zeke was deployed, I came home from school and Gram was sitting at the kitchen table waiting for me. "Danielle, can you come sit down for a minute, please?" she asked. I did a double take and really looked at her. She looked upset about something, so I walked over to the table and took her hand as I sat.

"What's wrong, Gram?" I hoped she wasn't getting sick again. It seemed like she was sick more often than not nowadays.

"Sweetheart, I need to talk to you about something," she told me in a low voice.

I sat there and waited for her to tell me what was going on so I could get over to Zane's. I wanted to show him the picture I drew for Zeke this week. He loved my drawings. He was my biggest fan actually, so I tried to send him a drawing at least once a month. My grandmother broke me out of my thoughts.

"Miranda came over this afternoon." Miranda was Zane's mom, so I was trying to think of what she would come over to talk to my grandmother about.

"I've been good and haven't caused any problems when I'm over at their house. I swear, Gram." That was the only thing I could come up with for why she would come over to talk to my grandmother, but I always made a point to be good when I was there, because I didn't want to risk not being allowed back.

"No, sweetheart, I know. That's not why she came over." She paused for a minute and put her head down. I was starting to get a really bad feeling.

Whatever the reason for her visit, it couldn't be good. "Danielle, she had some news about Zeke," she said as she looked up at me.

I smiled. "Does he get to come home early? I should go over and talk with Zane, we can plan a party for him." I got up to run over there, excitement taking over, but before I got to the door, Gram stood up on shaky legs and stopped me.

"Danielle, no. I'm sorry, but he's not coming home." She had tears in her eyes.

"O-Okay…Well, I guess it's only a couple more months till he'll be home anyway," I told her, still not understanding why she looked so upset. I could wait a couple more months. Or maybe Miranda had news that when he got home he'd be stationed somewhere else in the States. I wasn't really sure how the military works, but we could plan trips to go see him wherever he was.

"Sweetheart, listen, something happened…." she started with a broken sob, but I shook my head.

"No, Gram. No! Don't say it! He's coming home!" I shouted, finally beginning to understand. I could feel the tears coming, but I wouldn't let them fall. He was fine and he was coming home. He promised he would come home. I got a letter from him a couple days ago and talked to him on the phone last week.

"Danielle, something happened. There was an accident…Baby, he's gone, I'm so sorry," she finally finished, with tears rolling down her cheeks.

I shook my head again, which made my tears overflow. "*No*! You're lying!" I yelled and turned to run up to my room. By the time I got to the top of the stairs, my tears were falling so fast that I could barely see where I was going. Zeke was gone; he was never coming back. I would never see him again or get to hear him say he loved me like a little sister and that my drawings were amazing. I'd never be able to give him his football back. Zane would never get to play football at college with his brother. Oh no, Zane!

I ran down the stairs and out the door before my grandmother could stop me. I had to get to him and be there for him. He would be devastated!

I ran over to Zane's house and banged on the door. I waited a minute, but no one answered. Where were they? I knocked again, but still no one came. I started to walk back to my house to grab my phone to call him when I smelled it. Smoke. It was coming from the back yard.

I walked back to see what was going on. As I got closer, the smell got stronger. Someone was definitely burning something. Once I cleared the fence and walked into their back yard, I spotted him. Zane was sitting on the ground by the fire pit, tossing in what looked like papers. I walked over and saw what he was burning.

"Zane, what are you doing?" I asked, wiping the tears off my face. I had to be strong for him; he needed me now more than ever.

He didn't answer or even glance my way, so I sat down and looked at the stack of papers about the University of Texas sitting in front of him. He was taking them one by one, crumbling each into a ball and throwing it into the flames. He'd wait till it was nothing but ashes before he'd repeat the action.

"What are you doing?" I asked again.

Instead of answering me, he grabbed the whole stack and threw them all into the fire. Then, finally, he turned to look at me. His eyes were bloodshot, but no tears fell.

"Why did you burn the information you got about playing football at the University, Zane?" My voice broke at the end, but I continued on. "You got those with Zeke before he left."

"He was supposed to come home and meet me there. We had it all planned out; did you know that? I'd be in my third year when he would've gotten out, but he was going to enter the open tryouts. And he would have made the team too, because he was an even better player than I am. But now that's never going to happen. He just had to go and sign up to be a Marine. He couldn't stay here and do what we both talked about for years. He ruined everything!" he yelled at the end. After a couple of calming breaths, he continued, "He's not coming home, so I'm not going…how can I go without him?" He started angry, but by that last sentence, it was barely a whisper. He looked so broken and defeated.

I reached over and took his hand. "You have to go, Zane; he would want that for you."

He stared at me, not even blinking. He finally looked away and said, "I'm not sure if I can. Without him, there is nothing there for me."

A single tear slipped down his cheek. I reached up and wiped it away, then turned his head so he was looking at me again. "I know it's hard right now to see it this way, but I know that he wouldn't have wanted you to quit. You have to go, Zane, if not for yourself, then go for him. He may no longer be able to be here with us the way we want him to be, but he'll always be with us in our hearts. Play for him." I don't know where my words of wisdom came from, but they flowed out of me and felt like the right thing to say.

We sat there for an unmeasurable amount of time, staring at each other. We didn't have to say anything else, because there was nothing else to say in that moment. I squeezed his hand, then got up and walked back over to my house. I cried myself to sleep that night.

The next couple of months were hard, having to attend the funeral and learning how to go on without Zeke. Things started to get better, though. It was gradual, but what do you expect? Zane and I started to hang out more. We leaned on each other to help with the loss we shared. Losing Zeke was devastating for both of us, but I think in the end it brought us closer. We started hanging out every day after school, tossing the football around, talking about my drawings and the bike he wanted to buy for his upcoming birthday, and going out on the town. Zane become my best friend, and we forged an unbreakable bond.

After he finishes his senior year in a couple months, he will be going to the University of Texas like he and Zeke always talked about. I'm going to miss him a lot, but I'm so happy that he will be living out their dream. He seems more at peace with his decision to go to college since he went back for a tour of the campus a couple weeks ago.

***

I just finished with Zane's graduation present and plan to give it to him tonight. I'm so nervous, unsure what he will think. After his brother died, I decided I wanted to draw a memorial for him. Zeke always liked my drawings, so doing this for Zane only seemed right. And since he's turned eighteen and has been talking about getting a tattoo, I decided a design for a tattoo would be perfect.

I wanted to draw something that I could incorporate his brother into. So I did some research and came up with an idea; it would be mostly military themed, but with a little twist. I drew the boots, rifle, and helmet for the memorial. Then I added the Texas Longhorns symbol on one side and a motorcycle on the other. I figured since they both wanted to play football together and loved motorcycles, it would be the perfect combination. On the top in big block letters I wrote **'He Gave His Life For Me'**...and on the bottom, **'I Live, Play & Ride For Him.'**

Tonight is the party for all the seniors who graduated this year. I have an hour before Zane will be ready to go, so I jump in the shower to wash my hair and shave my legs. After I dry myself off, I go over to my closet to figure out what to wear. I decide to go with my favorite pair of jeans. They are old and faded but they fit me perfectly and are comfortable. I throw on a plain white tank top that shows a hint of my midriff, then complete it with my cowboy boots. I don't have time to do anything with my hair, so I just throw it up into a messy bun and call it good. I'll add a bit of makeup, and I'll be ready.

Just as I'm finishing with my mascara, I hear Zane honk his horn outside. I grab the folder with the tattoo sketch in it and run down the stairs. I stop to give my grandmother a kiss and tell her I'll be back later. She looks up from her book and gives me a tired smile. "Have fun, and be safe."

Concerned, I force a smile and ask, "Are you feeling okay, Gram?" She looks so worn out. She is barely able to get around anymore.

"I'm fine, sweetheart, just tired. I'm going to go to bed early. Don't you worry about me." She gets up and starts to head for her room.

"Okay, Gram. I love you!" I tell her as I head outside.

Zane is waiting for me in his driveway. I take a good look at him, and holy shit does he look good. He's wearing his favorite black boots, an old pair of faded jeans that have tears in the knees, a black t-shirt, and the cap I got him for his birthday, on backwards. His dark brown hair is cut so short that it's hidden by the hat. His green eyes, which are so deep they almost look gray, sparkle with mirth. Add his signature smirk, and damn that boy is H.O.T.

"Hey, Baby Girl!" he says as I run up and give him a hug. He's been calling me Baby Girl for the last couple months. I'm not sure why he does it since I'm sixteen now, but I like it anyway.

"Looking good, college boy!" I tell him with a smile and give him a wink.

He laughs at me and opens the passenger door. "Get in the truck, smartass."

"I'd rather be a smartass than a dumbass," I say with a chuckle as I slide into the truck and wait for him to walk around to his side. Once he's in, he starts the truck and cranks up the music.

***

We pull into the field by the lake a little after seven. There are a lot of people here already, but I guess I shouldn't be surprised since Zane is the most popular guy in the senior class. Star quarterback on our football team, champion for the last three years in wrestling, and he was also nominated Prom King this year.

We head over to where his friends from the football team are all standing around the keg. Most of them are seniors like Zane. There are a couple that will be taking their place next year, but I don't really recognize them except for a guy I know whose name is Jaxon. Someone hands Zane a red Solo cup filled with beer, which he passes over to me. Now that's what I call service! I smile at him and start to walk away to see who I can find to sit with while he talks with his buddies. Before I even get a couple steps away, someone is pulling me back by the waist.

"Where do you think you're going, beautiful?" I recognize the voice as Zane's best friend—Kolby.

"Well, I was going to go find a place to sit down and drink my beer away from you circus clowns," I tell him with a laugh and go to remove his hands so I can get away.

"Oh, come on, at least have a drink with us first.

14

It *is* our party, ya know."

I turn around to look at him and then over to Zane. At first when I glance at his face, he's staring at Kolby's hands around my waist with a glare of utter hatred. But before I can really think about it, he looks up at me and puts on his trademark smirk and winks.

"Fine, I'll have one drink with you guys, then I'm going to see if I can find some girls to hang with." I glance back over at Kolby, who is holding his hand over his heart.

"You wound me, babe!" Whatever. I lift up my cup and say cheers to them all.

After finishing my drink with the guys, I get myself a refill, then head off to see who's here. I spot Becca, Leanne, and Tori over by the lake sitting around a small fire. I pull up a chair beside Tori.

"Hello, ladies!" I say with a smile. We aren't close friends by any means, but they are usually the ones I hang out with at these parties. They are seniors this year as well, so if I decide to come to any parties after this year, I'll have to find new people to drink with.

After chatting with them and nursing my drink for an hour, I head over to the keg for another refill. As I'm filling my cup, Zane comes over holding a brown paper bag. "How about we break out the good stuff? What do ya say, Baby Girl?"

I drop my eyes down to the bag, then lift them back up at him. I tip my full beer to my lips and chug the whole thing. "Abso-fucking-lutley!" I yell.

He pours us each a shot, then we hold our cups

up in the air. "To Zeke," he says.

I share a sad smile with him and clink my plastic cup with his. "To Zeke," I reply. We down the shot, then fill it with another. "To new beginnings," he says for his next toast. "To college boys," I say next, with a laugh when he gives me a look that says "Really?" Then we down that shot too.

We spend the rest of the night drinking the bottle of Jack Daniels and sharing memories of the good times we had with Zeke and our plans for the future. When the bottle is empty and the keg is gone, we head back to his truck. Once inside, we sit there trying to sober up a bit before heading home. We're staring out into the night and listening to music from the radio.

"Thank you for tonight, Zane! I think that was the most fun I've had in a long time. I don't know what I'm going to do when you leave," I tell him after a couple minutes of silence. I'm really going to miss him when he leaves.

"I'm glad you had a good time, Baby Girl. And don't worry, I'll be back," he says as he turns and looks at me. I flinch a little at his last words, remembering that his brother said those exact words before he left. It never happened, but I'm hoping this time will be different. Zane will come back to me. At least I really hope he does.

"Your gram is going to be so pissed," he says after a while.

I laugh and tell him, "Nah, she told me to have a good time. She knows you're leaving soon, and since I don't go out much anyway, she wanted me to get out of the house and have fun." After the words leave my mouth, he stares at me. I can't look away. I feel like I'm under a spell. There's something about the way he's looking at me that is making my head spin.

I shake my head and am finally able to look away. What was that? It felt like I was floating, as if I couldn't breathe. I hear him clear his throat, then he puts the truck into gear. "I better get you home."

I don't want to leave, I want to stay here in this moment forever. It feels almost perfect, but it scares me too. I have no idea what I'm feeling right now, but it feels like more than the brother/sister/best friend bond we have had for the past couple years. Like my feelings for him are growing, changing.

He pulls up into his driveway, so I get out to walk over to my house. When I'm almost to the porch, I turn around. "Oh, hey! I can't believe I forgot to give this to you." I pull the folder out of my purse that holds my drawing and walk up to hand it to him.

I watch his face as he opens the folder. He looks at it for the longest time with a blank expression on his face.

"It's for a tattoo. I thought it would be something you could get, sort of as a memorial for Zeke," I whisper with a small smile on my face. I'm so afraid that I did a horrible job and he'll hate it.

After about a minute of him not saying anything, I start to get uncomfortable and feel worried. Maybe I should take it back so he doesn't feel like he has to keep it. I shouldn't have given him anything that would make him remember he lost his brother. I should have drawn something different or given him something else.

Finally, he looks up at me and a blinding smile takes over his whole face. Wow…just wow. He is so beautiful. That smile, it's like I told him he won the lottery. I have to look away because it's too much.

"It's amazing, Baby Girl. I love it," he says. Then he walks over and tips my face up to look up at him. "You're amazing. Thank you for making this for me."

Oh my God, I think I'm going to pass out. He's so close, and he's touching me. The way he's looking at me is like I hung the moon for him and it's making me feel crazy things. It's like I have a swarm of bees in my stomach.

I step out of his reach and look away again. "You're welcome. I thought it would be something you might like," I say with a shy smile. I look in his eyes for a second and then start walking backwards. "Well, thanks again for tonight. I'll see ya later." I give him a little wave and jog up to my porch.

Once in my room, I quickly undress and jump into bed. I lie there thinking about the night. I go over every detail—the fun we had, the way he touched me, and the feelings I got when it seemed like he was staring into my soul. Just as I'm on the verge of sleep, a thought passes through my head.

I'm falling in love with Zane Hendricks.

CHAPTER 2

The sun is shining brightly and I'm with Zane on his motorcycle. I'm pressed up against his back with my arms wound tightly around his stomach, and my thighs are squeezing his hips. I can feel the vibrations from the bike underneath me and his hard abdominal muscles under my hands. It feels so real and natural, like I was meant to be here with him like this.

He pulls over by the lake; then suddenly the sky turns dark and not even the moon can be seen over the water of the lake. He reaches back and pulls me over his leg so I'm straddling him on the bike. I should be nervous or stop him, but it feels so right, like we've done this exact thing a million times before.

I look into his eyes and I see not just his love for me as a friend, but something new, something that builds a fire deep down inside me. I lift my hand and run it along his jaw. "I love you, Zane." It comes out smooth, as if I've said it to him before. He looks deeply into my eyes, like he's searching

19

for something.

Then, suddenly, in the distance, thunder booms and lightning flashes. It scares me so bad, I jump in his lap. I look off into the distance and see a storm brewing. I turn back to tell him we should go, but when I do, he's not my Zane anymore. He's this hardened version of himself, and he's looking at me with such contempt and hatred that it makes me fall off of him and the bike. I get to my feet in front of him and reach for him, but he turns his head in disgust. He turns the bike around and leaves me there, alone.

It starts raining, and I hit my knees and my arms reach out to him automatically like it will make him return to me. "Zane! Come back! I love you! I need you, please don't leave me!" But he doesn't even look back, and then he's gone completely from my sight.

***

I gasp and sit up in bed. I can't breathe and my body is trembling so hard I can almost hear my bed shaking. My clothes are sticking to my skin, soaked from my sweat. What the fuck was that?

I'm so far in my head, I barely register that someone is walking up the stairs. It can't be Gram; she hasn't been up here in years. Then there's a knock at my bedroom door.

"Baby Girl, you awake?"

Zane. What the hell is he doing here?

"Um…yeah, give me a minute." I jump out of bed and toss my drenched clothes on the floor, then slip into a pair of yoga Capri pants and a sweatshirt. "Uh, you can come in now." I sit back on my bed with my arms wrapped around my knees and wait for him to walk in. When he opens the door, he looks around my room and then his eyes land on me.

"I didn't wake you, did I?" he asks with a sexy smirk on his face.

"No, um, I've been up for a while. What are you doing here?" I glance at him and then lower my eyes. I can't even bear to look at him; all I can see is the face I saw in my dream. The one before his expression hardened.

"Well, it's past lunch time, but I was wondering if you wanted to go get some breakfast with me." He wiggles his eyebrows.

He comes over and sits on my bed. I'm suddenly nervous, even though I shouldn't be. I mean, he's been in my room numerous times before. We've even lain in my bed and he's held me while I've slept. Why does it feel so different today? Oh yeah, maybe because last night I realized I'm falling for him. "Um...I should really stay here. Gram wasn't looking well last night." *Please don't question me, please don't make this into a big deal. Walk away, Zane, just walk away.*

"Oh no. I talked to Gram when I got here and she said she must have just been tired last night, but she feels fine now. She said I should drag you out of your bed if I have to. So, come on, get up. I'm hungry, and I'm not taking no for an answer. End of discussion." He gets up and strides to the door. Before exiting my room, he glances over his shoulder. "If you aren't downstairs in five minutes, I'm coming back up here. And trust me, it will not be pleasant. For you, anyway." He mumbles the last part and I almost don't catch it. Then he walks out of my room and I can hear him whistling as he goes down the stairs.

Well, shit! This is just what I need today, hanging out with him after last night and that fucked-up dream I had. But I know how stubborn he is when he has his mind set on something. I quickly get up to get dressed. The sooner I go and get it over with, the sooner I can come back home to try and figure out what the hell I'm feeling.

I head down the stairs, stop to give my grandmother a kiss, and head out the door with Zane not far behind me. He walks over to his bike, hops on, and hands me my helmet. This just isn't my day. Of course we would have to ride his bike after the dream I had.

On the way to the diner I try to figure out what the hell is going on with me. Could I really be falling for him? I mean, we have always been close, like brother and sister. But after last night, it's like there is a shift in our relationship. Or maybe it was just me and all the alcohol I consumed at the party last night. Maybe I need to stop thinking so much and forget about it.

***

The past month has flown by, filled with softball practice and games, and spending as much time as I can with Zane. At the same time, I've been going back and forth in my head on whether to keep distance between him and me. Or maybe I should continue on like I didn't have that mind-numbing epiphany the night of the party. Not only is it stressful, but it's exhausting, both physically and mentally. I don't know what is going on with me. I can't get the idea out of my head that there has been a shift in our relationship, but I can't put my finger on it. Maybe things are changing because he's going away soon and I'm getting older? But what I fear the most is that I'm actually falling in love with him. I don't know what I would do if that is the case; there is no way he returns those feelings, and I don't want to lose him as a friend by bringing up that I may feel more for him than just friendship.

On top of all of that, my grandmother hasn't been herself since she got back from one of her doctor's appointments a couple weeks ago. It seems like she is always sleeping. Today I even found her asleep in her recliner. I'm trying to get her to make another appointment with Dr. Tatum, but she says there is nothing wrong with her but old age. I don't believe her, but what else can I do? I worry that I'm losing her, that it's been too hard on her taking care of me for the past thirteen years.

I'm in the middle of cooking some soup for my grandmother, since she hasn't been getting around well and I want to make sure that she is at least eating, when the doorbell rings. I go to the front door to see who it is. When I peek through the curtain, I see Zane on the other side. When he sees me looking at him, he makes a funny face at me, which has me laughing. I open the door and head back into the kitchen. "Hey, I'm making Gram some soup. Ya want some?" I ask.

"You know I can't pass up food when you're cooking, Baby Girl." That makes me laugh even harder, because he and I both know that I'm a crappy cook. I'm only even *attempting* to make something because I feel I have to for my grandmother's sake.

"Ha ha, you're so funny. One day my cooking skills will be amazing, and you won't get to eat any!" I stick my tongue out at him, loving the way he can make me forget all that has been getting me down with only a few simple words.

After I take my grandmother her lunch, I sit at the table with Zane sitting across from me. "So what's up?" I ask him. He's been coming over every day for the past week to see if I want to hang out, but I haven't wanted to leave Gram.

"I was thinking about going swimming at the lake, and you're coming with." He doesn't ask, he tells me. "Then we're going to a party tonight."

Swimming does sound fun, and with today feeling like it's going to be the hottest day in recorded history, it'd be great to take a dip in the lake to cool off.

"Oh my God, that sounds amazing! Who's all going?" I get up to put my empty bowl in the sink and turn back toward him.

"Just you and me. I asked Kolby if he wanted to go, but he's busy finishing up some last minute things before he leaves for California in a couple weeks." Whoa, what? I thought Kolby was going with Zane and a couple others to the University of

Texas. He must have read my mind, because he says, "Yeah, he was going to come with me, but I guess his dad really wanted him to go to California. Says he wants him to follow in his footsteps, or some shit like that."

"Well, let me check in with Gram quick and then I'll go put my swimsuit on. I'll meet you outside in say, twenty minutes?"

He stands up and walks over to me. "Sounds good, Baby Girl."

I follow him to the door, but he stops abruptly, which causes me to run into him. He reaches out to steady me.

"Did you forget something?" I ask, not sure why he stopped.

"Yeah. I forgot to tell you to wear your red swimming suit," he says with a smirk.

Why would he say that? And not only did he say it, but he's also still holding my waist from when he caught me from falling after colliding with him. And his hands aren't *just* on my waist for balance anymore, his thumb has worked my shirt up a little in the back and it's now caressing the skin that he exposed. Add that to the way he is looking at me, like he's been told he's on death row and I'm his last meal. My head is spinning out of control and I have to reach out to steady myself. Except this time, it has nothing to do with running into him and everything to do with *him*.

I'm speechless. I mean, what the hell do you say to that? He must realize that he caught me off guard, because he quickly adds, "I mean it's a perfect day to catch a tan, right?" If he only knew how badly I wanted to wear my bikini for him. Then have him slowly strip it off my body.

Dammit! So much for trying to get over what I thought I was feeling that night of the graduation party. My emotions for him seem to grow stronger each day, and he's not helping by doing things like this. It's like falling in love with him is inevitable, like it's a part of me. But would he feel the same way? It could be *my* fate to fall for him, but what if it's really destiny being a stupid cunt again and he doesn't feel the same way? What if he's the only person I'll ever love but he'll never be mine?

I wonder what he would do if I jumped him. That would solve the problem of not knowing what he feels toward me *really* quick. He would either catch me and meet me in the middle for a steamy kiss. Or he would reject me. Sometimes I swear from the way he looks at me that he wants me too, but maybe I'm reading way too much into it. Maybe this is how friends act. It's not like I have an abundance of friends to base this on, and I don't have a lot of experience with guys and flirting, either. Shit, I'm so out of my league here!

I have no idea what to do. I want him, but at the same time, I don't *want* to want him. There's also that little fact that he leaves in a month for college, and I still have two years left of high school. And when he gets to college, there will be parties and lots of girls that would probably do anything to have him. Let's face it, I don't have any experience when it comes to sex, but Zane is no saint. I know he's slept with at least two girls, but probably even more than that. So if it came down to it and he felt the same way, would he be faithful or would a relationship with him be doomed right from the start?

I feel his hand stroke my cheek. "You still with me?"

I shake my head to clear my thoughts and say, "Uh yeah...I-I'm good. I'll see you in a few." I nervously laugh and push him out the door. I have no idea if he was just messing with me or not, but maybe I should wear the red bikini and see how he reacts. Who knows, maybe he'll make a move and I won't even have to think about it.

God, I hope he does, because if he teases me any more I'm going to combust. *Wait, stop! He's leaving in a month. You need to forget about it, Danielle, it's never going to happen!* But I'm still going to wear my red bikini, not because he told me to, but because it happens to be my favorite one.

I head over to my grandmother's room to check on her and to let her know I'm leaving with Zane. When I walk in, I see that she barely touched her soup and she is now sleeping. I don't want to wake her, so I write a quick note to tell her I'll be back later.

I head up to my bedroom and hunt for my bikini. I put it on in a rush, then throw on a pair of cut-off jean shorts. I forgo a shirt since it's so fucking hot out and grab my beach towel and sunscreen and put my flip-flops on. I take a quick look in the mirror, put my hair in a loose side braid, and head out to meet Zane by his truck.

He's already waiting for me when I get outside. Holy shit, he's not wearing a shirt! He's got his aviator sunglasses on, black swim trunks, and black flip-flops. Yum! I just want to lick him all over. I swear, I've never fantasized about any guy, ever, until last month. Now my thoughts are consumed with all things Zane. I'm still holding on to my v-card, but if you had someone as sexy as Zane as your focus, your imagination would go wild too.

I walk up to him and throw my sunglasses over my eyes. I don't want him to be able to see what he does to me. I'm sure my cheeks are bright red, but I can blame that on the heat.

"I can't wait to get in the water and cool down," I say as we walk down the driveway toward his truck. But when I get to the door, instead of opening it for me like he usually does, he just turns around and rushes over to his side. I jump in and roll the window down. It takes him a little longer than it should to get in, but once he does, he doesn't look at me or say anything. He only starts the truck and takes off. Well, I guess I can see how today is going to go…

Once we arrive at the lake, we get out and head over to the spot we always set up with our stuff. I lay my blanket down and unbutton my shorts, figuring I'll catch some sun first. Just as I'm pulling my pants down, Zane gives me a look that is both lustful and angry. "What the hell are you doing?"

What? "Um…I'm taking my shorts off so I can lay out before taking a dip in the lake. What does it look like I'm doing?" I add with a little attitude at the end.

He literally growls at me and takes off at a fast pace for the water. That was weird and uncomfortable.

Not sure what his deal is, but not wanting to piss him off more, I lie down and close my eyes. Something must have happened since he asked me to go to the lake, because the way he is acting now just doesn't add up. He never takes anything out on me or carries over any attitude, so I guess with everything he has going on he is probably having a bad day. Hopefully relaxing in the sun and swimming will take his mind off of whatever is bothering him.

About twenty minutes later, I hear him make his way back over toward me. Cracking open one eye, the first thing I notice is that he is dripping wet, which makes me instantly wet without even stepping foot into the water. The next thing I notice is that he is staring down at me with a hard face. I can't even read his expression because of the sunglasses covering his eyes. I lean up on my elbows and stare right back at him.

"Let's go." His voice is ice cold.

We haven't been here nearly as long as we usually stay, so I'm not sure why he wants to leave already. "What's the rush?" I ask, hoping he loses the attitude or at least opens up to me about what's going on with him.

"I forgot I have some things to do before the party tonight. Let's go." He doesn't even wait for my reply, just grabs his stuff and heads to his truck.

Well, so much for taking a swim. I get up, slip my shorts back on, and catch up with him. "Are you okay?" I can't piece this together. Even if something happened before we left, he has never taken his shit out on me.

"Yeah, I'm just fuckin' peachy." His reply has a hint of sarcasm, but is overflowing with anger. I should let this go, but for some reason I can't.

"Ya know, if you didn't want me to come to the lake with you, you should have just said so. There's no reason you need to be an ass," I throw back at him as I jump in the truck. Now I'm pissed as well. At least he doesn't have a comeback today, like he usually does when we argue on occasion about stupid shit. Fine by me, he can brood all he wants for all I care. Neither of us speak at all on the way home, and by the time we make it back to my house, I've figured out that something is seriously wrong. The silent treatment bothers me more than the attitude he was throwing at me earlier. I wish he'd talk to me about it instead of stewing and letting it get to him more.

I barely say goodbye to him when we pull up to my house because he seems to be thinking the same thing I am—*make a hasty retreat*. I have no clue what that was today. When we talked about going swimming earlier, I never thought it would end like this. And let's not forget that comment he made about my swimsuit.

I walk into the house and head straight up to my room. I know I shouldn't sit and nitpick over what happened at the lake, but I can't help it. With everything that has happened since the graduation party, things seem to keep getting more strained between Zane and me. If it isn't me worrying about my feelings for him growing into something more than friendship, then it's him acting really strange.

When he doesn't think I'm watching, I catch him looking at me in weird ways. I can't describe the looks or even figure out what they mean. One thing I know for sure, things are changing between us. I can only hope it's not for the worse.

CHAPTER 3

Since it's the weekend before Zane leaves for college, there is a huge get together tonight, sort of like a going away party I guess. I'm not really excited about attending, but want to be there and spend as much time with him as I can. Hopefully his attitude will be better. I hate where we are right now in our relationship. I just want to have my best friend back.

I almost want to say something to him, try to get him to tell me what is going on. I don't want to mention my feelings for him, just that things have seemed a little weird between us lately and I want to fix it. It's bad enough that he will be leaving for college in a matter of days, but if he leaves without us fixing our friendship, I fear I will lose him forever.

I'll have to see what tonight brings. It should be easy for me to sit down and talk with him at the party, and the fact that there will be an unlimited supply of alcohol should make things easier. That will loosen us up, and we can both talk freely. Then we can take it from there, and hopefully come out the other side with our friendship stronger than ever.

***

I'm not really in the mood to dress up too much tonight. I'm strung too tight not knowing what's going on with Zane and me, so I throw on a black tank top that fits like a second skin and shows about an inch of my midriff, and some skinny jeans. I fix my loose side braid, add some light make-up, and I'm ready to go.

I grab my phone and put it in my back pocket, then head down the stairs to say goodbye to my grandmother. "Bye, Gram, I'll see you in the morning." I give her a quick kiss on the forehead and walk to the door.

When I get outside, Zane isn't waiting by his truck like he usually is, so I head over to his house and knock. After a couple of seconds, Mrs. Hendricks answers.

"Oh, hello, Danielle. Are you looking for Zane?" she asks me.

"Yeah, is he ready to leave yet?"

She gives me a sad smile. "I'm sorry, honey. He left about fifteen minutes ago. Were you supposed to ride with him?"

Wait, what? Who did he leave with? His truck is still on the street and he would never ride his motorcycle to a party. "Oh, um…yeah, I thought he said he wanted me to ride over with him." I frown, not sure what to do.

"Well he didn't say anything to me before he left. He just ran out the door when a car pulled up outside."

Looks like I'll be driving myself tonight. Great. "That's okay, Mrs. Hendricks, I can drive myself. Have a good night." I turn around and walk back over to my house.

I don't understand why he would leave without me and not even say anything about riding with someone, even if it was last minute. We always ride together to parties, so I'm not sure why he thought this one would be any different. I walk to my car and hop in. Once I get to this party, I'm going to find him and we are going to have words. I'm going to settle this, even if the outcome isn't what I want.

***

When I get to the party, I walk over to the keg, since that is usually where he is. I see some of his friends, but no Zane. I know he's already here because he left before me. Maybe he's over by the bonfire? I grab a beer, then head that way.

At the fire pit, I look around to see if I can find him. Nothing. Where the hell would he be? Oh well, I'm not going to walk around all night searching for him; I'll run into him at some point.

I finish my first beer quickly and head in the direction of the keg for a refill and to see if I can find a bottle of something stronger. I have a feeling I'm going to need it tonight.

I pass a couple of parked cars and I'm stopped momentarily by what sounds like a girl moaning.

Holy shit! Is someone really having sex out here in the open where anyone can walk by and see? I don't care how horny I was, I don't think I could ever have sex in public. That would be embarrassing; I wouldn't be able to show my face in this town for a long time.

I start walking again to get away to give the couple some privacy and before someone catches me spying, but as I get past the next car, I see where the action is taking place. Some chick is pressed against a truck with her legs wrapped around the guy's hips. She has her head thrown back, eyes closed, and has a look of pure ecstasy on her face. Her arms are around the guy's neck, holding his face against her throat. He looks to be devouring her while his hips are rocking forcefully into her.

I can't look away. I know I should be disgusted or embarrassed on their behalf, not turned on by this, but holy shit is that hot. They both must be near their release, because the girl starts moaning louder and the guy is pumping into her faster and with more force than before. You can hear his own moans and grunts every time he drives into her. I really need to walk away before they finish and catch me watching.

I take a step back so I can go a different route to the keg when I hear her scream in completion, "Oh God, Zane, yes! *Yes*!"

Oh. My. God. She's fucking Zane? I just watched him screw some chick up against a truck? I can't believe this. To top it off, I wanted to watch and listen, thinking it was hot. I feel like my world came crashing down around me in less than ten seconds. I need to get out of here, but my legs won't move. I can't believe what I saw. I can't breathe. I mean, I knew he wasn't a saint, but to witness that shit firsthand? I think my heart broke into a million pieces and it'll never be whole again. It is painfully obviously now; I'm in love with him. If I weren't, I don't think it would hurt this bad.

I finally get control of my legs to walk away, hopefully unnoticed, but it's too late. Just as I'm starting to turn, they step out from where the cars are parked and are right in front of me. The girl sees me first and gives me a satisfied smile. Then Zane looks up from buttoning his jeans and his eyes land on me. I quickly try and school my emotions so he doesn't know that I witnessed their sexcapade.

"Baby Girl, when did you get here?" he asks nervously, though I can't fathom why. Even if he knew I had front row seats to the show that they both starred in, he would have no reason to be nervous. Embarrassed, yes.

"Um…h-hey. I just got here and was on my way to get a beer. I'll see you later." I quickly walk away before he can say anything else. I don't know what he would say, but I couldn't stand there anymore and see at the two looking freshly fucked.

When I get to the keg, I fill my cup and chug the whole thing. I've been such a fool. Even knowing that Zane could never see me the way I see him, I could have never prepared for the gut-wrenching pain that I'm experiencing now. It's not like we are dating, and I doubt he even knows how I feel, but fuck, I still don't want to think about him being with another girl, let alone to fucking see it with my own eyes.

I fill my cup again and then I head over to the picnic table that holds various bottles of hard liquor. I don't see a bottle of Jack, but there is a full bottle of vodka. Fuck it. It's not normally my choice of drink, but it will have to do tonight. People may be pissed with me for taking the whole thing, but they can kiss my ass. I think I need it more than they do. I need to erase these pictures I have in my head of the two of them going at it. It's too much to handle, it hurts so fucking bad.

I find a log close to the lake and take a seat. I need to be alone right now. I have to get my emotions in check before I face Zane again tonight. I refuse to let him see how much this is tearing me up inside. I have no claim on him, but it still cuts deep.

I drink the vodka slowly and sit quietly under the serenity of the quiet night sky. It's a full moon tonight and the sky is clear so you can see all the stars. The vodka doesn't burn as much as Jack Daniels, but I know it will fuck me up fast if I don't drink slowly. I have to make this bottle last a while anyway because I'm not ready to go back to the party.

By the time I feel like I can head back, the bottle is more than half gone. I am definitely feeling the effects of the liquor. I want to continue drinking, but I know I need to stop so I don't pass out or get sick, so I'll switch to beer. That should allow me to keep the buzz but ensure I don't puke either.

I set the vodka on the table and grab a new cup for my beer. Then I walk over to the bonfire to sit in an empty seat by some guy I've never seen before. He tells me his name is Gunnar and that he will be a senior this year. He recently moved here from Florida and will be attending my school. He is tall, tanned, and gorgeous, but not as hot as Zane. He has hair so dark it almost looks black and he has it cropped really short. His eyes are a deep blue, and he has a chiseled jaw and a sexy smile. And the best part: he seems to like me.

He plays baseball, which is a nice change of pace since Zane and I usually only talk about football. And since I play softball, I understand the dynamics of the game. We talk about our school's team and how we think next season will be for both of us. I find myself looking forward to going back to school, which I thought would be impossible. It's nice to have something to look forward to again, with Zane leaving for college, and with what I witnessed earlier tonight, it's a pleasant feeling.

A couple hours have passed since I sat down and starting talking with Gunnar. I haven't seen Zane since the show he put on by the truck, but maybe that's for the best since everything still feels raw. I've slowly been sobering up and drinking water because I should head home soon. Having Gunnar here making me laugh makes it so I don't need the alcohol to numb the pain. Looking into his eyes and talking with him feels like having a nice cool ointment over an open wound; I can still feel the cut, but it isn't glaringly obvious now. We actually have a lot in common. Maybe I should see where this goes with him if he is interested like I think he is. I did say that I should get out more and possibly start dating. This could be my chance.

I take a look at my watch and see that it is almost three in the morning. I'm pretty sure I've sobered up enough that I can drive home now. "I should probably get going, I have to be up early tomorrow." I get up and look down at Gunnar to say goodbye. He surprises me when he stands and reaches out to take my hand in his.

"Do you really have to leave?" He's looking at me like he doesn't want to let me go.

I open my mouth to answer him when Zane walks up. "Where the hell have you been? I've been looking everywhere for you. Let's go." He takes hold of my other hand and pulls me toward him, which causes me to break the contact I had with Gunnar.

Zane's attitude instantly pisses me off, so I break the hold he has on me. "What are you doing?" I hiss.

He turns around and stares at me, then glares over my shoulder at Gunnar, who I feel come up behind me and takes my hand again. Zane doesn't say anything for a moment, he only looks where my hand is joined with Gunnar's.

"Let's go, Danielle, I'm taking you home," he says through his teeth.

If he thinks that he can come over here and demand that I go with him after everything that happened tonight, he'd better think again. "I didn't come here with you, Zane. I drove myself, remember? So I'll leave when I'm ready."

Oh shit, he really looks pissed now. Well, he can get over it; I'm tired of his shit. One minute he acts like he doesn't want anything to do with me and the next he acts like there is nothing wrong.

He walks up to me and leans down so he is at eye level. "You've been drinking. You aren't driving tonight," he almost growls at me.

"Thanks for your concern, but I can take care of myself." I turn to walk around him, pulling Gunnar along with me, which pisses Zane off more. He yanks my hand out of Gunnar's grip and takes off toward my car, dragging me along after him.

Gunnar must have finally had enough, because he pulls me away from Zane and steps between us. "Listen, man, I'm not sure who you are, but she said she doesn't want to go with you. Leave her alone, all right?"

I lean to look around him, but he blocks me with his arm to keep me behind him. The move kind of pisses me off because I don't need protection from Zane, but in a way, it's sweet since he doesn't know what he is dealing with. He doesn't know our history, so he is being cautious. Like I said, not necessary, but sweet all the same.

"Who the fuck are you?" Zane is toe-to-toe with him now. Shit, this is not good. I need to stop this before something happens.

I step around Gunnar and between the two, and face off with a furious Zane. "Not like it's any of your business, but if you must know, his name is Gunnar." As I say this, Gunnar grabs me around my waist and pulls me up against his front. Wow, his stomach feels like steel!

"Look, I don't want any trouble. But if she doesn't want to leave with you, I'll make sure she gets home safely. I was going to offer to give her a ride home anyway," Gunnar says calmly.

I look up at him and smile, then back over to Zane. "Baby Girl…" he starts, but doesn't finish. He still looks upset, but now defeated.

"I'll be fine, Zane. I'll even text you when I get home, okay?" I add the last part so he can relax a little. I know he cares about me and doesn't want me to get hurt, and since Gunnar is new around here, he thinks he is a threat. Little does he know that the threat to my wellbeing is himself.

He looks me in the eye and finally agrees. "If I don't hear from you in an hour, I will come looking for you. And you." He points to Gunnar. "If anything happens to her, I will hunt you down and bury you where no one will ever find you. You got me?" Fuck. Zane is hot when he is pissed and in protective mode. I need to stop thinking like that, though, because Zane and I will never be.

"I said I would text when I got home and I will, but you will not threaten Gunnar." He makes me so angry sometimes!

"It wasn't a threat, Baby Girl. It was a promise." He gives one last glare to Gunnar, looks at me, and then walks away.

"Well, that was fun," Gunnar says as he squeezes my side.

"I'm sorry about that. He's a good friend and worries about me," I whisper to him. I'm so embarrassed right now. I wouldn't blame him if he never wanted to see me again.

"Hey," he says and grabs my chin to force me to look at him. "I completely understand. He doesn't know who I am and wanted to make sure you were safe. I would have done the same thing if I were in his shoes."

I look at him doubtfully. "Well, I still feel horrible that he acted that way toward you."

He gives me a small laugh. "Don't worry about it, beautiful. Let's get you home." He called me beautiful. No one has ever said that to me before.

We start walking in the opposite direction from my car, which has me a little worried. Maybe I should have gone with Zane. "I'll give you a ride. I'm sure your car will be okay here until the morning." We stop at a black truck. Holy shit, this thing is huge! He opens the door and I stare up inside. I'm suddenly nervous and unsure if I should go with him, but I really want to spend more time with him. I look at the truck, then up at him. "That's a long ways up." I laugh nervously.

He grabs me by the waist and hoists me inside. "Up you go, beautiful." He gives me a wink and closes the door before walking around to his side.

Once he is settled in, he starts the truck and turns the music down. "Where to?" he asks. I smile and give him directions to my house. We keep a steady conversation going the entire time. I can't stop staring at him, waiting for the next time he'll glance my way.

When we pull up to my house, I turn to thank him for the ride and grab hold of the door handle. Before I can open the door, though, Gunnar grabs my hand. I turn to look at him.

"When can I see you again?" he asks.

I give him a nervous smile. "Um…I could give

you my number if you want?"

He reaches over and cups my cheek, then slowly leans in toward me. Oh God, is he going to kiss me? "I've wanted to kiss you since you first sat by me."

He doesn't wait for my reply, just presses his lips to mine. I close my eyes, wanting to experience my first kiss fully. It's a gentle kiss, nothing earthshattering, but makes me feel good.

He pulls away slowly and I open my eyes to look at him. "Wow…" I whisper to myself.

He gives me a sexy smile and pecks my lips briefly once more. "Give me your phone."

I hand it over and watch as he programs his number. Then he sends a text to himself so he can save my number. "Call me tomorrow, and I'll take you to pick up your car."

I nod and turn to get out of the truck. "Goodnight, beautiful," he says when I'm out the door.

"Night, Gunnar," I tell him. I turn around and walk in a daze to my front door. He waits till I'm inside before he drives away.

I walk up to my room, get into my pajamas, and slide into bed. I can't believe he kissed me! It was really sweet. I can't wait to see him again tomorrow.

I close my eyes, but a couple seconds later I hear my phone chime. I grab it and see I have a new text message.

Zane: Where are you?!

Me: Home. In bed. I'm fine.

Zane: You were supposed to text me as soon as you got home!

Me: I forgot, so sue me.

Zane: Smartass

Me: Jerk!

Zane: Night Baby Girl ;)

Me: Night Zane :)

Well, at least things seem better with me and him now. I still can't believe I saw him having sex with some random girl, but I don't have any say in what he does. Tonight wasn't as bad as it could have been, and I have Gunnar to thank for that. Remembering what I saw still hurts, and I don't think any guy will be able to take that away fully, but it's a start I suppose. Maybe with time things will grow with Gunnar and me, and then everything won't be so awkward with Zane. I'm glad I still have him as my friend, and in the end, that's all I really care about.

Suddenly, my phone goes off again. Zane is the only one I really talk to, but we already said goodnight so I have no clue who is messaging me now. I pick up my phone again and open up my messages.

Gunnar: Sweet dreams, beautiful. I can't wait to see you tomorrow.

Me: Goodnight. Tomorrow can't come soon enough!

I close my phone and fall asleep with a smile on my face. Things may be looking up for me. I only hope that I can get over whatever was going on with me and Zane so it doesn't ruin what I might have with Gunnar. No one will ever compare to Zane, but it's time I get over him and move on with my life. There's no point in pining over a guy that I could never have.

CHAPTER 4

As soon as I got up this morning, I had a message from Gunnar telling me to text him when I was up so we could go get my car. I let him know to give me an hour and I would be ready to leave.

I went downstairs to make sure Gram was doing okay, and that she ate something for breakfast, and then headed up to my room for a shower.

I throw on my white halter dress with the brown braided belt and slip on my brown cowboy boots. Then I curl my hair and put some makeup on. I don't want to look like I'm trying too hard, but I still want to look good.

I hear the doorbell, so I run downstairs to answer it. When I open the door, I'm surprised to see Zane instead of Gunnar.

"Oh, hey, Zane. What are you doing here?" I ask.

He looks me up and down and a slow smile creeps onto his face. "Hey, Baby Girl. You look beautiful today."

I smile shyly and tell him thanks. It's so strange that I've never been called beautiful before in my life by a guy, and now I've heard it twice in less than a day—once from a guy I hope to have a relationship with, and once from one who I'm in love with but will never have.

I step outside on the porch and sit on the swing. "So what's up?" I say as I push myself a little.

Zane just stands off to the side and regards me quietly. "I came by to take you to get your car. I assumed you left it at the lake last night. Then I was thinking we could order some pizzas and watch movies."

Well, that's surprising. I didn't think I would see him today, let alone have him offer to take me to pick up my car.

I open my mouth to answer him when I see Gunnar pull up to my house. I get up and give Zane a small smile. "Thanks, but actually Gunnar already said he would take me." As I finish saying that, Gunnar comes up behind me and wraps his arms around my waist.

"Hey, beautiful," he says before I feel his lips brush the top of my head.

I giggle—yes giggle—and turn around to face him. "Hey." He's dressed in a black shirt and a pair of faded blue jeans that fit him like a second skin.

I look back and notice Zane staring at me with an emotion I can't quite read.

"Hey, man. Zane, right?" Gunnar asks and offers him his hand.

"Yeah," Zane says as he stares at the offering for a couple seconds before taking it in a firm shake. They both seem to be putting way too much strength behind their handshake, almost like they are testing who is stronger.

"Well, we should get going," I say and start walking down the steps. "I'll call you when I get back to make plans for tonight."

They release each other's hands, and Gunnar turns to follow me.

"Yeah…I'll see you later, Baby Girl," Zane says, then walks over to his house.

Once Gunnar and I are in his truck and driving back to the lake, he finally asks the question I've been dreading. "So, what's the deal with you and Zane?"

God, how in the hell am I supposed to explain this to him when I barely know how to describe our relationship myself lately?

"Well, it's kind of a long story," I say, not really knowing where to start.

"I've got all the time in the world, beautiful," I can hear the smile in his voice, and when I look up to confirm my suspicions, he winks at me.

Okay, well, I guess I should just start at the beginning. It's not like there's anything to be ashamed of or that I need to hide. But maybe I'll keep the part where I may have feelings for him that go beyond friendship to myself. Yeah, I'm definitely keeping quiet about that.

"Zane and I have been friends since I was thirteen. And, as you can see, we're also neighbors. I started going over to play at their house when Gram had things to do or when I wanted to give her a break. It didn't take long for us to build a close relationship. We were like the three musketeers; Zane, Zeke and I," I tell him.

"Who's Zeke? I don't think I've met him yet."

Zeke…God I miss him. So much. I look down at my hands, and figure now is as good a time as ever to tell him what happened. "Zeke was Zane's brother, and has been gone a little over a year now. He was a Marine stationed over in Iraq…" It's still so hard to even think, let alone talk about him. I haven't done it in a long time, and when I do, it's only with Zane.

A tear slides down my cheek and I go to wipe it away. "He, um, he was doing a routine security check when they were ambushed. He was shot and died before a medic could even make it over to him," I whisper.

Gunnar reaches over, rubbing his thumb along my hand, comforting me. "Baby, I'm sorry."

I don't reply because I never really understand why people say they are sorry anyway, like they had a hand in what happened.

After a couple minutes of silence, I continue. "After Zeke died, Zane and I became even closer. He's always been there for me, and I've always tried to be there for him. He took the loss of his brother pretty hard." I stare out the window and try to clear my head a little. It kind of feels like I'm betraying Zane by telling Gunnar about Zeke, but hopefully now that I've told him what happened, we won't talk about it again.

"And that's pretty much it. He's my best friend, well, I should say my only friend." I look over and give him a little smile.

"You mentioned you started going over there because of your grandmother. Do you live with her?" Of course he wouldn't miss that part. Now he's going to want to know about my parents. I guess it's better to get all of the sensitive subjects out of the way right away.

"Yes, I've lived with Gram since before I can remember. My mother died when I was three, and right after, my father signed his rights over to her. She's been raising me ever since." There, now it's out there and he knows everything. Well, almost everything. As much as I'm willing to tell.

He starts to say something, but I cut him off. "I really don't want to talk about it, if that's okay. It was a long time ago, so can we please drop it?" I turn to stare out the window. My words came out a little harsher than I wanted them to, but I can't stand talking about my past. It brings up too many emotions and feelings of being unwanted. I hope he understands, but I don't want to dwell on the past anymore.

"Yeah, baby, sure. What would you like to talk about?" he asks and squeezes my hand. I glance over at him to gauge his reaction. He doesn't look upset or disappointed, which makes me let go of the breath I didn't know I was holding.

"Tell me about Florida," I say, since I've always wanted to go there. I'm even thinking about applying to college there when I graduate. Gunnar smiles and tells me about where he used to live, his family and friends from back home. It's nice hearing about his life.

When we pull in by my car, I turn to thank him for taking me. "What are you doing tonight?" he asks. Tonight is Saturday and I didn't have plans before, but now I'm not so sure. I should check with Zane first, since I want to spend as much time with him as possible. He leaves Tuesday for college.

"Well, Zane mentioned possibly hanging out tonight." I hope this doesn't upset Gunnar. I know sometimes guys get jealous when girls have guy friends, but he only smiles and leans over to give me a chaste kiss.

"Of course, beautiful. I understand. You should spend time with him. Why don't you call me later if you want to hang out, okay?" I smile back at him and nod, then head over to my car.

He ends up following me to my house to be sure I make it there without problems. When I pull in my driveway and get out to wave him off, he surprises me by getting out of his truck. He walks over to me, grabs my hips and pushes me back against my car. Then he grabs my face with both hands and devours my mouth. Holy. Fucking. Shit. Where last night his kisses were soft and sweet, now they are hard and demanding.

By the time he pulls away, I'm a hot, breathless mess. I slowly open my eyes, gasping for air. "What was that for?" I finally ask.

He smirks at me and kisses me one more time on my forehead. "I wanted to make sure my girl doesn't forget about me tonight." Did he really just call me that? I must say, I like it.

"Your girl?" I ask nervously. I don't know why I'm so nervous around him, but I feel almost giddy at the thought that he wants me. It's foreign to me. Besides my gram wanting to take care of me, and Zane and Zeke wanting me as a friend, I've never been wanted before. And for some reason, knowing that Gunnar wants me as more than a friend tops it all.

He reaches out and grabs both my hands in his. He stares deep into my eyes, like he is looking at my soul. He must be able to tell that I'm nervous and unsure, because he drops my hands and cups my cheek. "I know we only met last night, but there's something about you, Danielle. I want to get to know you better. So, will you be my girl?"

I smile up at him and decide to be bold. Reaching up on my tiptoes, I kiss his lips. "Yeah, I'll be your girl."

He gives me a blinding smile and another mind-blowing kiss. After he has me breathing hard again, he tells me to text him later. I walk up to my door in a daze. I have a boyfriend. Oh my God, I have a boyfriend! I have to tell Gram!

***

After talking with Gram about Gunnar and telling her that he asked me to be his girlfriend, I decide to text Zane to see what he has planned for the night.

Me: Hey you! What you doing?

Zane: Hey yourself. Finishing packing up my room.

Me: :(I'm going to miss you when you leave!

Zane: Oh yeah? Seems to me like you'll have someone else to fill your days with…

Does he really think that I would replace him, or that I even could? No matter where this relationship goes with Gunnar, there will always be a place in my heart for Zane. Yes, I think I may be in love with him, but that love can go nowhere. He'll always be my best friend, though.

Me: Please don't be like that. No one could ever replace you if that's what you're thinking…

Zane: Sorry, it's just weird. I mean, what do you even know about this guy?

Me: I know it's weird, but I think I really like him. He moved here a few weeks ago, and he is really nice. Can you please give him a chance? For me?

Please say that you understand and you are willing to get to know him. I don't think I would be able to do anything that Zane is against. It will break my heart to not have him behind me.

Zane: I'll try, but only because you asked. So what are your plans for tonight? Going out with the new guy?

Me: Well, you mentioned earlier you wanted to hang out, so I thought I'd check with you first.

Zane: Well, what are you waiting for? Get your ass over here…

Not like he has a choice; I would have told him I was coming over regardless of what he said. Even though I can't wait to see Gunnar again, I know he will understand. I'll have the whole year to see him, whereas Zane…not so much.

I send a quick message to Gunnar, letting him know I'm hanging out with Zane and that I'll text later. Then after I let Gram know where I'm going, I head out the door, excited for tonight.

I don't bother knocking on the door because I know his parents are out and he knows I'm coming over anyway. I walk in and go upstairs to his bedroom. The door is open so I walk right in.

The first thing I notice are the boxes everywhere. All the things Zane has collected over the years are now packed away. This is too different. I hate seeing his room like this. It's so empty. He's really leaving me. I know he's only leaving to go to school and will be back to visit, but it hurts my heart knowing I won't see him every day anymore.

Suddenly Zane is in front of me, wiping tears that I didn't even realize were falling. "Don't cry, Baby Girl. I'll be back, I promise. And you know you can always come visit me anytime you want," he whispers. His words only make me cry harder. I reach up and hug him hard.

"I'm going to miss you so much. What am I doing to do without you?"

Zane rubs my back and holds me tightly. I hardly ever break down like this, at least not in front of people, so I'm sure this is hard for him to see. But ever since Zeke died, it's been him and me, and I honestly don't know how I'm going to deal with him not being here.

I finally pull myself together enough to stop crying and look up at him while wiping the last of my tears away. "I'm sorry. I didn't mean for that to happen." I give him a small laugh and pull out of his embrace.

"Danielle, you don't have to hide from me. I don't know what I'm going to do without you around either, if it makes it any better."

I wouldn't say it out loud, but I don't think he'll have any trouble filling his time without me, if what happened last night was anything to go by.

I clear my throat and look in his mirror on the closet door to make sure my face looks okay. "So, what should we do tonight?"

He smiles and finishes putting the rest of his books in the last box. "Well, there's not much we can do here, so I was thinking we could chill at your place," he says, taping the box he filled.

"Why don't we go get that pizza you suggested earlier? And then we can pick up some movies and head over to my house to watch them. We can make popcorn too!" I suggest. I don't feel like going out, but I'm so hungry that I think it would be a good idea to stop and get something to eat. Plus, that will save me from trying to cook something.

"Sounds good to me."

We jump in his truck and head over to the pizza place in town. After ordering, we sit in the booth and talk. At first, it's stupid stuff, but then he brings up Gunnar again. Why did I think we could get through this night without him bringing up my new boyfriend? Wow, I have a *boyfriend*. It's going to take some time getting used to saying that. Zane doesn't know that it's official, though, so I better tell him before he hears it from someone else.

"Well, he asked me to be his girlfriend, and I said yes. I really like him, Zane. Do you think I'm stupid for starting something with him this soon?" I can't help but ask. I need him to say he understands and is happy for me, but I also need him to tell me the truth.

"Well, it does seem a little fast. But, if it's what you want to do, what can I do to stop you? Doesn't mean I like it, though."

I smile. That's his way of saying he is not going to make it into a big deal. He may not like it, but he won't stop me.

"But if he hurts you, I will hunt him down and make him wish he was never born." Of course he would have to say something like that.

"Okay, *Dad*!" I scoff, like he is irritating me, but I secretly love the fact that he is acting so protectively. At least it shows he cares.

The rest of the night is amazing. After finishing our pizza, we rent a few DVDs, then head back to my house. We only talk about the good times we've had and everything we are looking forward to in the future. We eat popcorn, watch lots of movies, laugh, and even cry a little until he heads back over to his house around 4 a.m. I'm so glad we hung out tonight. It was like old times.

CHAPTER 5

As soon as I wake up Sunday morning, I send a text to Gunnar, letting him know I'm going to be busy for the next few days. I feel bad at first, but if he doesn't understand, then it's best to find that out now. Zane is a huge part of my life and always will be. Thankfully, though, Gunnar isn't upset and just tells me to message him when I could.

The weekend passes in a blur, and before I know it, it's Tuesday morning and I have to say goodbye to my best friend. Even though we spent the rest of the weekend together, I'm not ready for him to leave. I don't think I would ever be ready for that, but whether I like it or not, in an hour he'll be off to college and starting the rest of his life without me. I'm probably overreacting, but I hate the thought that after today, things may never be the same. Sure, I'll see him on holidays and maybe a couple times here and there in between, but it will never be the same.

Once I'm out of the shower, I put on a new purple summer dress and head downstairs to grab a bite to eat before I go to see Zane off. Gram is already at the kitchen table drinking a cup of tea. "Good morning, Gram. How are you feeling today?" I ask as I grab the orange juice out of the fridge and pour a small glass.

"Good morning, sweetheart. I'm feeling pretty good today. I slept real well last night."

After finishing my OJ and putting my cup in the sink, I give her a kiss on the cheek. "I'm heading over to see Zane before he leaves. Will you be coming over shortly to see him off?" I ask. I know she was talking about going over, but I'm not sure if she is still up to it. If not, I know Zane will come over before he hits the road to give her a hug.

"I'll be over before he leaves."

Nodding, I give her a small smile and head out the door.

I can already feel the tears forming in my eyes because this will be the last time that I run out of my house to go to his.

I need to get myself together though, I don't want today to be anything but smiles and well wishes. I just can't help thinking about my last goodbye to his brother. Even though I know deep down this is nothing like last time, it still feels final in a way. After today, Zane and I won't be the same. He's not going to be only a short walk and a door away anymore.

As I'm walking up his porch steps, the door opens and Zane storms out.

"Whoa, where's the fire, college boy?" I force out a laugh, but as soon as I get a good look at his face, my smile falls. "Zane, what's wrong?"

He grabs my arm as he walks past me without even breaking his stride. He doesn't stop till we are in his back yard. Letting go of my arm, he starts pacing back in forth. I have no idea what would have him this upset.

I don't say anything because I can tell he needs time to figure it out in his head before he talks. Finally, after what feels like hours, he stops in front of me with his head down. He runs his hands through his hair before raising his head. The look in his eyes is pure agony with a hint of anger. I have to turn away because it breaks my heart to see him like this. I still have no idea what happened, but I need to take a minute to gather my thoughts before I face at him again. Whatever is going on, I have a feeling it's really bad.

Once I meet his gaze again, I take his hand in mine. "What's going on?" I whisper. I don't have the strength to speak louder.

I know he hears me, though, because he squeezes my hand before answering. "It's nothing for you to worry about, Baby Girl. Just not seeing eye to eye with my parents." He blows out a breath and then runs his hand through his hair again. He must be all out of sorts because he only does that when he is really pissed off or upset.

"Talk to me. What don't you see eye to eye about?" I'm trying to figure out what would make them fight the day he leaves for college, but I'm coming up empty. I mean, they are thrilled he is going to the University of Texas and playing football. It's a great college, but they thought after Zeke died, that it would never happen. I also know he still isn't sure on what he wants to major in, but I don't see why that would upset them. Not everyone knows what they want to do when they go off to college. Sometimes you need to take some general classes before it hits you. I don't know what I want to do, though I'm pretty sure it will have something to do with art.

He hasn't answered me, and I can't figure out if that's good or bad. We are usually open about everything, though we haven't been lately with all the strain on our relationship. Maybe he doesn't feel like he can talk to me anymore. Regardless, I won't push him; I know that he'll talk to me about it when he is ready. I only want to be able to help him. "Anything I can do?" I ask after a couple minutes of silence. He understands this is my way of letting him know he doesn't have to tell me, but that I'm here for him.

"Nah, it's all good. They'll get over it," he says, and pulls me into him for a hug. "I'm going to miss you, ya know that?"

He kisses the top of my head, and suddenly I can't stop the tears. He thinks he'll miss me, but he has no idea what he means to me. I try to compose myself before I speak, because I don't want to make this worse for him. "I'm gonna miss you too. Who am I going to annoy now that you won't be here?" I say, trying to make him feel better with a joke.

He laughs and tickles my side before letting me go. "I'm sure you'll find someone."

Grabbing my hand, he leads me back over to the front of the house and takes me upstairs to his room. It looks so different, even from the last time I was up here. His desk has been cleaned of all his belongings and his bed is made up with two boxes sitting on top. No personal touches are left except a couple of motorcycle posters on the wall and some football and wrestling trophies on a shelf.

I walk over and sit on the edge of his bed. "When do your classes start?" He's told me before, but I need to hear him talk right now. The silence in the room is making me feel edgy.

He sits down next to me and lets out a long breath. "Next Monday."

I still don't understand why he needs to leave a week before his classes begin, but I suppose it would be good for him to get settled before everything gets busy. I want to be selfish and keep him here as long as possible. I know it wouldn't make a difference, because he's leaving no matter what, but at least I would have him here with me for a couple more days.

Zane turns toward me and takes hold of my hand. "You know I'll always be here for you, don't you, Baby Girl? Doesn't matter how far away I am; I'll always be there for you."

I look down and try to push the tears back, but I can feel them fall anyway. If I didn't know better, I would say this sounds like he is making his final goodbye. Like I won't ever see him again. I know that is nonsense, but it's the way I feel. My heart hurts so much I can't stop the sob that takes over me. He wraps me in his arms while whispering reassurances into my hair. He gently rocks me, running his hand up and down my back until I can pull myself together. It's while he is holding me in his arms, getting ready to say goodbye that I realize that I've truly fallen for him. There was never really a choice or anyway around it. I'm madly in love with Zane, and things are never going to be the same again. He's walking out the door today, and even though I know I'll always have him as a good friend, he'll never be mine. But even with this knowledge, I also know that no matter who I am with, I'll never feel for them what I feel for Zane.

I do my best to dry my tears so I can see him off. I can break when he's gone, but right now I need to show him I'm okay. If he knew how much it is killing me to watch him go, it would make it so much harder for him to leave. And he really needs to go, to live the life Zeke would want for him. I won't stand in the way of their dreams. I would rather live in hell for the rest of my life knowing that Zane is happy and doing what he and his brother wanted most, than hold him back so I don't lose him. When you love someone, sometimes you have to let them go.

I follow him down the stairs and out the door. We put the last two boxes in his truck, and make sure everything is secured in the back. My grandmother has just stepped outside, but before she can walk down the steps to come to him, Zane jogs up so he can say his goodbyes. I watch the exchange, but when I see Gram kiss his cheek I have to look away. Zane is such a big part of our lives, I know she will miss him dearly. After saying one last goodbye and giving her a final hug, he turns around and walks back to me. His parents aren't out here, but I'm sure they've already said their goodbyes this morning.

Once he reaches me, he pulls me in for one last hug. He's holding on to me so tight I can barely breathe, but I don't want him to ever let me go, even if it kills me. At least if I die right this second, it would be in his arms. He kisses the top of my head, gives me a final squeeze, and lets me go. I look up into his eyes and see something I've never seen before: desperation, but it's gone before I can think any more of it.

He leans down and presses his forehead against mine. With his eyes closed, he takes a deep breath and slowly releases it. His warm breath hits my face and sends chills down my back. "Take care of yourself, Baby Girl." Before I can answer him, he releases his hold on me and gets in his truck. I'm in a daze as I step back onto the sidewalk before he pulls away from the curb. I stand there until I can no longer see him, then drop into the grass and stare at my hands. He's gone.

I'm not sure how long I sit outside, but eventually I make my way into the house. I walk right past Gram and up to my room. As soon as I open my door, I strip out of my dress, grab my sleep shorts, and throw on an old shirt of Zane's. I grab Zeke's football and my phone before slipping under the covers.

I send a quick text to Gunnar to let him know I'm not feeling up to doing anything tonight and that I'll call him tomorrow. Before I turn my phone off, I type a message to Zane. One last goodbye.

Me: I miss you already…

CHAPTER 6

You'd think that staying in bed all day and feeling depressed would make the days tick by slowly. But instead, I woke up this morning and it was already Thursday and first day of my junior year. As soon as I opened my eyes, I knew today was going to be a horrible day. Not only have I not been able to sleep since Zane left, but also knowing I wouldn't be riding to school with him or even seeing him at some point today is almost enough to break me.

We haven't talked since he left except for his reply to my text that he would see me soon. And a couple hours later when he let me know he made it. I couldn't bring myself to reply, even though I probably should have. I thought I would need a couple days to get used to the idea of him not being here, but now it's Thursday and I still haven't replied. I need to get over it and call him already. I don't want him to know how much I'm suffering, or risk him thinking I don't miss him.

After getting out of the shower, I grab a pair of

cutoff shorts and a tank top, then slip on an old sweatshirt I stole from Zane last year. It's huge on me and almost covers all of my shorts so it looks like I'm not wearing anything underneath, but I don't give a damn; I want to have something of his with me today. I should care what I look like, since it's the first day of school and I'll see Gunnar at some point, but I can't bring myself to be concerned. I toss my hair up into a messy bun, throw on my tennis shoes, and run downstairs. As I'm pouring myself some OJ, my phone goes off.

My heart starts beating so fast I think it's going to jump right out of my chest. I run over to my bag to pull my phone out and unlock the screen, eager to get to my message. I'm not sure why I thought it was from Zane, but I am sorely disappointed when I see it is from Gunnar.

Gunnar: Good morning beautiful. I was wondering if I could pick you up for school…

Me: Good morning to you too. I wouldn't mind a ride if you are offering. What time will you be here?

I put my phone down to grab my OJ and put a bagel in the toaster for breakfast, but I barely manage to get across the kitchen before my phone is going off again.

Gunnar: I'm outside your house now ;)

Not sure if that should make me happy or a little

freaked out, I decide to go with the former. I type a quick reply that I'll be out soon and finish making my breakfast.

Once I have my bagel in hand, I give a quick wave to Gram and grab my book bag.

"Hey," Gunnar says and then leans in to kiss my cheek. That one action has me smiling and my mood lifting a little.

"Hey, yourself," I say as we walk to his truck. He opens my door and once I'm situated inside, he jogs over to his side and hops in. Before he pulls out onto the road, he leans over and kisses my lips softly.

"Mmm, this is what I've been missing for the past five days." I haven't seen Gunnar since the day he came over to take me to pick up my car. With trying to spend as much time as I could with Zane before he left, then saying goodbye to him, I didn't have the energy for anything else. I feel bad, but when I talked to Gunnar Wednesday morning, he assured me he understood.

"I've missed it too," I say shyly. This whole having a relationship deal is still new to me, but it feels nice. He grabs my hand and starts the drive to the school. He's able to navigate through town, heading in the right direction. I almost ask how he knows where he's going but dismiss it. I'm sure he's been there since moving here to fill out paperwork. Plus, this town is small. It wouldn't be hard to figure out even if he has never been there before.

Five minutes later, we are pulling into the parking lot. He finds a spot in the middle, then jumps out and walks over to my side. I've already got the door open and I've started to slip out when he grabs me by my waist. "I've got ya, babe." Once I've got both feet firmly on the ground, he leans in to give me a quick peck on my nose and closes the door. We both grab our bags and start the trek to the front doors of the school.

On the way, we pass a couple of the popular groups that hang out outside until the first bell rings. I'm usually not so self-conscious, but walking into the school with Gunnar has me feeling not so sure of myself. Maybe it's because this is the first year I'm without Zane by my side, or at least close by. Or it could be that I've never had a boyfriend before, so everything seems so weird. Whatever it is, I try not to let it get to me. I lift my chin and we continue on our way.

Once we are through the doors, I walk with Gunnar to the office to grab his schedule and locker arrangements.

"I'll see you at lunch, if not before?" he asks me.

I smile at him and nod. "I'll see you at lunch."

He leans in to give me a quick kiss before I walk down the hall to my locker. He sure likes to kiss a lot. I'm not sure yet if this bothers me or not, but I figure I'll get used to it. Feeling wanted by anyone besides my grandmother and Zane is new to me, so it will take time.

My first class of the day is English, so after dropping my bag off in my locker, I head that way. Since I don't have a lot of friends, I have no reason to delay getting to the classroom. At least this way I can try to get a seat in the back so I don't have to worry about being called on often.

I walk in, and thankfully there are only two other students there, who have both chosen seats in the front row. I don't know who they are except for their first names, and I really don't care. I accepted the fact early on that I don't need friends. I have people that I talk to every once in a while, and then there are a couple of girls that I hang out with at parties, but no one that I confide in or look forward to talking with. It makes choosing a spot much easier, since I don't have to try to save seats. My days in school are boring, but I'm not there to do anything but learn, so I don't care.

Ten minutes later, Mr. Murray starts class by doing roll call and handing out our books. He jumps right in to what he expects of us this semester. English isn't my favorite class, but it's one I excel in. I don't mind reading or writing papers, so when he tells us at the end of the semester we have to write a ten-thousand-word essay on a book from a list he gives us, it doesn't faze me.

Second period I have Phys Ed, third period is Geometry, and the last class before lunch is Chemistry. The morning goes surprisingly fast, which I'm grateful for. I'm a little nervous about meeting Gunnar at lunch, though I'm not sure why. I get to my locker and drop off my books. Then I head to the cafeteria. Once I'm in line, I spare a quick glance through the room to see if I can spot him. By the time I make it to the food I still haven't seen him, so I grab what food I want and head to the table outside, where I usually sit. I like eating outdoors whenever it's possible, since I'm inside all day.

I've barely sat down and started to open my soda when someone joins me at the table.

"Hey, Danielle. How has your first day been going?"

The guy is not someone I've talked with much before, but I've seen him around hanging with the rest of the football players at parties. Jaxon Reynolds is a quarterback, but has never seen any game time because Zane had been first string since his sophomore year. I'm really not sure why Jaxon is sitting by me, which makes me a little uncomfortable.

"Um, hey, Jaxon. I, uh, guess my day has been fine so far. H-How has your day been?" I have no idea what to say to him but don't want to be rude. Who knows, maybe this will be a year that I will come out of my shell and maybe even make some real friends.

"Well, it was going good, but recently tipped the scale to great," he says with a smirk that makes me think I'm missing something.

Not knowing what else to say, I nod. "That's good to hear." Then I go back to opening my soda and start picking at my food.

Thinking he'll just get up and leave, I don't pay him any more attention or say anything else, but a minute later he's still there. I look around to see if there is a group of his friends pointing and laughing like this is some dare he's been put up to, but I don't notice anyone even looking our way. I decide to let it go for now.

He asks me what classes I have this year, and

how softball was last season. I politely answer his questions, and since he asked me about softball, I ask how the start of the football season is going. I'm half-listening and half trying to decide if this is something that should concern me or not. Since he has never made an effort to socialize with me before, I feel like this is a big joke and the laugh is on me. As he's in the middle of telling me about how good he thinks the team will be this season, he looks up at something behind me and stops talking. He gets this confused expression on his face as he glances at me, and then at whatever caught his attention. Before I can turn around and see what he's looking at, someone wraps their arms around me. I stiffen at first because I'm not used to having anyone grab me like that, but then I remember Gunnar.

"Hey, beautiful," I hear him say close to my ear. I smile and turn toward him to return the greeting, but notice his attention isn't on me; it's on the person sitting across from me.

I don't think they have met each other yet, so I decide to introduce them. "Jaxon, this is Gunnar. He moved here from Florida. Gunnar, this is Jaxon. He's a senior as well."

After my awkward introduction, they still stare at each other, almost like they're sizing each other up. Like I said, I'm new to this whole relationship thing, but if I didn't know better I would say that Gunnar thinks Jaxon is stepping on his territory. I'll have to tell him later when we're alone that he doesn't have to worry about anyone trying to steal me away from him. I've been going to this school all my life and no one has ever shown any interest in me until he came along.

After a few more tense moments between the two, they finally seem to loosen up. "Hey, man, nice to meet you," Gunnar says. Then he sits down next to me and pulls me closer against him.

"Yeah, you too," Jaxon replies, as he looks at Gunnar and me like he's trying to figure us out. "Uh, how do you guys know each other if you're new here?"

Before I can answer him, Gunnar gives a small laugh. "We met about a week ago at a party out by the lake. I saw her and decided I better make my move. I wasn't sure if she was with anyone, but figured if she was, I would have to change that and claim her as mine. And have I told you lately how glad I am that I did, babe?" He finishes by looking down at me with a smile on his face.

I don't like the way this conversation is going, but I don't know if this is a normal thing for a guy to do when he sees another guy talking to his girlfriend. I wish I could ask Zane, but that's not going to happen. And I especially don't like the way Gunnar is staking a claim on me, like I'm a possession. I've seen plenty of guys go caveman on girls before, and it has never been something I thought I would want. Turns out, I was right. It makes me go from feeling wanted and cared for to ashamed and pissed off. I'll definitely be having a talk with him sooner rather than later. I don't want to become one of those girls that lets a guy control her; I've heard how relationships like that end. It starts off almost innocent, like this seems now, then turns controlling and in most cases becomes violent. There is no way I will let that happen to me.

Instead of answering, I give him a little smile and finish my sandwich. Lunch is almost over, and I want to get to my next class. "Well, I better get going. I'll see you later," I say as I stand.

He grabs my hand and stands with me. "What class do you have now?" he asks, pulling me closer to him.

"Uh, I think I have Government," I tell him. This day seems to be going from bad to worse. I just want to get to my next class so I can be over and done with this.

"I've got English with Ms. Liner, I think. Then I've got a free period, so if you want to skip out early, come find me," he says with a wink. I have no clue whether he is joking or not, but decide to not comment on it.

"Okay, well, I'll see you later. Nice talking with you, Jaxon," I throw over Gunnar's shoulder and walk toward the door to head back inside. But again, before I can get too far, Gunnar wraps his arms around my waist and pulls me back to him. I'm so surprised that I slam into his chest. He doesn't give me any time to recover before he grabs my face and kisses me. I'm too shocked to kiss him back, but he soon lets me go and walks away. I think I may start taking my lunch in the art room like I used to do before Zane got me to start sitting with him. At least that way I would be able to eat in peace and not have to worry about getting in the middle of a pissing contest that I have no interest being involved in. Maybe this whole relationship deal isn't for me, or maybe just not with Gunnar. I need time to think this through.

My last two periods are both in the art room. I have a free period, and instead of taking a study hall, I asked Mr. Tillman if he would be okay with me helping him out. He's always been my favorite teacher, and he has never had a problem with me. In fact, he has told me numerous times that I have an amazing talent and if there is anything I need, to let him know. So it came as no surprise that he was okay with letting me be his T.A.

Since art class isn't really a class with homework and most students use it as a free period anyway, there isn't much for me to do to help out around the classroom. Mr. Tillman says that I can use that time to work on my homework or draw. I figure at least until I know what the work load will be this year, I should take advantage of having extra time for my drawing. My free period bleeds into the next, and since I don't have to change classes, I continue at my easel in the corner of the room to get as much done on my drawing as possible.

Since I've been taking art since my freshman year, Mr. Tillman lets me draw whatever I want now. Sometimes I choose to do what he tells the other students to draw, but today I want to draw freehand. I've had a lot on my mind these last few months, and since I've been trying so hard to spend time with Zane this summer, I really haven't been able to draw much lately.

When I started this picture, I wasn't sure what it would turn out to be. I just let my pencil flow. When Mr. Tillman says to start clean up because class is almost over, I finally step back to look at what I have drawn. It's a bunch of lines and swirls around the edges, but as you get to the middle, you can make out the back of a truck. As I stare at it, I finally realize what it is: it's Zane driving away.

CHAPTER 7

Today was the last day of school before Thanksgiving break. In some ways, the time went at a slug's pace. I think the only reason it felt so slow was because I was counting down the months, weeks, and then days before Zane would be home again. He hasn't been back since the day he left, and we barely get to talk on the phone. Mostly, I get short text messages asking how I am doing, how Gram is feeling, how things are going with Gunnar, and if he is treating me okay. Since I don't want to get into my relationship, I keep my answers short and turn them around on him. Though when I ask how college life is going, I get one word answers like "good" or "fine".

Then when I ask about football and when I can come see one of his games, he quickly changes the subject. It seems the only time he talks about football is when I ask if he is coming home or if I can visit him. He'll say that he is too busy with practices and training that he can't come home or that I shouldn't make the trip because he won't be able to spend time with me. I'm not sure if it's because Zeke isn't there and maybe his emotions are all over the place when it comes to football, or maybe he really is busy, but it's like he's trying to keep me away. It doesn't sound like football is as important to him anymore, but it is always there as an excuse when he needs one. I hope that's not the case, because it's the one thing that should make him feel closer to his brother.

My relationship with Gunnar has been touch and go since school started. I find myself ignoring him more often than not, and I've noticed that he has gotten more arrogant and aloof as the days pass. When we do hang out, I long for the way we were that first night we met. Conversation came easy, and I could feel that he cared about me. Now, it seems like it's all a front. I want to ask him what we are doing, but I'm scared to hear the answer. Even though I don't feel for him what I probably should or wish I did, I fear that he will tell me he doesn't want me, and it will cut me deep to hear that yet another person I've gotten close to feels that way. Like I'll never be good enough to keep or stay with.

I am just getting in the door from school when I hear my cell phone ping, but before I can check out the text message, it starts ringing. Gunnar.

"Hello?" I answer as I start walking into the kitchen to grab an apple.

"Hey, beautiful. What are you doing tonight?"

Not really in the mood to go out, I try coming up with a viable excuse. "Um, well, I have to clean up the house and get ready to make pies for tomorrow." That is better than telling him I don't want to hang out with him.

If it were Zane asking me, I would drop everything to spend time with him. I thought after a while I would stop comparing or dropping Zane into scenarios where Gunnar and I were concerned, but Zane is still all I can think about. I know it's not fair to Gunnar, but Zane is my everything. I only wish I could tell him that and have him return those feelings.

"Can't your grandma do that? There's a party tonight." There's always a party he wants to go to. But since Zane is no longer here, parties just aren't the same for me. I end up sipping on one drink, wishing I was at home or that Zane would walk up with a bottle of Jack for us to share like he always did. But then I remember he's away at college and I feel the crushing grief of him not being here all over again. The pain hasn't lessened even a little since I watched him drive away.

"You know she hasn't been feeling well lately. I'm sorry, but I can't go," I say, irritated. He should know by now that Gram is more important to me than anything else, and I have been taking on a lot more to make things easier for her. I shouldn't even have to explain it; it's a given. Zane would never question me when it comes to my grandmother. Maybe it is time to break it off with Gunnar. With all the thoughts in my head still about Zane, what we are doing feels like a charade. It's not real, and it's not going anywhere. It would be better for both of us to end it.

"Yeah, okay, whatever. I guess I'll just talk to you later." I can tell he's pissed, but what's new?

"Bye, Gunnar," I say into the phone, but I barely get that out before the line goes dead.

I don't want to ruin this Thanksgiving break for either of us, so I decide to wait till we get back to school to have a talk with him. Sit down and explain to him that it would probably be better if we were only friends. Maybe then we can go back to the carefree relationship we had at the beginning. He really is a great person, but he's not who I want to be with romantically. Not like we have done anything more than make out, even though he's tried. I haven't told him I'm a virgin, but he must know. Every time his hands wander, I pull back from him. I can tell he gets upset, but he's gentleman enough not to push or say anything.

After I take my bag up to my room and eat my apple, I run downstairs to check in with Gram. She has felt under the weather lately, but she won't go to the doctor. She's sleeping more than usual, and whenever she is doing something more than sitting, she gets short of breath. I'm no doctor, but even I know this is more than a cold or old age. I just need to convince her of that.

"Hey, Gram, I'm going to start making the pies for tomorrow. Then I'll clean up. Do you need anything before I get started?"

She's in her chair in the sitting room with her latest cross stitching project. Without even looking up, she says, "No, sweetheart, I'm fine. Would you like help with the pies?"

I'm not the best cook, but these pies should be pretty simple. I don't think there is much room to go wrong when I have her recipes. "I got it, you just relax. I'll bring your dinner in later."

By the time I finish making one apple and two pumpkin pies, get supper done, and then clean up the kitchen, it is past ten. I jump in the shower and put on my yoga pants and a tank top, then lie on my bed to draw a little. Except for what I draw in art class, I haven't done much else lately. I forgot how relaxing it can be, and a great way to free my mind when I have so much going on. Tonight is no different. I just clear my head and put my pencil to paper and let go.

When I'm done, I finally look at what I have drawn: a girl facing away from me with long, dark hair. Leaves are falling all around her, and down the road, you can see a bright red door. Flowing out of her hair are birds, flying away. It's a picture of the girl walking away from what she's known, and going toward the door that leads into the unknown. And the birds signify that she's letting go of all her shame, all her hurt, all of her hopes. If someone were to look at this picture, they'd probably say the girl is sad and it's depressing. But when I look at it, it looks like freedom.

After I put all my drawing stuff away, I get under the covers and check the time on my phone. I see a text notification. Between talking to Gunnar, making pies, and cleaning, I forgot I got a message earlier. It's from Zane. With a smile on my face, I open it up to see what he has to say, but as I read the message, my smile fades.

Zane: Hey Baby Girl. I hate to do this, but I won't be able to make it home for

Thanksgiving. We have extra practices with big games coming up. I'm so sorry…

He's not coming home? I don't care if they have state championships the day after Thanksgiving, I need him here. I haven't seen him since the day he left. I hoped with him home, I'd finally start feeling like myself again and things would be clearer. I wipe the tears I didn't even know I was shedding, and pull up my contacts to call him. It rings five times before going to voicemail. "Hey…I just got your message. You really can't come home? Even for a day? I really miss you…I need to see you. Call me when you can, please."

I hang up the phone and stare at the ceiling. Knowing he won't be here this weekend, I doubt I'll be able to sleep. The nightmares will come tonight; I can feel them already sneaking up on me.

Since Zeke died, whenever I'm upset about something, they come. It started out with reliving my grandmother telling me about Zeke and the funeral, but then they progressed into my fear of losing Zane. It happens differently every time; sometimes instead of Zeke, it's Zane who went overseas and I'm getting news that he died. Or Zane tells me he doesn't want me and I watch him walk away. Sometimes it's a combination of the day he left for college and losing him the way we lost Zeke. It doesn't matter what scene takes place in those dreams, the outcome is always the same. Me, alone, feeling broken and unwanted.

Ten minutes into my staring contest with the ceiling, my phone pings. I quickly grab it, hoping it's Zane.

Zane: Can't talk right now, in a study group.

A study group at midnight? And on the night before a holiday…if I didn't know better, I would think that he's making excuses and lying to me, but he would never do that to me. Would he?

Me: Study group this late?

Zane: Yeah, we've got a project due for a class the first day back from break, that's why I can't make it home.

Me: I thought you couldn't make it home because you had football practice…

His reply doesn't come for a couple minutes. I worry I've upset him, but I can't find it in myself to care. If he is lying to me, it would be the first time. And the fact that he felt he couldn't just tell me the truth hurts worse than if he would've said he doesn't want to come home. Sure, that would hurt like hell too, but lying to me…that's a knife to my heart.

Zane: Look, I have practice AND a big project due. I shouldn't have to explain myself to you like you're my mother. I said I can't make it home, end of story.

I can't believe he's talking to me like this. Even

when he's been at his worst, he has never taken anything out on me. The way he's being right now makes me want to throw my phone or drive to where he's at and throat punch him. Then the beeping of my phone brings me out of thoughts of violence.

Zane: I'm sure you'll be busy enough with your boyfriend anyway. Look, I have to get back, I'll talk to you later.

I think about what he said and how I should reply. It's not only that he seems to be ignoring me, but he's upset that I'm dating Gunnar. He doesn't know that I'm ending it with him, but that doesn't mean anything. I've always put Zane before Gunnar, even though he isn't here. There's no reason he should be like this toward me.

I give up. I'm done being the only one trying to keep our friendship on track. I'm done with feelings of hurt and disappointment. I slowly type out my response. Then I stare at it long and hard before hitting the send button.

Me: I get it, Zane. I hope practice and your project go well...I'll leave you alone from now on. By the way, I broke up with Gunnar.

I turn my phone off without waiting for a response. Instead of burying myself under my covers, I decide to go to the party Gunnar mentioned. Since it's a warm night, I slip on my jean skirt and change into a black tank top. I head into the bathroom to fix my hair and put on some make-up. Since I'm in a dark mood, I use a heavier hand with my eye shadow, eye liner, and mascara. I put my hair in a messy pony tail and give it more volume. Once finished in the bathroom, I sit on my bed and put on my black combat boots.

I quietly walk down the stairs so I don't wake Gram, and get in my car. I don't need to call Gunnar to ask where the party is; they are always at the lake. Tonight, I'm going to drown everything I'm feeling in a bottle of Jack.

***

The first thing I notice when I arrive at the party is that there are more people than I expected. Considering how late it is and that it's the night before Thanksgiving, I assumed that nobody would be here. Not that it matters; I'm here for one thing and one thing only: Jack Daniels.

I head right over to the table where the drinks are usually set up. I hope there is still something left since the party has been on for a few of hours now.

I pass a couple kissing by the fire, another stumbles over to the vehicles, and there's a group of guys from the football team huddled around the keg. That sight alone makes me smile. That hasn't changed since Zane left; you can always count on the football players guarding the keg. When I used to come to parties here with Zane, I would hang with him and his friends on the team before branching off to sit with some girls. But most of them graduated when he did, leaving Jaxon the only one who I've spent some time with.

I spot a half bottle of Jack, so I grab it and then walk over to the guys by the keg. When I'm a few feet away, I notice Jaxon has spotted me and has a look in his eye that would normally make me want turn and run, afraid of what caused it, but I hold his stare and continue forward. I'm not sure where my confidence and attitude are coming from, but I kind of like it. Maybe I've found the new me. Kickass, take-no-prisoners Danielle.

He intercepts me before I make it all the way to the group. "I take it someone told you," he says when he reaches me.

"Why else would I be here?" I reply. Not like I would need someone to tell me about a party to show up, but I suppose it helps.

He puts his hand on my shoulder and gives me a look of apology. "I'm sorry, Danielle. I tried to reason with him, but I think he is too drunk to know better."

Looking at him in confusion, I try to laugh it off. "What are you talking about, Jax?"

He lowers his hand from my shoulder and shakes his head. "Wait, you're not here because someone told you about Gunnar?"

What would Gunnar have anything to do with my being here? Sure we're dating, but he isn't the only reason I would come to a party. "Tell me about what? Gunnar called me earlier to tell me about the party. I wasn't going to come, but I finished what I had to do at home so I decided to show up to have a couple drinks."

He doesn't say anything for a few seconds, and

the look he is giving me is a look of confusion, anger, and pity.

"What's going on, Jaxon?" There has to be something more to this.

He runs his hand through his hair and gives a nervous chuckle. "Uh…nothing. Just didn't know you were coming. Gunnar said you weren't, is all."

"Jax, spit it out already. I know something is going on, and if you don't tell me, I'll find someone who will."

I turn to walk away, but he grabs my hand to stop me. "Look, Danielle, I thought you already knew. I don't want to be the one to tell you, but you should know."

I wait for him to continue, but he says nothing. I go to walk away again, but he pulls me back. "Just say it, Jaxon!" On top of everything else I've dealt with tonight, I don't need to add any more. Everyone wants to beat around the bush instead of being straight with me. I'm sick of it.

"Okay, okay…Gunnar, he uh…he left with Sophie." He doesn't say anymore.

So what if he left with Sophie? I would rather have him catch a ride home than…Wait. He left with Sophie… "As in…he left with her to get a ride home or…" I don't finish. I think I already know the answer.

"Exactly." I can tell Jaxon is upset on my behalf, but surprisingly, I'm not. I don't know if it's because I'm already feeling numb inside from my conversation with Zane, or because I was planning on breaking up with Gunnar after Thanksgiving anyway. Regardless, it doesn't bother me.

I start laughing, which makes Jaxon look at me like I'm losing it. Maybe I am, but I don't care. Finally, I calm down enough to speak. "Look, Jaxon, I can tell you are upset for me, and I appreciate it, really. But it's okay. *I'm* okay."

This has him staring at me like I'm certifiably crazy. "You're okay with the fact that your *boyfriend* left with another *chick* and is doing *God knows what* right now with her?"

Having him break it down for me out loud should have me flinching or at least making me want to cry, but I feel nothing.

"I was going to break up with him anyway. So he can do whatever he wants. I'm fine, really. Let's just drink and have a good time, all right?" I sidestep him and head over to the rest of the guys. I don't really talk to any of them except Jaxon since that first day of school when he plopped himself down across from me at lunch, but I don't care. I came here to have a good time, and what better way to do that than to lose myself with a bunch of football players and have a few drinks?

I no longer feel like I need to get wasted, but I can still have a good time and drink socially. In a way, hanging with the football players makes me feel closer to Zane. Closer than I've felt to him in a long while. So tonight is going to be about reminiscing about the good old days, and thinking about me for once. I'm not going to worry about my grandmother, what I'm going to do with Gunnar, or missing Zane. Tonight is about me, myself, and I for a change. Everything else can wait till tomorrow.

CHAPTER 8

It's early afternoon when I finally get out of bed and head downstairs. My grandmother is in the kitchen slowly moving around and making the stuffing before putting our small turkey in the oven. When she looks up, I see her smile. "Morning, sweetheart. You look happy today." She winks at me before resuming her preparations for our Thanksgiving dinner.

I guess I am happy, or at least happier than I have been the last couple months. After the revelations of last night, I feel lighter almost. Maybe I should feel down and depressed or even pissed off that Gunnar most likely cheated on me last night, but I don't. I feel relieved that now I have a viable reason to end our relationship. Though I would have ended it anyway, I think it will go smoother now that there is a reason. To be honest, he was probably thinking the same thing, and that's why he cheated.

Since it's always just my grandmother and myself, we don't have to make a lot, but we make plenty to stuff ourselves to the max for dinner and have plenty of leftovers. Thank goodness I made the pies yesterday, otherwise it would be hell getting it all done after I slept in. I didn't drink too much, but I stayed out till five this morning joking and talking to Jaxon. He really is a nice guy. I think we will be good friends.

With the turkey in the oven, we don't need to do anything until we make the potatoes, green bean casserole, gravy, and the dinner rolls about an hour before the turkey is done. I tell Gram to sit down and relax, then head upstairs for a quick shower before cleaning the rest of the house.

After everything is cleaned, I get everything set up for the rest of our dinner, then sit in the living room to watch the Macy's Thanksgiving Parade. It's a tradition that Gram and I do every year. I love watching all the floats and listening to the different kinds of music. It makes me feel happy, no matter what mood I wake up in. I can always count on the parade lifting my spirits.

I decide to take the pie I made for the Hendricks' over to their house before finishing dinner; that way I won't have to worry about it later. We always make a pie for them on Thanksgiving. Gram taught me that this holiday is about giving, and what better thing to give than a yummy pie? I know it's going to be weird going over there without Zane, but I'll get over it.

With the pie in hand, I walk to the door, but Gram stops me. She says she could use the fresh air and will take it over instead.

"Okay, Gram, I'll finish dinner while you're

gone." I hand her the pie and return to the kitchen. Once everything is in the oven, I head upstairs to change into a new dress I bought for today. It may be silly since no one will be coming over, but I want to look nice. I usually wear a dress for all our holiday dinners, whether it's just us here or we have guests over. It feels right to do so on special occasions.

As I turn to walk out of my room, I spot the football Zeke left. I should have given it to Zane after Zeke died, but I wanted to keep something of his for myself. I know that was selfish, but it's the only thing I have of his except for a couple of old shirts. This football is more personal, though, and it was something he specifically gave to me to hold on to.

I walk over and hold it in my hands. I remember all the times the three of us played catch, and all the times I watched the boys play a friendly game of tag football in their back yard. Those days were the happiest I'd ever been. I had a best friend and a big brother. But those days are long gone, and I'll never have that feeling back. With a heavy heart, I put the football back where it was on my shelf and head downstairs to check on the food.

***

Dinner was delicious, as always. There's something about Thanksgiving that I love; it could be the food, or maybe it's the fact that I have my grandmother to be thankful for. Being here with her all these years has been great. I can't say that I wish

I didn't have my parents with me, because who knows, maybe if my mother hadn't died, or my father hadn't walked out on me, my life would have been different—perfect, even. Or maybe things happened the way they were supposed to. Let's face it, it could have been worse. I could have been placed in foster care and ended up with strangers. Instead, I got to grow up with a family member who loves me. Even though when I was young I was resentful that I didn't get to do some activities or go places the other kids got to, now that I'm older, I appreciate the little things like helping my grandmother do yard work, working in the kitchen with her, and listening to her tell me bedtime stories. Those memories are priceless, so yeah, I have a lot to be thankful for.

I finish cleaning the kitchen, tell Gram goodnight, and head up to my room for a hot bath. After last night and a day full of cooking, I could use a nice long soak.

While I'm sitting in the water, I close my eyes and try to clear my head, but I keep thinking about Gunnar and Zane. It's like a broken record going back and forth, skipping between the two: how much I miss Zane and where things are going with Gunnar. I can't believe that I haven't heard from him yet. I thought someone would tell him I showed up at the party after he left, or that he would feel guilty about what he did. It's possible it was all innocent, but I find that hard to believe. Jaxon said they were pretty cozy even before they left the party. I'm almost one hundred percent positive something happened. They may not have had sex, but it was far from innocent. Not like it matters; we were doomed from the beginning. Which brings me back to Zane. I thought my feelings for him would have diminished, but they seem stronger than ever.

I get out of the bath, grab a pair of panties and a tank top, then plop down on my bed. I reach for my phone to see if I might have missed a call or text from Gunnar, but realize I never turned it back on after I sent that last message to Zane. Shit, maybe he *has* been trying to get in touch with me all day and I didn't even know it.

As I turn my phone on, there's suddenly a sound at my window. It almost sounds like the glass is cracking or a tree branch has hit it. I look outside and stay quiet to see if it happens again. After a moment, I hear it, but this time I can tell it's a rock being thrown at my window. It must be Gunnar. If he tried calling me and I never answered, he probably decided to come over to see what was going on. I was planning to wait to end things with him, but I suppose the sooner I can get it over with, the better.

I open the window, and lean out to tell him I'll be out in a minute. It takes my eyes a couple seconds to adjust, but once they do, I'm stunned to see who is staring back up at me. I almost fall out. "Zane? What are you doing here?" Am I dreaming? I can't believe after all these months and the excuses for not being able to make it home, he's here. Outside my bedroom.

"Hey…can I come up?"

I'm so shocked that he's here that before I can answer, he's walking around to the front of the house. He's no stranger to sneaking in. We used to do that a lot after Zeke died and I was having nightmares. He would sneak over, and we would stay up all night talking so neither of us had to go to sleep, afraid of what we would see in our dreams. Then, when I finally passed out, he would hold me till the early hours of the morning before he'd sneak back out.

I am still at the window when I hear the door open. He closes it and stares at me with a look I can't quite place. I glance down and notice that I'm only in my panties and tank top, so I rush to my dresser for some sweatpants. Zane has seen me in almost every state of dress or undress except complete nakedness over the years, but tonight it feels more intimate somehow. Or maybe it's the fact that I haven't seen him for months that makes me suddenly nervous around him.

We stare at each other across my room for what feels like hours, but in actuality, it's probably only a couple of seconds. Finally, I find my voice. "W-what are you doing here?" I can't figure out why he came back after he made such a big deal that he couldn't make it. Did he send a text to let me know plans had changed and I didn't see it because my phone was off? I feel like I should pinch myself, like I'm dreaming he is here with me. But if I'm dreaming, I don't want to wake up, because then he will be gone.

"Well, after your last text last night, I tried messaging you back to see what was going on. You said you and what's his name weren't together anymore, so I wanted to make sure you were okay.

But you never answered me, and then when I called, your phone was off."

I forgot I had told him that I was breaking up with Gunnar. "Wait a minute. You mean to tell me that you came all this way because I told you I broke up with Gunnar and then didn't answer you after you pretty much bitched me out for asking why you couldn't come home?" Why would that warrant a trip home? Especially since he said he had so much going on that he couldn't make it.

"I don't get it. You told me you had practice and a project so you weren't coming. Then all of a sudden, I tell you I broke things off with Gunnar and turned my phone off so I could forget about everything for a night and have fun. You try to get ahold of me, and when you can't, you decide to rush to the rescue?" It's actually kind of sweet that he would drop everything to make sure I was okay. "Ya know what, forget it, it doesn't really matter why you came back, I'm just glad I finally get to see you. How long are you staying?" I don't have any plans for tomorrow because I hate going Black Friday shopping. I would rather stay away from all the crazies and not lose any sleep.

"I'm only here to make sure you're okay. I have to go back tonight, Baby Girl." He says this like it's causing him physical pain.

"You drove all this way to make sure I was alright and then you're going to leave again? But you just got here!" I turn away so he can't see the tears that I know are coming. I've missed him so much, and now that he's here with me, I'm not sure I can watch him drive away again. It's going to hurt worse than the first time I had to watch him walk out of my life. The only difference is now I know things are different, and going off of the way things have been the last few months, this could be the very last time I see him.

I hear him come up behind me. Then his arms slide around my waist and he turns me around. "Don't cry, Baby Girl. I can't stand it when you cry," he whispers into my hair as I let the floodgates open and stain his grey shirt with my tears.

I'm not sure how long we stand there, me crying and him rubbing small circles on my back while murmuring assurances, before I finally get ahold of myself enough to look up at him. What happens next comes out of nowhere. I have no explanation and I could not tell you who leaned in first, but the next thing I know, my arms are around his neck and his are so tight around my waist that I guarantee there will be bruises in the shape of his fingertips tomorrow. I don't care, though; I want his mouth on mine. I have dreamed of kissing him, but even my wildest fantasies don't come close to this.

He walks me backwards toward my bed without breaking the kiss. I feel lightheaded from our connection or it could be that we hadn't come up for air yet. Either way, I wasn't going to complain. If I died right now, I would be happy.

Suddenly, we are falling back onto my bed. Fuck oxygen! I don't need to breathe when I have Zane kissing me like this.

He is the first one to break the connection, but it isn't long before he moves his lips down my neck. "Please don't leave me," I beg. If he leaves tonight,

I think I may die, because not only is he here with me, he's making all my dreams come true with a couple strokes of his tongue.

He doesn't answer me with words, but his actions are enough. He kisses down my neck, across my collarbone, and up the other side of my face. God, his mouth is magic. I feel like I could come from his kisses alone.

His hands are still in safe areas, but fuck, I want him to touch me everywhere. I want to strip him of his clothes slowly, and feel all the ridges of his abdomen with my hands and then my tongue. I want him to make love to me. The thought alone should scare me, or at least make me nervous, but it doesn't. I'm ready, and I want him to be my first—my only.

He makes his way back up to my mouth, but his hands are slowly moving down. His finger slips under my shirt, and he draws tiny circles on my stomach. He's driving me crazy, and he's barely touched me. I turn my head to the side to catch my breath, but grab his hand to move it up toward my chest while keeping the skin on skin contact. He hesitates for only a second before he starts to massage my naked breast, then runs his fingernail over my nipple. I gasp at the feeling that travels down my stomach to my core. Fuck, I'm so close to coming.

He lifts his head and looks at me with hooded eyes. "Fuck, you're so beautiful."

I reach out for him and run my hands up under his shirt. Holy shit, his chest feels better than I had imagined. I've seen it a million times, but touching him like this is unbelievable. I move my hands back down to the bottom of his shirt, and push them up gradually. "Please, take it off." I don't even recognize my own voice. It's thick with lust and desire.

I don't have to tell him twice. He leans back on his knees, reaches one hand behind his neck and pulls it off. His muscles flex in a way that has my mouth watering. He throws the shirt on the floor and reaches to take mine off. His eyes meet mine like he's asking permission. I nod slowly and bite my lip. That draws his eyes to my mouth and makes his eyes heat. Before I know it, my shirt is ripped off and thrown somewhere behind him, then he's on me again. I cradle him between my legs while he has one hand on my breast and the other fisted in my hair, pulling me into another dizzying kiss.

I can feel his hard length pressing into my core and it feels so good I let out a long, dragged-out moan. "Oh, God." I rock my hips to meet him, which causes his grip in my hair to tighten almost painfully.

"Fuck, baby, you feel so fucking good." He moves his head down and latches his hot mouth on my nipple. His teeth scrape against it with the right amount of pleasure and pain.

His hand slides down my side and inside my panties. *Oh my God, yes, please touch me!* He doesn't disappoint. I feel the tip of his finger make contact with my clit first, then he starts to slowly rub in small circles. I've never touched myself before, so the feelings his fingers are bringing out in me are overwhelming to say the least, but in a good way.

I start to move my hips in rhythm with his movements, making the sensation triple in strength. Oh shit, this feels so good.

Zane moves his hand further into my panties, then brings the tip of his finger to my entrance. He slowly starts to push inside until I let out a loud moan. Hearing that, Zane starts to pump into me faster, then adds another finger. I feel so full and complete with him inside me, though I wish it were something else instead of his fingers.

Not wanting to be the only one feeling this good, I slip my hands down his pants. I must be bolder with the pleasure flowing through my veins. I start to stroke him, causing him to curse, then pick up speed with his fingers.

"I'm gonna come, Zane. Oh my God, it feels so good, please don't stop!" He makes a sound that's a cross between a moan and a growl, and it's so sexy I think the sound alone makes me come.

As my orgasm starts, he lets go of my nipple and drowns my screams in his mouth. It feels like a live wire is connected to my lower limbs and fireworks are going off behind my eyelids. He slows his thrusting fingers, but doesn't stop kissing me.

I can't believe I just had my first orgasm. Not only my first orgasm, but it was given to me by Zane. It's lame, but the only thing that keeps running through my head is that dreams really do come true.

My body goes slack and our kiss slows. "That was the hottest thing I've ever seen," he says breathlessly as he pushes hair out of my face. I should probably feel disgusting with my hair soaked with sweat, and embarrassed with his fingers still inside me, but the way he's looking at me, I don't even care.

We both catch our breath, and he rolls over to lie down beside me, my hand slipping out of his pants from the movement. My heart rate finally gets back to its normal pace and I turn on my side to look at him. Out of the corner of my eye, I can see he's still hard.

"Did you come?" Even though I had my hand wrapped around his cock, I have no idea if he finished or not, I was so caught up in my own pleasure.

He softly chuckles and shakes his head. "Unbelievably, no. I thought you were going to unman me there for a minute, though."

I'm not sure if that's a good or bad thing. "I'm sorry?" I roll onto my back and close my eyes. It's embarrassing enough that I had my first orgasm when we didn't even have all of our clothes off, but to add insult to injury, he didn't even come. Was it not good enough? Was *I* not good enough?

He interrupts my inner battle with myself by turning onto his side and gently caresses my face. "Hey. What's the matter?"

What do I say? This is so new to me, but it feels wrong that I got off and he didn't. Don't guys get pissed if they don't get their rocks off too? I'm not sure how this is supposed to work; it's so frustrating. I want to lie in my afterglow and share it with him, not worry that I did something wrong. "What's going on in that gorgeous head of yours?"

I look into his eyes and see they don't look upset. "Did I do something wrong? I mean…for you not to, uh, for you not t-to get off?"

He looks at me like I've grown two heads. "Are you kidding me? It felt so fucking good I was worried I was going to come in my pants."

I still don't get it. "So why didn't you? Didn't you want to come?"

I try to keep my eyes on him, but I'm too embarrassed. He doesn't let me stop, though. "Look at me, Danielle. Yes, I wanted to come, but I wanted to watch you lose control more. It was the sexiest thing I have ever seen, so I wasn't even thinking about myself."

I consider what he said, and then come up with a plan.

I sit up and put my hands on his shoulders to push him back onto the bed. He opens his mouth to say something, probably to ask what the hell I'm doing, but I put my finger to his lips, silencing him. "Shhh…I want to do this for you." I don't let him answer; I just kiss him, then work my way past his collarbone, spend a little time playing with his nipple, then kiss down toward his stomach.

"Danielle…"

I start to unbutton his pants. He must be too stunned to speak, because before he can even get words out, I have his cock out of his pants and in my hand.

His head drops back as I start to stroke him again. I take the time while he isn't paying attention to me to get a good look at what he's been hiding in his pants. I've never seen a guy's penis before, but

Zane's could be a work of art. I almost want to get my drawing pad out and capture it on paper, it's so gorgeous.

I'm not really sure what I should be doing; I just keep stroking him, long and hard. If the grunts and his heavy breathing mean anything, I think I'm going a pretty good job. But I want to make him lose control, like he made me.

I glance up and notice he still has his eyes closed, so I use that to my advantage and lower my mouth to his cock. There's a drop of moisture at his tip, so I run my tongue along the top to see what he tastes like, taking him by surprise.

"Oh fuck!"

Now I have his full attention. His eyes are no longer closed, but staring heavily at me. Holding his stare, I run my tongue around the top of his cock, then take him fully into my mouth. He hisses, and I'm not sure if it's in pain, so I pull up to make sure he's okay.

"Oh God, don't stop. Fuck, please don't stop."

Loving how I've reduced him to begging, I enthusiastically take him back into my mouth, but he's so big, I have to adjust. When I have him all the way in the back of my throat, I thank God I don't have much of a gag reflex, because that wouldn't be sexy at all.

"Oh fuck yeah, baby."

Hearing that he likes it makes me get more creative. I've never given a blowjob before, but I've read enough books that I should be able to make it good for him. I reach down and massage his balls and start to work my mouth in a twisting motion while hollowing out my checks to get better suction.

He tangles his hands in my hair. "Shit, Danielle that feels so fucking good."

I speed my pace up a bit and bring my other hand around to work the bottom of his shaft, adding a couple turns to my strokes. He grips my hair harder and starts pumping his hips. "Fuck, I'm going to come."

He goes to pull away, but I really want to taste him, so instead I suck him harder. I remove my hand and take him as deep as I can.

"Fuck, baby, you need to stop or I'm going to come in your mouth."

I push him all the way to the back of my throat and try to swallow him whole.

"Fuuucccckkkk!" he shouts softly. I feel warm, salty liquid hit the back of my throat, so I swallow again, which makes him growl. "Shit! Fuck, Danielle!"

A couple more spurts hit the back of my throat before I feel him soften in my mouth. I lick him clean, then sit back and look up to see he's got his arm over his eyes and is breathing heavily. Not bad for my first blow job, I think. I crawl up beside him and cuddle into his side.

"Holy shit, where did you learn to do that? Wait, don't answer."

I don't really want to tell him it was my first time, but the way it sounds, it may ease his thoughts. "I've never done it before," I say quietly, still a little embarrassed, but happy that he seemed to have enjoyed it so much.

We don't say anything for a while. We only lie

there, side by side. I yawn and snuggle closer to him.

"Go to sleep, Baby Girl."

I want to stay up and spend this moment with him, but I can barely keep my eyes open. Before I drift off to sleep, I hear him say, "I love you, but I can't lose you." I fall asleep before I can decide whether I heard him right or if it was just my imagination.

CHAPTER 9

I wake up lying on my stomach with the sun warming my back and the covers tangled around my feet. I reach my hand out behind me, but feel nothing but cold sheets. My head snaps up, seeing nothing but an empty bed where Zane was only a few hours ago. I look around my room and over toward my bathroom door, thinking maybe he's taking a shower, but the door is open and the light is off. Where is he? Would he have gone downstairs?

I sit up and grab my phone when I see a note lying underneath it. I pick both up, check the time quickly and see it is a little after noon, and then open the letter.

Danielle,

I don't know what to say besides I'm sorry. Last night shouldn't have happened. You are my best friend, and I have no excuse for what came over me. I hope you don't hate me and that what *happened doesn't ruin our friendship. I had to head back to school, but I'll call you later. I'm sorry...*

    Zane

He regrets what happened last night. What I thought was a turning point for us was nothing but a mistake for him. Tears slip down my face, but I don't even care enough to lift my hand to wipe them away. I can't believe that what we shared meant so little to him. I thought watching him leave again would hurt, but my heart feels like it's broken into a million pieces and someone set fire the remains. I should have known better than to think that my dreams were coming true, that destiny was finally going to make up for the shit life has thrown me.

I don't know how I'm going to get over this. It was hard enough being around him when I knew I had feelings for him, but now actually getting a taste of what I so badly wanted and having it taken away, I feel like I'm dying inside. No, death would be too easy; I'm being tortured.

I fall back onto my bed and push the letter under my pillow. I want to keep it as a reminder to myself that he'll never want me. Last night was a mistake. Our emotions got the best of us and one thing lead to another. No matter what I feel for him, he will never feel the same way. I don't know how I am going to act like nothing happened; I'll have to pull my big girl panties on and get over it. Or at least pretend I'm okay until I'm behind closed doors. That should be easy enough considering I have done a lot of pretending in my life. It's either that or the alternative, not having him in my life at all, and I'm not sure I can handle that.

***

When I got back to school after Thanksgiving break, I pulled Gunnar aside and told him it wasn't working between us. I never mentioned I found out about him and Sophie and he didn't say anything either. I think deep down he knew this was coming regardless of what happened between them. He didn't argue with me or even ask me to reconsider, he just said that he understood and hoped we could still be friends. What is it with guys and saying "Let's still be friends?" Regardless, I told him I'd really like that and left it. I didn't want to get into an argument or go into detail with him; I only wanted to move on with my day and get through the rest of the school year.

I didn't go to any more parties, and I barely left my room. Gram kept asking if I was all right, but finally gave up when I would say I was fine. She knew there was something wrong, but figured I would talk about it when I was ready. I never wanted to talk about what happened between me and Zane, though. I was stuck between wanting to forget it ever happened and wanting to relive those few moments over and over again when he was mine.

It took us a while to get back to even a fraction of the friendship we had before, but we're slowly getting there. It will never be the same, but I've found that I'm becoming even better at pretending. We never talked about that night, just left it in the past. He's only been back once since then, at Christmas, and let's say that we brought a whole new meaning to the word awkward.

As much as I miss the way we used to be, I don't think I could go back to that even if I tried. Knowing what could have been and remembering the way he tasted makes that hard, but at least I still have him in my life and that's all that matters in the end.

Today's the last day of school and Gunnar has been asking if I'll come to his graduation party. It took us a while, but we have come to be good friends. I don't really want to go to the party, but since I've grown close to both him and Jaxon, I feel like I need to.

Jaxon got a full football scholarship at the University of California and Gunnar got a full baseball scholarship to the University of Florida. He's excited to go back to his hometown and play the sport he loves. I think he may actually go pro, he's that good. I'm proud of both of them, and decide to go to the party and have a good time, even if it kills me.

***

By the time I make it out to the lake, the party is in full swing. I'm wearing a pair of holey jeans and what has become my signature black tank top and black combat boots. Since the last party I went to, the night before Thanksgiving, I've found I've been wearing a lot of black. I guess it fits my mood better than anything else.

Jaxon and Gunnar stop me immediately, one with a red Solo cup filled with beer and the other with a bottle of Jack. Yup, these boys know how I like it.

"Hey, Cupcake. It's about time you got here. Now the party can really begin!" Jaxon says as he pulls me into a hug. He's taken to calling me Cupcake lately, and though it's a little weird, I don't mind it.

Once he lets me go, Gunnar pulls me in for a hug.

"Yeah, sorry I'm late." I wanted to make sure my grandmother was in bed before leaving. She has been getting worse lately, but still refuses to go to the doctor. But if she isn't better by next week, I'll drag her there if I have to. I hate feeling like I'm slowly losing her and there is nothing I can do.

We sit by the fire, passing around the bottle of Jack and sipping our beers. We talk about stupid, unimportant shit, not wanting to talk about anything of significance. I'm not in the mood to talk, so I let them do most of the talking. They don't push me and don't seem to mind my lack of keeping up my part of the conversation. I'm letting them do most of the talking anyway, not in the mood to keep up with my part of the conversation. Eventually they start talking about how excited they are to go to college and I space off, not wanting to think about them leaving soon.

After about an hour of sitting and drinking, Sophie comes over and plops herself down on

Gunnar's lap. They started dating about a month after we broke up. I'm really happy for him; they seem to make a great couple. Though Sophie is going to school in New York, they want to try and make things work. I honestly do wish them the best and hope it works.

Mary, Sophie's friend, walks up behind Jaxon and starts to rub his shoulders. Not sure what the deal is with those two, but they seem to always be hot and cold. One week they are all over each other, and the next they want nothing to do with each other. Unfortunately, tonight is a night that the former option is true. Not wanting to be the fifth wheel and witness such gross public displays of affection, I get up and head over to the keg for a refill. Once my cup is full, I turn around to survey the party. There are a lot of people here, but they all seem to be coupled up. I don't want to spend the night watching people practically fuck in front of me, so I down my beer and decide to call it a night and go home.

I walk over to Gunnar and Jaxon and tell them goodnight. They are a little upset, but once I tell them I'm heading home to make sure Gram is okay, they let me pass. It also helps that Sophie and Mary are both distracting them with lap dances. Yup, it's time to head home.

Once I walk in the door, I make my way to my grandmother's room to check in on her, then head up to my room. I change into my pajamas and slip into bed. As I'm staring up at the ceiling, my phone pings.

Zane: Hey, Baby Girl, how was your last day of school?

Me: Same shit, different day. You coming home for the summer at all?

I know he won't, because it seems he never has the time to make it home anymore, but I can't help but ask. Hope can sometimes be a bitch. Plus, I figure if I get a heads up, I can make sure my walls are up.

Zane: I may be home here and there, but have a lot going on here. I'll let you know as soon as I know more.

Me: All right. I'm going to bed, talk later.

Zane: Okay, Baby Girl, sleep good.

I hate that one night has seemed to ruin everything we built over the years. I wonder if we will ever be the same again.

That night, I dream of the days when Zeke was still alive and all the fun the three of us had. It's the first dream that I've had of him that I haven't woken up from screaming. I wish I had more dreams like this. As much as I miss Zeke, I think I miss Zane more, which is crazy considering the difference between the two; Zeke can never come back and Zane chooses not to. There's something about missing someone even though they are right there with you that makes it worse.

***

Five Months Later

It's the last day before Thanksgiving break of my senior year of high school. I've applied to and been accepted to a bunch of schools, but I'm going to go to the community college here in town. Gram has only gotten worse over the months, and the doctors haven't been able to tell her what is wrong, so I've decided to stay close so I can take care of her. It's the least I can do after all she has done for me, plus, it will help me out too. I won't have to stay in the dorms or find an apartment that is close.

After school, I stop at the grocery store to grab some last-minute items for our dinner tomorrow and then head home. I put everything away and start making the pies. Once I get those in the oven, I make grilled cheese sandwiches and tomato soup for supper and bring a bowl to Gram's room. She's been spending the majority of her time in bed, but will sometimes come out and sit in the living room. I wish there was something I could do for her; I hate seeing her like this. Her skin has become pale and since she doesn't eat much anymore, her face seems almost sunken in. Every time I look at her I want to cry.

I clean up the pie and supper mess, then head upstairs to take a nice long bath. I want to go to bed early tonight. As I pass my desk, I see my sketch pad. I haven't had much inspiration to draw lately, which makes me even sadder. Drawing has always been my escape, my passion. And lately, I really need an escape, so I pick it up and carry it over to my bed. I lie down, open to a fresh page, and can only stare at it. I have no idea what to draw.

After staring at the paper for over ten minutes with no ideas, I start to doodle instead. I hate doodling, and only do it when I'm in class, but I think that's all I'm going to get out tonight. Oh well, there is always tomorrow for inspiration to hit me.

I put my supplies away a little while later, crawl into bed, and think about the last year. Things have changed so much that I barely even recognize myself. Last year around this time, I was heading to a party, not knowing that the next day my world would come crashing down around me. I wish I could go back and change what happened. As much as I don't want to, I would, knowing that it inevitably caused me to lose Zane. I would have never turned my phone off so he wouldn't have worried about me and driven all the way here for one night full of regrets. I'd rather not know what it felt like to be in his arms and his lips on mine than know what it was like and then be crushed even more when I lost it all. That's the last thought I have before I drift into a dreamless sleep.

***

April 5—My Eighteenth Birthday

I wake up a little earlier than usual, get in the shower, and decide to take a little extra time on my appearance. I haven't gotten dressed up or given much thought to my looks for a while. I mean, what's the point? I don't have a boyfriend, Zane is no longer around, and I don't really care what anyone else thinks. But since it is my eighteenth birthday, I want to go the extra mile. Maybe if I look better, I will feel better.

I shave my legs and wash my hair, then grab my towel and get started on my long locks. It's going to take me at least a half an hour to blow dry it. Then I want to curl it to give it some texture before putting it in a ponytail.

With my hair dry, I turn on the curling iron and walk into the closet to pick out my outfit. I'm not sure if I should go with my new favorite style of the darker, edgier look, or if I want to soften it up and wear a dress. I decide to stick to my new look because it makes me feel better about myself, so I grab a pair of skinny jeans with a couple holes in them and a white tank top. I pair it with the new leather jacket I bought last week with the money my grandmother gave me for my birthday. Now I just need to decide whether I want to wear my combat boots or heels. Since I'm going to do my hair and makeup extra special, I decide to wear my black heels.

I walk back into the bathroom to curl my hair and put on my makeup. I still want to keep it on the darker side, but not as edgy as I have been doing. I do a dark smoky eye shadow, line my eyes with eyeliner, use a generous amount of mascara, and put on red lipstick to make everything pop. I take one more look in the mirror before I put on my heels, grab my book bag off my desk, and head downstairs.

The first thing I notice is that Gram is still in bed. I wish there were more I could do for her, but it doesn't seem like she is getting any better. Instead of waking her up, I let her sleep. I write a note and leave it on the table to let her know I'll see her after school, then head out the door.

No one at school knows that it's my birthday today because there isn't really anyone that I talk to anymore. I make it through the whole day without anyone finding out, but do get a few lingering gazes from the guys and some hateful stares from a couple of the girls, no doubt because of the stares I'm getting from the male population. I don't even let it faze me because I'll be done with school in a little over a month's time. Then most of these people will be going off to university, while I stay here and go to community college.

I could have gone to any college I wanted, never needing to worry about money to pay for tuition since my sperm donor has a college fund for me. But I don't want to use that money—blood money is what it feels like. Gram asked why I didn't go to one of the other schools I was accepted into, but I showed her how great the art program was here so she'd back off. It really is a nice school.

When I arrive home, I don't see my grandmother anywhere.

"Gram, are you here?" I call out as I walk into the kitchen for some water. She isn't home, so I run upstairs to put my bag away. After I do a quick check in the mirror, I head back downstairs to see what we can do for supper. I would love to go out to eat, but I doubt she'll feel up to it. Maybe I could

113

order a pizza and have it delivered. We could pop some popcorn later and then watch a movie.

An hour later, she walks in the door with a bag that looks to be from the pharmacy.

"Hey, Gram, whatcha got there?" I walk over to take the bag from her, but she shakes her head and pats me on the hand.

"I've got it, sweetheart, but thank you. Happy birthday, by the way! Why didn't you wake me before you left for school? I would have made you a special breakfast."

I give her a quick hug, follow her into the kitchen, and jump up to sit on the counter. "That's okay, Gram, I was running late anyway," I lie.

"Well, what would you like for dinner, then? I bought cake mix to make your favorite cake," she says with a smile.

"Mmm, can we just have cake for supper?" I ask like I am five years old again.

She laughs and shakes her head. "No, we cannot, young lady. Now go upstairs and get cleaned up. I'll figure out what to make you for dinner."

I jump down and start walking out the door, but turn around when I remember what I wanted to do. "Actually, I was hoping we could maybe order in pizza and then watch a movie tonight."

She looks up from taking stuff out of the bag and I give her the special smile that I used to give her when I was young and wanted to get away with something. She could never resist that smile.

"Okay, sweetheart, whatever you want. Why don't you call in the pizza in and I'll start the cake?"

I run up the stairs and grab my phone off the charger as soon I close the door. I eagerly look down, hoping to see a missed call or at least a text message from Zane, but there's nothing. I sit on my bed and stare at my phone. I can no longer keep the disappointment and heartache at bay. If he was going to wish me a happy birthday at all, he would have by now. Last year I only got a text message, and now I don't even get that. I know things have been different between us since what happened, but to completely forget about my birthday? And my eighteenth birthday at that? I don't think I can do this anymore. It may be time to let him go completely.

I go back downstairs when the pizza arrives, but no longer have a smile on my face. I feel tired now. My grandmother and I sit at the table and quietly eat. She can tell something is wrong, but thankfully doesn't say anything.

I barely taste my cake, and make up the excuse that I am starting to get a headache so I can just go to bed. I should feel bad for skipping out on her, but I honestly can't even make myself care. I am so tired and want to be done with everything. I cry myself to sleep that night. But hey, it's my birthday and I can cry if I want to.

CHAPTER 10

May 30—Graduation Day

I wake up early to make a big breakfast. I want to try and be happy today, if only for my grandmother. Since my birthday, I've hardly spoken, and I know she is starting to worry about me. I need to forget about everything that happened. I mean, so what if Zane never told me happy birthday? Not like we've really talked that much lately anyway. Actually, we haven't talked at all since a couple weeks before my birthday. I was going to text him a million times, ask him what is happening to us? How could he forget my birthday? Why can't he love me? But there's no point. I just need to move on with my life, and if he doesn't want to be a part of it, then that's on him.

As I'm putting the last piece of French toast on a platter, my grandmother walks in. "Good morning, Gram," I say in what I hope is a cheery voice. "I made us some breakfast. I hope you're hungry. It's going to be a big day today!" I smile as I look up at her and almost drop the platter of food. The woman in front of me doesn't look like my grandmother at all. She's even paler this morning and seems to be holding on to the counter like she doesn't trust she can stand on her own.

"Gram, are you okay?" I say, more scared than I care to admit. I walk over and take her arm to help her to the table so she can sit down. Once she's settled, it still takes her a couple moments to get her bearings and to catch her breath.

Finally, she pats my hand, which is still hanging on to her for dear life, and gives me a weak smile. "I'm fine, sweetheart. I think I just overdid it a bit, picking up my room this morning. I'll be fine after I rest for a minute."

For some reason, I don't believe her. It seems no matter what she does or doesn't do, she keeps getting worse and worse. Something is most certainly wrong with her, and I need to find out what it is. "Gram, you should have told me and I would have picked up your room for you later. You don't need to be working yourself so hard. That's what I'm here for." I walk to the sink to get her a glass of water.

"Oh, don't be silly, child. I'm more than capable of cleaning my own room. Plus, you have more things to worry about today than your old grandmother."

I know it won't do any good to argue with her, so I'm going to have to do a better job of making sure everything is done so she doesn't have to do it. I'll sneak into her room if I have to. I drop the subject and sit down to eat my breakfast.

"What time do you need to be at the school for the ceremony today?" she asks me before she picks up her fork to take a small bite of her food. I know exactly what she's going to do before she does it. She'll chew what little bit is in her mouth, then put her fork down and take a drink of her juice. Then she'll pick the fork up again to start cutting the rest of her meal, and then she'll just push it around until I'm done. She will then try to get up to take my plate, which will then jump start my argument that I will take care of the dishes. Then she'll dump her plate and insist on helping till I kick her out of the kitchen. Every time we sit down for a meal, it's the same thing. No wonder she doesn't have energy for anything; she never eats, but Heaven forbid if I argue with her about it. I know I should push more, but there's really no use. At least she snacks during the day, so she's getting some nutrients.

"Um, I think I need to be there at one o'clock to get my cap and gown, then start getting in position. I was thinking you could go with me when I leave so you can get a spot in the front." And so she doesn't have to drive herself, but I leave that part out. I also don't mention that I want her to ride with me so I have an excuse to leave when everyone asks if I'm going to the party tonight at the lake. I don't want to go, there's too many memories out there that I don't want to confront tonight. It would be nice to get out and maybe have a drink or two, but I know I won't.

"That sounds good, honey. I'm going to go lay down a bit, but wake me up at noon if I'm not up already, okay?" She doesn't even wait for me to reply before she gets up and starts her slow walk out of the kitchen. I make a mental note to stop somewhere along the way to get her a snack, and start to clean up the kitchen. Once I have that done, I head up to my room to get a little drawing time in before I have to start getting ready.

Before I know it, the morning has passed me by and it's time to make sure Gram is up and to get myself together. I'm going to wear a simple sun dress since I'll have my gown over the top. I decide to leave my hair down also, since I have to wear my cap anyway. After waking Gram, I'll only need to get dressed and I'll be ready.

I run down the steps and walk into my grandmother's room. She's lying peacefully on her bed napping and I almost want to leave her be, but that's not an option today. I gently shake her and softly tell her it's time to wake up. She slowly opens her eyes and gives me a little smile. I help her sit up and see that she has her dress lying on the other side of the bed, so I walk over and pick it up.

"Do you need help getting ready, Gram?" I know she's going to say no, but I ask anyway. If there is anything I can offer to make things easier on her, I will do it.

"No, sweetheart, you go on and get yourself dressed." I nod and lay her dress beside her, then head upstairs.

I took a shower last night, so to the only thing I need to do is freshen up a bit. I look in the mirror and instead of leaving my hair hanging limply around my shoulders, I quickly do a side braid. It will still be easy for me to take my cap on and off, but it will look nice with my dress as well. It's a little country, but hey, I do live in Texas, so why not? I put on light eye shadow and some mascara, then add some lip gloss. Then I head into my room and get my dress on. It's a little short, but it's one of my favorites, with lots of greens, yellows, and white. I pair it with my cowboy boots and am ready to go. I toss my phone in my purse and head downstairs.

Gram is sitting in her chair with her eyes closed. I wait to see if she notices I've come into the room, but when she doesn't, I walk over to her and gently lay my hand on her shoulder. "I'm ready to go, Gram."

She slowly opens her eyes and it seems to take her a minute to focus on me, but once she does, she looks me up and down and a slow smile graces her tired face. "You look so lovely, Danielle. Just like your mama."

I take a minute to breathe through my nose, hoping the tears I feel gathering in my eyes don't fall. I manage a stiff nod and walk into the kitchen for a bottle of water.

By the time I've composed myself as best I can, I head back out to the living room to help her up. We slowly walk out to the car, and once she's situated, I head to the gas station to grab us a quick snack. Then we head toward the school. Traffic is more hectic than usual because of graduation, but once we make it to the parking lot, I manage to find a space close to the doors. It helps that I have a handicapped sign in my car for when Gram rides with me.

I walk her into the gym and make sure she's comfortable before I head off to the music room to wait till it's show time. Thankfully, everyone is too excited to notice my entrance, so I manage to find myself a quiet corner to sit and wait.

A half hour later, Mr. Tate whistles to get everyone to quiet down. "Okay, everyone, please be quiet. I know you can't wait to be done with this place, but until you have that diploma in your hand, you are still under my control." He says this with an evil smile. We know he is only giving us shit, though. "Now, I want everyone to line up by the door in alphabetical order, and wait for my signal. We will then quietly walk into the gym. Once we get there, I will introduce our special guest, Mayor Gilmore, and he will give a brief speech. Adam will then proceed to give his Valedictorian speech and after that it will finally be time for you to receive your diplomas. We will call each of you up to the stage one at a time. Once you have received your diploma, please make your way quietly back to your seat. Once everyone is seated, I will announce you as the class of 2010 and you can toss your caps into the air. You will then make your way back here and wait to be released. Don't worry about your cap, we will have them all brought back so you can take them home. Is everyone ready?"

Everyone either nods their head or says yes. "Okay then, get lined up." He walks out the door, probably to notify whoever is in charge of the music that we are ready. A few minutes later, he returns. "Okay, let's go. Remember! You will be quiet or I will make you all stay an hour after the ceremony for your last detention!" Some laugh while a few say things like "I'd like to see you try!" or "Just admit it, you're going to miss us, Mr. Tate!"

Our class song, or what I assume is our class song, starts when we get closer to the gym. I couldn't even tell you what the song is called, that's how much I have been out of it the past year. I know it's a country song, and it sounds like it could be Luke Bryan, but I'm really not sure.

When we arrive at the gym, we start the long walk to our seats. Once everyone is seated, Mr. Tate makes his way to the podium. I don't hear anything after he thanks everyone for coming today. I don't really care what he or the mayor says, and I probably won't even listen to what Adam says. All I want is to get my diploma so I can get out of here, and never look back at this place. I wouldn't have even walked in the ceremony if it weren't for my grandmother.

Thankfully it doesn't take long for everyone to give their speeches, and before I know it, I hear my name being called. "Danielle Rose DeChenne." I stand up and make my way to the stage. When I reach Mr. Tate, he holds his hand out to shake mine.

"Congratulations, Ms. DeChenne." He passes me my diploma with his other hand and I turn to look at Gram. She has a smile on her face and what looks like tears in her eyes. It means everything to me that she is here for me today. Before I look away, I notice Mr. and Mrs. Hendricks sitting next to her. I don't know why they are here, but I give them a small smile before walking back to my seat.

Did my grandmother invite them, or did they

come on their own? But the most important question that keeps going through my head: Is Zane here too? I force myself to look straight ahead and not around the room to see if I can spot him. I know if I do see him I will crumble, and I can't afford that. But the main reason is because I don't think I could stand the disappointment if he isn't here. I lose no matter which way I slice it.

It doesn't take long for all one hundred and twenty-two students to receive their diplomas, and soon Mr. Tate is walking back up to the podium. "I give you the class of 2010!" Everyone stands up and tosses their cap, except me. I just let it fall to the ground. I never really understood the point of tossing your cap. Why even have a cap if you are only going to wear it for a short period of time and then toss it in the air? Doesn't make sense, but whatever. To each their own.

Once the chaos has settled a bit, we walk back to the music room. Well, we're supposed to walk, but most everyone is jumping around, riding on someone's back, or literally running. I stay with the crowd, but I am not as enthusiastic as everyone else.

It takes about twenty minutes for the janitor to bring a big bag full of caps back to us. Everyone has taken their gown off and is waiting to be released. Mr. Tate comes back in soon after and says we can all leave. I find my cap pretty quickly and start to walk back to the gym. I'm not sure if my grandmother will still be sitting there waiting for me, or if she has gone outside already. With a quick glance through the doors, I see she isn't in there, so I head outside to the front of the school were everyone is congregating.

I spot my grandmother sitting at a picnic table off to the side, but she is not alone. Mr. and Mrs. Hendricks are with her. I guess I was going to have to talk to them sooner or later, but I've been hoping I wouldn't have to do it with my grandmother right there.

When I reach them, Mrs. Hendricks pulls me in for a hug. She holds me tight and congratulates me. Then Mr. Hendricks pulls me to him and gives me a hug as well.

"We are so proud of you. I hope you don't mind that we came, but we couldn't miss this." Mrs. Hendricks is a sweet lady, she really is. Now that they are here, I think I might have misjudged the situation. It's not as uncomfortable as I thought it would be. At least until my grandmother asks the one question I don't want to know the answer to.

"Where's Zane? I didn't see him in there."

Looks like whether I want it or not, I'm going to get the answer.

"Ah, well, he's not here actually. He, uh, he's pretty busy with school right now," says Mrs. Hendricks. If I wasn't staring right at her, I would have missed the brief look of pain that crosses her face before she covers it up. So it seems like I'm not the only one who he has been ignoring. Or maybe they are still tense from the fight they had before he left for school. He never did tell me what happened that day, and never mentioned if things were better.

"Oh, I thought for sure he'd be here. With this being Danielle's big day and all." There is no malice behind my grandmother's words; she is genuinely shocked that he hasn't come. I wish I could say I am too, but I guess I knew deep down that he wouldn't be here. I mean, I haven't even spoken to him in almost two months. It is like he dropped off the face of the earth, or he forgot about all of us. If my heart didn't hurt so much, I would be majorly pissed off.

Mr. and Mrs. Hendricks give me another hug, hand me an envelope, and congratulate me again. Instead of opening the card right away, I stick it in my purse and turn toward my grandmother. "Are you rea—?"

I don't get a chance to finish my sentence before someone is picking me up and twirling me around. I honestly have no idea who it is, and Gram has a look of confusion on her face, so it's someone she hasn't met or doesn't remember.

After a couple of spins, whoever has ahold of me puts me back on my feet and turns me around. Jaxon. "Congrats, you are officially an adult!" Before I can answer he pulls me into his arms for a hug.

"Jaxon, what are you doing here?" I ask him once he releases me. I can't believe he's here.

"Well, I came to watch you take your first step into your future, why else would I be back?"

I chuckle at his remark and playfully punch him in the stomach. "Oh, I don't know, maybe for the party that's happening tonight?" If he's here for any reason, it would be the party, not for me. Jaxon loves going to parties, but I'm sure there is an even better one at his college, so why he came back here is lost on me.

"Well, that too." He chuckles, then turns toward my grandmother. "Hi, I don't think we've ever met. I'm Jaxon, I went to school with Danielle last year." Leave it to Jaxon to introduce himself; he can't wait for anyone to do it for him like a normal person.

"Oh, it's nice to meet you, darling." My grandmother smiles and then looks at me. "Are you ready to go home, sweetie?"

I nod and turn back to Jaxon. "It was great seeing you. Have fun at the party." I help Gram up and start toward my car.

"Aren't you going? I mean, it is in your honor after all." Of course he would turn it around and try anything he could to make me feel guilty. But it's not going to work this time.

"Technically it's not for me, but the whole senior class. It's nothing special anyway; they'd use any excuse to party." When I turn back toward my grandmother, she has a slight frown on her face. "Gram, you okay? Do you need to sit down?"

She shakes her head and pulls her arm out of my grasp. "I'm fine, Danielle, but I don't understand why you don't go to this party. Like Mr. Jaxon here says, it's in your honor. It doesn't matter that it's not *just* for you. You should go."

Ugh, now I have my grandmother pushing me to go? Does it ever stop? "Gram, it's okay. I don't really want to go." I try to take her arm again, but she evades me. For being so slow lately, she sure is quicker than I thought.

"No, you are going and that's final." I open my mouth to argue, but she cuts me off before I can get anything out. "Bite that tongue, young lady. If I

126

have to lock you out of the house, I will."

So much for using my grandmother as an excuse not to go.

"Great, it's settled then. I'll pick you up at nine," says Jaxon.

I start to shake my head when my grandmother speaks. "That's so sweet of you, darling. She'll be ready." Then she grabs my hand and we start toward the car.

"Gram, I really don't want to go. Plus, I thought we could watch a movie since we didn't get to for my birthday." Maybe if I work this the right way, she'll cave.

"Nice try, but you're going. I will hear no more of it."

I close my mouth and shake my head. Add on the fact that Jaxon is picking me up now too so I can't even leave early. Tonight is going to suck!

CHAPTER 11

I've been in my room since I got back from the ceremony, trying to come up with a way to get out of going tonight. Why did Jaxon have to come over and mention the stupid fucking party in front of my grandmother? I mean, most people would shy away from talking about drinking and such around old people because it would be uncomfortable. But Jaxon? No, not him. He has to go balls to the wall and not only mention the damn party, but pretty much use my grandmother as a means to make me go. Did he know my grandmother would do that? No, probably not, but I'm going to blame him for it anyway.

I finally get up and change out of the summer dress I wore for the ceremony. I put on my pair of jeans with the most holes; they are everywhere—the knees, the thighs, and even the ass, but I'm wearing black leggings underneath. I throw on my signature black tank and combat boots, and put my hair up into a high pony tail. I fix my makeup, keeping with my dark look, then grab my phone and head downstairs.

I look at my phone and notice I still have about five minutes before Jaxon will be here to pick me up, so I go to the kitchen to grab an orange and a bottle of water. On my way back into the entryway, I hear my grandmother's voice. "Sweetheart, can you come in here a minute?"

I set my water and orange down on the counter, grab my leather jacket on the way, and go in search of her. She isn't in the living room, so I head back to her bedroom.

She's lying in bed with a bunch of photo albums and pictures spread out all around her. I don't know what she's doing, but I don't want to upset her by taking my anger and irritation out on her, so I put a smile on my face and squat down beside the head of the bed.

"What is it, Gram?" I look around, trying to figure out what it is she could need, but find nothing. I turn back and lock eyes with her. She sets aside the photo she has of me, Zane, and Zeke playing outside the first Fourth of July after they moved in next door. It's then that I notice all the pictures surrounding her are mostly of me; pictures of Zane and me, Zeke and me, and some of all three of us, a couple of her and me, and then pictures of my mother and father with me as a baby.

"What are you doing?" Maybe it's because I graduated today or maybe she does this all the time and I never noticed.

"Just wanted to have a look at some old pictures before I went to bed." She clears a spot for me to sit beside her and pats the blanket. I straighten from where I was squatting and sit down on her bed. She takes my hand in hers and lovingly caresses it. She doesn't speak for a couple of minutes. She only looks from our joined hands to my face, and then at a couple of the pictures that surround her.

"Are you okay?" I don't know if she's sad that I'm growing up or happy for me. Right now, it's looks to be a mixture of both.

"I'm so very proud of you, Danielle, and I know your mother and father would be too."

I start to interrupt her. I want to say that my father wanted nothing to do with me so I highly doubt he would be proud of me, and even if he is, he can go fuck himself. But she shakes her head and levels me with a look that has me keeping quiet.

"Now let me finish. I know both your mother and your father would be proud of you. Things haven't been great for you, I know. You lost your mother way too early and your father couldn't deal with the loss of his wife. He really thought it was best for me to take you in, and I think he was right. Sometimes, a broken man needs time to heal and he couldn't do that with a child. I'm not trying to make excuses for him or to even say that it was right, but maybe for him, it was." She takes a couple of minutes to catch her breath and then continues. "I want you to know that I don't regret a single day of having you here. I have loved every second and wouldn't change it for the world. I love you so very much, Danielle, and I'm so proud of you. You are an amazing young girl and I know with every fiber of my being that you will grow up to be an amazing woman."

I wipe the tears that have fallen down my cheeks, but can't say anything yet. I'm literally speechless. She reaches over to her nightstand and pulls open the drawer, then reaches in to pull out a small rectangular box.

"Happy graduation, sweetheart." She hands the box to me and I take it with shaky hands. I look up at her before I slowly open it. Nestled inside is a heart shaped locket. On the front, there's an inscription that reads *'Ma Cheri Cheri,'* which I know means "My Darling Sweetheart" in French. I open it up to find a picture of her and me on one side, and on the other an inscription that says *'Always in your heart.'* After reading that part, my hands drop in my lap with the locket and I start to sob.

She pulls me down so my head is on her shoulder, and begins to rub little circles on my back while murmuring, "Shhh…it's okay, sweetheart, I've got you." It makes me remember all the times when I was little and hurt or sad, and she would pull me onto her lap and rock me back and forth until I calmed down.

It takes me forever to finally compose myself again before I sit up. "I love it, Gram. Thank you." Words cannot express how much I love this woman and what she has done for me. I will forever be thankful to have her in my life. I start to say she didn't have to get me anything when the doorbell rings.

"That must be Jax," I say with a sigh. I don't even try to ask her if she wants me to stay home because I know she already has her mind set that I need to go out and have fun. It's a day of celebration in her eyes.

"Go have fun, Danielle. I love you so much, I hope you know that."

I lean down to give her a kiss on the cheek and walk toward the door.

"I love you too, Gram. I'll see you tomorrow." As I walk out her door, I hear her say, "Goodbye, sweetheart."

I put on my new necklace on my way to the door. Once I have it hooked, I make sure I have my purse and walk out.

"All rea—Whoa, you okay?" Jaxon asks me once he gets a good look at my face. I forgot I had been crying a few minutes ago.

I wipe under my eyes and find black on my fingers when I pull them away. Great. "Yeah, I'm good." I add a little smile and we walk to his truck.

Once inside, I pull the visor down to look in the mirror. My face isn't as bad as I thought it would be, only a few smudges and my eyes are a little puffy. Nothing I can't fix. He takes one last look in my direction before putting the truck onto the road and starts driving toward the lake. He doesn't try to start up conversation with me, which I am grateful for.

Before I know it, we are at the party and getting out of the truck. "All right, let the party begin!" He takes my hand and we walk to the keg.

***

We have been at this stupid party for over two

132

hours, and every minute of it I have spent sipping my beer and trying to come up with a way to skip out. I just want to be home, in my bed, thinking about my life and where I go from here. Without Zane, I really don't know where that is. Yes, it wasn't like I had him as a huge part of my plan anyway, but he was still there as my friend. Now, all of that is gone. I need to get over it and come up with a way to get on with my life without him in it.

I bring my cup up to my lips. Empty. I get up and head over to the keg to get a refill. I haven't touched any of the bottles because I don't plan on staying long. I'm only trying to pass the time by sipping a couple of beers, make it look like I'm having fun, then tell Jaxon that I am ready to go. If he doesn't want to leave, then I'll find a ride home from someone else. There has to be someone here that will be leaving early, and if not, I'll bribe someone.

As I get my cup under the nozzle of the keg but before I'm able to get anything out, I'm being lifted up from behind and twirled around toward a table off to one side that wasn't there earlier.

"Put me down!" I yell at whoever is holding me. I don't care who it is as long as they let me go. They don't say anything, but they do as I say when we are beside the table. Before I can turn around and yell, I feel hands on my shoulders pushing me down onto one of the chairs. This person is really asking for it. I'm in no mood to be here, let alone being manhandled.

I open my mouth to give them a piece of my mind when Jaxon walks out from behind me to sit in the chair next to mine. I should have known it was him. Instead of voicing my outrage, I level him with a look that says it all; I'm pissed. You know that saying "if looks could kill"? Yeah, I was giving him one of *those* glares. Not only would he be dead, but scorched and in ashes right now.

"Oh, calm the fuck down. We have been here for a while and you have only had, what, maybe three drinks, and barely said ten words. I don't care if I have to suffer your wrath for an eternity, you are going to sit here and play drinking games and you will have fun. Do you understand me?"

So this is how he's going to play it? I want to hand him an ass kicking, but decide to go another route. "Fine. I'll make you a deal."

He gives me a look that says there is no deal in the world that he will make with me tonight, but he stays quiet to hear me out. Smart guy.

"I will drink, play stupid games, and be sociable. I will honest to God try to have a good time. But if in two hours I still want to go home, you have to either take me or not stop me from leaving. Deal?" There is no way that even after two hours of trying to let loose and have a good time I will want to stay longer. Sure, I can drink with the best of them, but I haven't been sociable in so long that I doubt tonight will be any different. But because Jaxon is my friend and he is making an effort to try and lighten my mood, I will try.

"Fine, but you better try one hundred and ten percent, otherwise the deal is off and you go home when I do." Like he would know if I'm really putting all my effort into it or not. According to him, we'll be playing drinking games, so the more we play, the less observant he will be.

"Okay, I'll give it my all, but at the end, you have to keep your word if I say I want to leave. No matter how wasted and upset you are."

He nods, grabs the stack of cards on the table, and starts shuffling.

"Okay. We'll start with beer, but we'll work our way up to Jack." I have no idea what we are playing, but drinking games can't be that hard, right? Even if I lose, it's still a good thing for me because I can handle any kind of alcohol.

"We'll start off with Fubar." As he starts telling me how the game is played, four guys join us at the table: Marc, Heath, Robbie, and Jon. I don't know if Jaxon told them that we were going to be playing or if they noticed that a game was about to start. Doesn't matter either way. The more people that are playing, the less I'll have to interact. Though I will have to jump into the conversations to show the effort I'm making to have a good time, the others should distract Jaxon so that he won't notice me too much.

Two hours later, we have played Fubar, Never Have I Ever, High/Low, and are getting ready to play Paranoia. They said that this is the best game, especially after everyone has a good number of drinks in their system. I've had more to drink than I thought I would, and surprisingly, this is fun. I still want to go home, but I'm no longer sorry I came.

"So…" Jaxon says smugly, knowing I've had a good time. He's had more to drink than me but he is holding his own. I thought for sure that he would be slurring and forgetting about me by now, but he has kept me involved and succeeded in helping me relax.

"You were right. I did have fun."

He starts to say something, probably "I told you so," or some other bullshit, but I hold my hand out to stop him.

"But…I do still want to go. I'm glad I came, but it's been a long day and I just want it to be over. I'm sorry."

He looks a little disappointed, but I see understanding in his eyes. "Okay, I respect that, but would you at least play this last game with us and then we'll go?"

What's another half hour anyway? "Sure. How do you play it again?"

He tells me the rules again. When it's your turn, you whisper a question into someone's ear and they have to answer it for everyone to hear with the name of the person in the group. The questions are general, like who's the hottest person here? The part the makes it fun is that the person named has to drink and then gets to flip a coin that decides whether the questioner has to reveal what the question was. This could get very personal and interesting, but it could also get ugly fast. And I thought Never Have I Ever was rough.

Since I'm the only girl at the table, I'm guessing that my name could be mentioned quite a bit, but I don't usually care what people think of me, so I doubt I will get very paranoid.

As it turns out, my name has only been mentioned twice, and I haven't cared when I flipped the coin to have them say the question out loud. Everyone else has seemed to really want to know what people think of them, especially when I say their name. It's really funny. They now know who in the group I consider my top friend, which is Jaxon of course. Who I would kiss if dared, which again is Jaxon. Who I'd have sex with, again it would be Jaxon since I don't know the others that well. And lastly, who I think could be gay, which was very awkward, but I answered with Robbie, who didn't seem all that upset, so maybe I'm right?

Someone asks Jaxon a question and he says my name. He hasn't said my name before, so I'm a little curious. This time when I flip the coin, I pray that I get heads so I can hear what the question was. Luck is on my side for the time being.

"Okay, spill," I say, eager to know the question.

"The question was…who I would take a bullet for."

Definitely not what I was expecting. It confuses me. I know we are pretty good friends, but I thought he'd for sure take a bullet for one of his guy friends and former teammates. Everyone around the table is silent, trying to figure out for themselves what that means.

Before the game starts up again, I take his hand in mine and give it a squeeze. I want him to know that I appreciate what he said. Even though I'm still a little confused, it makes me happy that he considers me worth saving, like a best friend or sister. Having someone care for me like that means more than wanting me as a girlfriend or a friend.

He looks down at our joined hands and then back

up to my eyes. "You're an amazing person, Danielle, and someone I consider family."

I push back my tears and squeeze his hand once more before releasing it. "Thank you." I don't know what else to say.

"You ready to go?" he asks as he releases my hand.

I'm feeling a good buzz but am more emotionally drained than anything. I am definitely ready to go home. "Yeah, if you don't mind." I stand up and wait for him to follow.

"Not at all." He takes my hand and leads me to his truck.

When we are outside my house, I turn to look at him. "Thanks for making me go. I really did have a good time."

He smiles in return, then waits till I'm in the house before driving away.

I head straight to my room and don't even bother changing before slipping under my covers. I barely have time to finish a full thought before I fall into a dreamless sleep.

CHAPTER 12

I wake up to my phone going off. I reach over to my nightstand and unlock the screen. It's a text message from Jaxon telling me he is heading back to school. I type a quick response and jump in the shower.

I dress in yoga pants and a t-shirt, then head down to find something to eat. Once in the kitchen, I notice that Gram isn't up yet. She wasn't in the living room and she's not in here, so either she went out for a bit or she's sleeping. It's after one in the afternoon so my guess is that she's napping, which she often does in the afternoon.

When I finish my orange juice and a bowl of cereal, I go back to my room to clean and gather laundry. It takes me a little over an hour to finish, then I head down to start the wash.

I still haven't heard or seen my grandmother up and about yet. I should to let her sleep, but really want to see what her plans are for the day. I'm thinking a nice lazy day is in order and what better than to lie around on the couch all day and watch movies?

I quietly open her door and see her in bed. I notice that she still has some pictures on her bed from last night. She must have fallen asleep while looking at them. As I step quietly into her room to pick them up to put them away, I notice how utterly still she is. She looks very pale too. I walk slowly up to the bed and gently shake her. But when my hand touches her shoulder, I feel how cold she is. "Gram, wake up."

She doesn't move or even attempt to open her eyes, and the only thing that I keep thinking about is how cold she is. "Gram, time to get up," I say again but a little louder. Still nothing. "Gram, wake up…please…"

I shake her again and again, but she doesn't move and she doesn't wake up.

"*Gram*!" I shake her one last time, almost violently and start to sob. "No no no no no! Gram, please wake up. *Please*!" But she's gone. She must have passed away last night while I was out drinking and having a good time. "Gram, please don't leave me…"

***

Today is the day of Gram's funeral. The past four days have been a blur of emotions and activity. I learned that she had heart disease and kept it from me. She knew she was sick for almost a year and declined any treatment. Her doctor said that he gave her medicine to make things easier for her and more comfortable, but she wouldn't let him do anything else for her. I don't understand why she didn't tell me, but knowing what I know now, everything makes sense. Her being sick all the time, arguing about which college to attend, making sure I went out and built a life of my own beyond the walls of her house, and even our talk the night before she died. I see now that it was her goodbye.

I also learned that she had planned her funeral and made all the arrangements, going as far as making sure it was all paid for. That means at least I don't have to worry about what needs to happen or what she would want. The funeral home even sent out all the announcements and said they would take care of all the rest. I'm thankful because I'm so lost right now I would probably mess it up, and she deserves to have a nice service and burial.

People stopped by the house and some called to give their condolences and ask if there is anything they could do. I tried to be polite, and though I'm not sure if I succeeded, no one commented on it. I just wanted to be left alone so I could come to terms with the fact that my grandmother is gone and is never coming back. It's so hard because she was my rock; she was what grounded me. What am I supposed to do without her? I don't worry about what I'll do financially, not like I'd have to since she left the house and almost $50,000 of life insurance. On top of that, I still have the college fund and trust fund from my father. Money was the last thing on my mind. But I honestly didn't know what I would do *physically* without her here. I would give all the money away if I could get my grandmother back.

I look at the clock and see that I only have an hour before I need to be at the funeral home, so I jump into the shower and put on the new black dress I bought yesterday. I didn't have anything that I wanted to wear on the day I have to say my final goodbye to my grandmother and I want to look nice for her.

I don't put any makeup on so I won't have to worry about ruining it when the tears come again, and I know they will. I thought I'd be all dried out by now, but I still cry every time I think about her or saying goodbye. I leave my purse because I don't need to take anything with me. I just want to go and get this over with so I can come home, cry myself to sleep, and then tomorrow start to figure out where I go from here. That's all I feel like I've been doing lately, trying to figure out what to do and where my life will lead me.

***

The ceremony was beautiful and so many people showed up. More than I thought possible. Some I didn't recognize, but mostly friends of my grandmother that I've seen from time to time and of course our neighbors; Mr. and Mrs. Hendrix, but no Zane. The only person who was really there for me was Jaxon. I don't know how he knew about my grandmother's death, but he showed up on my doorstep the day after, holding a bottle of Jack Daniels, chocolate, and pizzas. We didn't even really talk; he was just there for me.

I'm still standing at her final resting place in the

cemetery when I hear my name being called behind me. I don't turn around, but I feel someone stop beside me.

"Danielle?" I don't recognize the voice so I glance up to see who would be here, talking to me. I regret it immediately. I know from one look exactly who it is.

"What the hell are you doing here?" I try to keep my voice down but am so pissed off that my whole body is shaking. He looks at me in shock, but quickly recovers.

"Danielle, I know I'm the last person you probably want to see right now, but when I heard what happened, I had to come to make sure you were okay."

I can't believe this man. After everything he has done to me and put me through, he shows up here, the day I buried my grandmother. "Okay? Am I okay? What the fuck do you care?" I seethe.

"Danie—"

"No! Shut your fucking mouth. How dare you come here, today of all fucking days, and think that you deserve to even ask that fucking question? What? You think because you fathered me that you get to walk into my life anytime you want? That you could ever comfort me? If that's what you think, then you are even more of an asshole than I thought."

I turn to walk away but he grabs my arm. "Danielle, I understand that you're angry—"

"Angry? No, I moved past anger a long fucking time ago. Now, I'm just plain fucking livid!" I try to walk away again, but stop because I want to say one more thing to him. "I understand that you were hurt after my mother died. I get it. You gave me up. I get that too. You had to do what you did to make yourself better. And I had a great childhood and was raised by a woman who loved me enough to last a lifetime. So if it's forgiveness you need, fine, I forgive you for abandoning me. But you gave up the right to be my father the day you walked out on me, so do me a favor and leave me the hell alone. I never want to see or hear from you again." I don't wait for his reply. I turn and walk away. Now he knows how it feels to be rejected.

Instead of going to the car that is waiting for me, I walk home. I could use that time to cool off and get my thoughts straight.

When I get in the door, I drop to the floor and let all the pain and anger out. I've lost everyone I love: my mom, my dad, Zeke, Zane, and now my grandmother. I have no idea what I'm supposed to do now. I don't even know how to make it through the rest of the day, let alone the rest of the week, or year. Should I still attend the community college or should I go somewhere else? Or maybe I shouldn't even go to college at all.

I pick myself up off the floor, grab the bottle of Jack that Jaxon left, and head up to my room. Tonight, I only want to forget. I'll worry about everything else tomorrow.

* * *

I wake up the next morning with a massive headache. I drank the whole bottle but everything

144

still hurt, so I gave up and let myself fall asleep, praying for some peace. But of course that was too much to ask. I had nightmare after nightmare, but since I was so wasted, I wasn't able to rouse myself to get away from it all.

I go downstairs to get some water and Tylenol and head back up to bed. Soon after, I fall asleep again, but I'm woken up by someone banging on the front door. Sneaking a glance at the clock on my way downstairs, I take note that I've actually slept for four hours and now it is noon.

When I open the door, I see a very distraught Zane in front of me. "Thank fuck! Why the hell haven't you answered your fucking phone!" he booms.

I'm so shocked and confused that he's even here that I can't get any words out before he pushes his way inside, slams the door, and engulfs me in his arms. "Why didn't you call me? I had to hear it from my mother when she called last night to ask why I wasn't at the funeral. Why didn't you tell me, Baby Girl?"

The shock passes and is replaced with rage. "What do you mean, why didn't I call you? Why the fuck would I? You have barely even talked to me this past year. You didn't call on my birthday or even graduation. So ask me again why the fuck I didn't call you." I start toward the kitchen, then turn to face him and yell, "And excuse fucking me, but I was a little preoccupied with finding my grandmother dead and trying to get through the pain and shock of losing her, so I'm so fucking sorry that I didn't think to call you. Not like you would have answered your fucking phone for me anyway!" I walk away again without waiting for him to reply. I'm so pissed at him that I could care fucking less that his feelings are hurt or what the fuck ever is his problem.

"Look, Danielle, I'm sorry, okay? I know I haven't been around lately, but you should have called me. You shouldn't have had to go through that alone."

But I had gone through it all alone because I have no one. "Well, I did. I was the one who found her. I was the one who had to deal with people calling and stopping over to tell me they were sorry. I was the one who had to sit by myself at the funeral. I was the one who had to deal with my father showing up. And then I was the one who had to come home to this empty house that holds all of my dead grandmother's stuff. Maybe I shouldn't have had to go through all that alone, but I did, so I don't fucking need you." I end on a sob. I can't do any of this anymore.

He instantly steps forward and wraps me in his arms, and I can do nothing but cling to him while all my agony and grief washes through me. I cry harder now than I have the past five days. God, I've missed him so much! I thought I could do this without him, but I can't. I need him here with me, I need him to tell me it's all going to be okay and that he'll be there for me.

"Shh, it's okay, I've got you. I'm not going anywhere. We'll figure this out. I'm here, shh." He drops us down onto the floor and then starts to rock me back and forth, trying to soothe me. If he only knew what his presence alone does for me. I don't need his words, I only need him here to hold me.

***

Zane orders Chinese takeout, and after he gets over the shock of hearing that my father showed up, we discuss what happens next. I tell him that my grandmother left me everything and that I want to keep the house. I tell him that I'm still going to go to school in the area, but I might get an apartment. I don't think I'll be able to stay in this house without Gram, at least for a while. The pain is too fresh, the memories too much. It's more than I can bear right now.

"Why don't you come to school in Austin? You got accepted there, right?"

Yes, I got accepted there, but I don't think I should or could go. Sure, I've missed him and want to get back to the way things used to be before he left, but is that even possible? I mean, so much has happened over the past two years, I'm not so sure we can get back to the carefree relationship we had before. It would be too much to see him every day and know what I'm missing and that I'll never be more than just a friend to him.

"I don't know, Zane." I don't know how to explain it to him, but I'm sure he knows.

"Look," he says, "I know things have been different lately, and that's my fault. But hear me out. Spend the summer tying up loose ends and packing what you want to bring with you, and then put everything else in storage. Or shit, even leave it all where it is. I'm sure you'll come back from time to time and that would give you a place to go when you need to get away or need to be close to your grandma. Just say you'll come with me. I promise, we will work this out. We'll fix what needs to be fixed. Let me take care of you, Baby Girl."

Can we fix our friendship? Maybe...I guess. What do I have to lose anyway? "Okay, I'll call the schools next week and get everything switched over. It might be too late to get a dorm room, but I could use some of the money I got from my dad for an apartment." I don't want to have to use that money, but I will if I need to. This could work. Maybe we can fix what is broken with us and finally move on. At least I'd have him back in my life and I wouldn't feel so detached and alone anymore.

He gives me a smile and takes my hand. "Okay, good. I'll help you move your stuff over if you want, then show you around. This will be great, Baby Girl, I promise. Everything will be fine, you'll see." He says it like he's trying to not only convince me, but himself too. I don't know why, but I believe him. Maybe it's because I have nothing else to believe in right now or maybe it's because no matter what happened in our past, I could always count on Zane. We will always be together. It may not be a physical relationship or what I want, but it's something. And right now, I'll take anything I can get.

CHAPTER 13

I called the schools that following Monday to get everything switched over. After that, the summer flew by. I was consumed with packing away my grandmother's stuff and cleaning the house.

Now I have to get my shit together because I start classes in one week at the University of Texas. They were even able to set me up with a dorm, so that saved me some money and the stress of having to find a place to live close to campus.

I load my car with the bare minimum of what I need and leave everything else. I didn't clean out any of Gram's things or pack anything away in storage. I'm going to try to come back here at least once a month to make sure everything is still okay, and to get away from school. I take a long look at the house before heading off to college and hopefully a fresh start.

I arrive in Austin at about five in the afternoon. I send Zane a text to let him know I'm here and ask where he wants to meet. He said he'd help me unpack and then show me around campus once I'm

149

settled in my room.

By the time I make it to what I hope is my dorm building, I still haven't heard back from Zane. So I give him a call. Finally, on the fifth ring he answers.

"Yeah?" He sounds irritated, but I have no idea why.

"Uh, hey, everything okay? I sent you a message but didn't hear back. I'm here, sitting in front of my building."

I can hear him trying to calm himself down by breathing slowly and deeply. After about thirty seconds he replies. "Shit, I'm sorry, Baby Girl. It's been a fucked-up day. I'll be there in five." He hangs up before I can reply. Instead of getting out, I wait in my car.

When he pulls up alongside my car, I get out to meet him at the back of his truck. Instead of saying hey, giving me a hug, or even starting to unload my car, he leans against his truck, crosses his arms, and looks down at his feet, letting out a long sigh.

"Are you okay?" I ask. "If you were busy, you didn't have to come and help, I would have been able to handle it myself."

He looks at me and runs his hand through his hair. Yeah, there is definitely something bothering him, but what it could be is lost on me. It's not like I know a lot of what he has going on in his life anymore. "No, it's not that. I'm sorry. Like I said, it's been a fucked-up day. What do ya say we hold off on all of this and go grab some food first? I'm starving."

Instead of waiting for my answer, he walks over and opens his passenger door for me. I hesitate for a second before I lock up my car and jump in. He drives for a couple of minutes and then we are pulling up to what looks like a bar.

"It doesn't look like much on the outside, but they have the best burgers around." We get out and make our way inside.

We both order a burger and fries, and I sip on a diet Mountain Dew while Zane pretty much slams his Bud Light. I wonder how he is getting served, since he isn't twenty-one yet. Maybe a fake ID, or they don't care around here whether you are old enough to drink or not. I hear some college towns are like that.

We are almost done with our food when his phone rings.

"Yeah?" he answers. I can't hear what the other person is saying, but from the tone I can hear on the other end, I think it's a guy. "Yeah, all right. I got a friend with me, though. That cool?"

I focus on my food, acting like I'm not listening to his conversation.

"All right. See ya soon." He hangs up and takes a drink of his beer.

"Who was that?" I wasn't sure what the conversation was about, but it sounded to me like we were going somewhere.

"One of my buddies. He knows someone who is throwing a party and wanted to see if I was game. I told him you were with me but he said to bring you along. What do you think, want to go?"

Party on the first night here? I don't think that's a good idea. I'm not even moved into my room yet.

"Oh, uh, why don't you just drop me off at my

dorm? You go ahead. I want to get my stuff unpacked and go to bed early." I take a drink of my soda and then pick at the rest of the food on my plate.

"No, you gotta come. It'll be fun, I promise. You can crash at my place tonight, then tomorrow we'll spend the whole day unloading your stuff and touring the campus."

Looks like he's not going to take no for an answer. Typical Zane. "Okay, well, can we at least stop at my car so I can grab some different clothes to change into?" I'm wearing a simple summer dress because I wanted to look nice. Don't ask me why, though, considering I was only planning on moving today.

"You look fine, trust me. Don't worry about it." The way he emphasizes "trust me" has me thinking there's something behind his words, but I have no idea what it could be.

We finish eating and then climb back into his truck to head to wherever this party is. The house turns out to be only a couple blocks away. When we get inside, we walk right into the kitchen. Zane introduces me to a couple of people and grabs us some drinks.

"Yo, Z-Man, that you?" A guy walks in and pulls Zane into a one-armed hug.

"Hey, Liam, this is my friend Danielle. She got in today."

He looks at me briefly, then turns to look at Zane. He looks like he wants to say something, but refrains. Looking back to me, he says, "Hello there. Z didn't mention his friend was an attractive girl."

The way he says it doesn't sound flirty, it sounds concerned.

"Hey," I say, and then look over to Zane, confused and a little freaked out.

He takes my hand and leads me into the living room, where there are some tables set up with chairs. A couple more people come up to greet Zane, but he doesn't introduce me to anyone else, not that I mind. I would really rather go back to my dorm and unpack so I can go to sleep. Its been a long day.

I get up to go to the bathroom, and when I come back, there is a stunning blonde next to Zane where I was sitting a couple minutes ago. Zane catches my eye and gives me a smile and a look like he's asking if I'm okay. I give him a little smile back and what I hope is an expression that tells him I'm okay but want to go home. He must not read it right, because he turns back to talk with the blonde.

Over the next hour, I sit in a chair toward the back of the room while Zane and the blond get bolder with their touches. I don't want to stare at them and their wandering hands, so I either stare at the floor, the wall, or take short glances around the room. The last few times I did that, though, I saw Zane's friend, Liam, watching me. I've tried getting Zane's attention, but he hasn't even looked over at me for at least the last thirty minutes. I hope he hasn't forgotten I am here. With him.

I'm starting to get a headache and I feel flushed. Getting up, I head into the bathroom to splash cold water on my face to try and make myself feel a little better, but no such luck. I'm going to have to ask

Zane to take me back to my dorm or at least he could give me his keys so I can drive myself.

When I return to the living room, I don't see Zane or the blonde anywhere. They probably went to get more drinks. I don't feel like trying to make my way through all these people to find him, but figure he will be back shortly, so I sit back on the chair to wait.

A while later, I still haven't seen Zane, or any of the people he introduced me to earlier. My head is really starting to pound, so I go into the bathroom again in hopes of finding some Tylenol. I feel bad snooping in their cabinets, but I really need it. Unfortunately, there is nothing that I can take.

When I open the door to walk out, I bump into a solid wall of muscle. I look up and see a guy I've never seen before. Well, I guess I've never seen any of these people before, but he's not someone Zane introduced me to or that I remember seeing around the party. He must have been in a different room. "Oh, sorry," I mumble. I try to sidestep him but end up bumping into him again when he tries the same thing.

"Hey, that's all right, babe. You look a little lost. Can I help you with something?" He seems nice enough and like he knows the people and his way around this house, so maybe he'll know where Zane is.

"Uh, yeah, maybe. I'm looking for my friend Zane. I came here with him, but I can't find him. I have a headache and wanted to see if he'd take me home." That was probably a little too much information, but my head is pounding like a bitch and I'm so damn tired that I really don't care right now.

"Oh, yeah, I know him. Um, I saw his truck outside about ten minutes ago, but I haven't seen him for a while." He looks back at me and gives me a once over again, and then a reassuring smile. "Here, why don't you go wait in one of the rooms down the hall while I go look for him? With the music blaring and all the people yelling, I don't want your headache to get worse."

I'm not sure that's a good idea, but right now, I don't think I have much choice. "Uh, okay, thanks. That would be great."

He walks me a few feet down the hall and opens a door on the left. The room is dark until he turns on a side lamp. It's a neat room with a desk on one side with a chair, and a small dresser. A huge bed takes up the rest of the room, leaving little walking space. I sit on the corner of the bed since there are books and a bag on the chair. "I'll be right back," he says before walking out the door, closing it softly behind him.

I look around again, wishing this were Zane's room and we weren't at a party full of loud, drunk strangers so I could lie down and close my eyes. But it's not, and I don't think it would be very appropriate if I lay down on a stranger's bed. It's bad enough I'm sitting on it; it's weird.

It takes the guy—I just realized I didn't ask him his name—about fifteen minutes to come back in. I hope he found Zane because my head feels like it's going to explode.

"Here, I found you some aspirin and brought you

a bottle of water." He walks over and hands me the pills and the bottle.

"Thanks, uh, I don't think I caught your name."

He smiles and sits down next to me. "You're welcome, and my name is Nick."

I give him a half smile, which is all I can muster feeling the way I do, then put the pills in my mouth and wash them down.

"So, were you able to find Zane?" I ask, ready to head home.

He gives me a sympathetic look and shakes his head. "I didn't find him, but I was able to find out where he is." He doesn't continue, so I ask where. "He, uh, he left with some chick about an hour ago. But Liam said he told him to tell you that he left you his truck." He looks away for a second, then looks back at me.

"He left? But I came here with him. Why would he leave without even telling me?" I don't understand; I don't know a single person here and he just left me here to fend for myself.

"I'm sorry, he must have left with the girl he was with, his girlfriend maybe? Liam said they couldn't keep their hands off each other."

I can feel tears gathering in my eyes. I haven't even been here for one full day yet and he's already forgotten about me.

"Hey, it's okay. I'll make sure you make it home."

As I feel the first tear drop down my cheek, Nick brings his hand up to wipe it way. "Hey, don't cry." He pulls me into a hug and rubs my back. Even though I only met this guy twenty minutes ago, I take comfort in him. At least someone is here for me.

I pull back and look up at him. "I'm sorry. Thank you, I needed that."

He looks me deeply the in the eyes, and then leans into me. Before I know what is happening, his lips are on mine. I'm too shocked to stop him, but after a couple of seconds, I try to push him away.

"What are you doing?" I ask, and try to stand, but he holds me in place.

"Shh, it's okay." He leans back in to kiss me again, but I pull back even further.

"No! What are you doing?"

Without warning, he grabs me, lays me down on the bed and places his body over mine. "Come on, you know you want it." Then he presses his mouth over mine again but with more force. I try to push at his chest, but he grabs my hands and pulls them above my head.

"Stop!" I yell, and kick out, trying to get him off of me, but all that does is give him the perfect opportunity to situate himself between my thighs.

I can feel his hardness against my center and it makes me gasp in shock and fear while I struggle even more. He's turned on by my fear and struggle! The only thing that separates my most private parts from his advances are my panties, but even that barrier doesn't last long. He holds my hands in one of his and reaches down to yank them off roughly, ripping them at the seams.

"Please stop! No!" I try to yell again but he stuffs my torn panties into my mouth and covers it with his hand.

"You're such a tease," he growls as he grinds into me.

Tears are streaming down my face and I feel like my lungs are burning from lack of oxygen with my panties in my mouth and his hand over both my nose and lips. I try to bite down on his hand until he pulls it away and yells, "Fuck, you bitch!" He slaps me so hard across the face that I see stars.

I feel him reach between us to unbutton his pants, then in the next second I feel a burning pain in my lower region as he rips through my vagina, stealing my virginity. *Oh fuck, it hurts*. It feels like someone held a knife over a hot flame and then shoved it up inside me. I scream again, but he covers my mouth with his hand as he thrusts into me again, this time harder.

The pain ripping through me is almost too much to bear; I feel like I'm going to pass out from it. I almost welcome that; I don't want to experience this anymore. But the blackness never comes. He keeps thrusting into me harder and faster. I can hear him grunt and groan and all I can do is scream and whimper into his hand while I try to think past the pain and pray that it ends soon.

It feels like hours later when he thrusts one last time and then stills inside of me. I can see black spots in my vision, but before blackness takes me from lack of oxygen, he lifts his hand from my mouth and removes himself from me. I spit the panties out of my mouth and try to take in as much air as I can, but it's made difficult from the sobs ripping through my chest. I can feel wetness seep out of me and run down my buttocks as I lay broken and sobbing on the bed.

With shaky hands, I pull my dress down and roll over into the fetal position. It hurts so much. I hear him zipping up his pants and then see him walk in front of me. He squats down so he can look into my eyes. "You know you wanted it, so if you try to tell someone otherwise, they won't believe you." He smirks at me and leaves the room. As soon as I hear the door close, I lose it.

***

I pull myself together as best I can and open the door to see if anyone is in the hallway before making my way into the bathroom. I check myself out in the mirror and see that my eyes are bloodshot from crying, I have the start of a bruise on my cheek, and my lips are bruised and puffy. I glance at my legs and see blood running down them. I take some toilet paper and try to clean myself up as gently as possible. My crotch burns and the pain travels all the way up into my stomach.

Once I've cleaned myself up as much as I can, I open the bathroom door and look around again to see if anyone is there. As soon as the coast is clear, I make a beeline for the front door. Thankfully, I don't run into anybody and I don't think anyone even notices me.

I find my way to Zane's truck and see that his keys are on the front seat. I climb in and sit down as gently as I can. I start the engine and peel out of the parking space. I don't care how reckless I'm being; I only want to get out of there and fast. I don't even know where I'm going; my only thought is to get as far away from here as I can.

Ten minutes later, I'm in front of a Wal-Mart. I grab my purse and go into the clothing section to find some sweatpants and a shirt. Then I go to the pharmacy section, throw the morning-after pill into my cart, grab some wet wipes, and head to the checkout.

The cashier looks at me strangely, but doesn't comment on my appearance. She can probably tell what happened to me, but she doesn't ask if I'm okay. She rings me up and avoids eye contact.

I step into the bathroom, clean myself up with the wet wipes, and change into the sweats. Then I cup my hands under the faucet and take the pill. The guy didn't use a condom when he raped me and I'm not on birth control. There is no way I can allow myself to get pregnant. I'll have to make sure I go to the clinic soon to get tested for STDs too.

Once I'm back in Zane's truck, I try calling him. It goes straight to voicemail. I hang up and open my messages.

Me: Where are you? I need you!

I sit there for five minutes without hearing back from him. I call again, and get his voicemail. "Zane, where are you? I need you. Please call me back!" I try to hold back my sob but it breaks free as I hang up the phone.

After I wipe the tears and calm down a bit, I text him again.

Me: Zane, please, answer me. Where are you?

Ten minutes later, nothing. I drive to my dorm and go to my car. I get in and sit there. I don't want to go into my dorm. I don't want my roommate to hear me talking to Zane when he finally answers. But after twenty more minutes, he still hasn't called or messaged me back. I call and leave another voice message. "Zane, please pick up. Why did you leave me at that party? Please, call me back, I really need you."

A couple minutes later I text him again.

Me: Answer your fucking phone, please!

After what feels like hours later, I finally get a message back from him.

Zane: Jesus fucking Christ! I'm sorry, but I do have a fucking life ya know. I can't be there for you all the fucking time. You need to learn to take care of yourself at some point. I'm not always going to be around for every little thing you need! I'm turning my phone off. Maybe I'll talk to you tomorrow. Make sure to leave my keys on the console.

I can't believe him! He was the one that took me to that party. He was the one who told me I should come here to go to school. He was the one that said he would take care of me. I didn't ask for any of this! Fuck this and fuck him.

I start my car and drive the two hours back

home. When I arrive, I walk right into my grandmother's room without turning on any of the lights. The sun is starting to rise so I can barely make out her bed. I throw myself down and cry.

When I've calmed down enough, I look on her nightstand and see the picture of her I placed there. I reach out and grab it, holding it to my chest. "What should I do, Gram? I feel so lost!" I cry some more and keep asking her over and over again for answers. Of course she doesn't reply, but it doesn't stop me from asking, praying for some sort of an answer.

I fall asleep clinging to her picture. I don't know what I'm going to do, but I do know that I'm never going back to Austin. I can't face what happened. And I don't want to face Zane either. He wasn't there for me when I needed him the most. And when I begged him to answer me and he finally replied, he didn't even ask if I was okay or what was wrong. He just blew up at me. Well, I've had enough. I'm done. Done with him, done with everything.

I wake up a couple of hours later and come up with a plan. I can't be in this house anymore, and I can't go back to Austin. There's nothing left for me here. So I pack up my room and take the few things of my grandmother's that I can't live without. Then I take sheets and some plastic from the garage and cover all the furniture. Then I unplug all the appliances. I'll deal with the rest later, but for right now, this will have to do.

Once I pack everything into my car, I grab the football Zeke gave me. I sit on the floor with a pen and paper to write Zane a note and place it in the box with the football. It takes me forever to come up with what I needed to say to him, but finally I find the words:

Zane,

You really let me down. You told me everything would be fine and you would always be there for me. Not only did you break your promise, but you broke ME. I can't be here anymore, there is nothing here but pain. Everywhere I look, I see a reminder of my grandmother and remember the way things were when Zeke was still alive, but the thing that hurts the most is you. Knowing that you are still here but will never truly be there for me. You have constantly left me behind, forgotten about me, and have damaged my heart so badly it's beyond repair.

Inside this box is Zeke's football. I should have given this to you a long time ago, it was always meant to be yours. I hope it brings you peace. Please don't try to find me or contact me. If you ever cared about me at all, you will let me go so I can try to heal. There will always be a part of me that loves you, but I can never forgive you. I hope you are happy in your life and you get everything you ever wanted.

Danielle

I write Zane's name on the box, then walk over and place it in his parents' back yard where I know it will be found. Then I get in my car and head west. I don't yet know where I'll go, but I know I can't stay here. I need to make a life for myself somewhere else.

The old Danielle is dead, and in her place is a girl that I don't yet know.

CHAPTER 14

Zane

I wake feeling someone's hand traveling down my abdomen toward my cock. When I open my eyes, I don't know why I expect to see Danielle, but it's not her—it never was, no matter how much I dreamed it would be—it's the blonde chick from the party last night.

I have been in love with Danielle since the first time I saw her five years ago. Then what happened between us Thanksgiving night a year and a half ago changed everything.

After I told her I wouldn't be able to make it home for the holiday—I had decided I was going to join the Marines and had to get shit situated with school—she told me that she and her boyfriend had broken up. I tried to message her and call to see what the fuck happened. If he hurt her, he was a dead man. But she turned her phone off. I was beyond crazy with worry, so I decided to jump on my bike and go to her. I needed to know what happened.

When I got there, she laughed it off like it was nothing. Then when I told her that I couldn't stay, she broke down and I couldn't leave her like that. I only meant to comfort her, but what happened next I will never forget. I made her think that it was a mistake and that I was sorry, but I wasn't. She gave me something precious that night, something that I will always carry with me.

Bringing home the blonde chick last night was a mistake. I shouldn't have left with her, but I was so pissed off. I only wanted to get drunk and forget about this day from hell, well, everything really, for a few hours. And what better way to do that than lose myself in some random pussy? It also didn't help that as soon as Danielle showed up at her dorm, I wanted to bend her over my truck, she looked so sexy in the dress she was wearing. All I could think about was the way she tastes, the way she feels, and how much I love her.

The day had started turning to shit when I got a call from my Commander telling me that we're getting shipped overseas in two months. I haven't even been able to tell Danielle that I joined the Marines yet. How the fuck am I going to tell her I'm getting deployed for at least a year?

When I graduated high school, I wanted to follow in my brother's footsteps, but after a huge argument with my parents, I decided I would give myself a year to make the decision. But then four months into my schooling, I knew joining was what I wanted, what I had to do. I didn't tell Danielle because I figured it would bring up old memories about Zeke. She wouldn't understand that it's for him that I have to do this. Shit, my parents didn't even understand. Not only did we get into a huge fight when I told them what I wanted to do the day I left for school, but they pretty much disowned me the day I finally decided I was going to do it. I should have said something to Danielle the day I left, but I thought with everything else going on, she couldn't handle it.

Over the past two years, I've had lots of times to tell her, but really no time at all. When she would call me, I would ignore the calls because I needed more time to figure out what to say to her. I would always send simple text messages to let her know I hadn't forgotten about her, but it was never enough. Then, when I left for training, I had no phone to call or even text her. I know I missed her birthday and her graduation, but I figured she would understand when I finally told her. She'd be upset, but she has always forgiven me. And after the shock wore off, she'd be proud of me, like she was of Zeke. She would get it, and I knew that, but I still couldn't make the words come out.

Then it didn't help that she was dating that dipshit for a while after I left. I would love to be able to say that she was always with him and I never had the chance to tell her, but that would be a lie. She always made time for me, and if I told her I needed to see her or that I had something important to tell her, no matter where she was or who she was with, she would have dropped everything for me. That's just who she is—selfless and purely good. She would do anything for the people she cares about. But I couldn't bring myself to tell her.

After her grandmother died, I couldn't leave her there alone anymore. I knew I would have to tell her as soon as she got here since she would find out I was no longer in school eventually, but I wanted to find the perfect time. But a couple hours before she arrived in Austin, I got the phone call of the impending deployment. Time had officially run out.

***

When I drove to meet her at her dorm when she first arrived, the first thing I noticed was the dress she was wearing. It was white, short and made her look like an angel—my angel. I had to calm myself down before I did something I couldn't take back. So instead of unpacking her stuff right away, I figured we could delay for a bit and get something to eat first. Plus, I really needed a drink if I was going to make it through the night. I had to control myself because the alternative wasn't an option. I couldn't lose her, and I knew if I took what I really wanted—what I needed—I would, and I couldn't let that happen.

While we were at the bar eating, I got a phone call from a buddy of mine from when I was still at school, Liam, about a party his boy was throwing. I figured it would be fun for Danielle, and I would be able to delay telling her the news until tomorrow. Maybe this would work out for the better.

We pulled up to the house, and as soon as we walked in, I noticed the looks the guys were throwing her way. I was pissed off, but knew I couldn't do anything about it. She was bound to find someone soon anyway. I would have to get over it.

I only introduced her to a few people I knew, because frankly I only knew a handful of people there since I don't go to school anymore, then led her to the living room to sit with our drinks. She went off to the bathroom soon after we arrived, and the only thing I thought of while she walked away with her hips swinging from side to side was following her. I wanted to push her up against the wall and ravish her sweet body. It didn't help that I already knew what she tasted like, what she sounded like when she came. I knew I'd had too much to drink. I would have to slow it down and get a handle on this shit, and fast.

As I got up to clear my head of all the things I want to do to Danielle, this busty blonde comes over and takes Danielle's spot on the couch beside me.

"Hey, sexy, thought you could use a drink." She hands me a beer and starts talking, but I don't hear anything she says because I can see Danielle coming back into the room. I give her a look, trying to see if she is okay, but before I can make out her expression, the blonde starts rubbing her hand up my thigh. Fuck, that feels good. Since Danielle arrived today, I've had a constant hard-on.

Over the next hour or so, I am barely able to sneak a glance at Danielle, but she doesn't come over and she hasn't said she isn't having a good time. She's probably used to this anyway. It sure as fuck reminds me of a lot of the parties in high school—me having to let off steam in another chick's pussy while only thinking of Danielle.

Things with Blondie are starting to really heat up, and unless I want to fuck her here on this couch in front of everyone, we need to take this private party outside. I'm thinking we can have a quickie in my truck, and then I can come back in and grab Danielle.

I get up and try to find Danielle to tell her I'll be right back, but I don't see her. Before I can look around for her, Blondie sticks her hand down my pants to stroke my cock. I won't be long anyway, I decide. I'll find Danielle when I'm done. It will probably be better this way, because if I see a look of hurt or disappointment on Danielle's face, I probably won't be able to go through with it. And that's not an option. If I don't do this, I'll risk attacking Danielle and losing her.

Once out in my truck, things happen pretty fast. I barely get my jeans unzipped and a condom on before she is sinking down on my cock. "Fuck!" Damn, this is exactly what I needed. I grab her hips and start to pump harder and faster into her, racing to the finish line. I don't care if she gets off or not, I just need relief.

I close my eyes and picture Danielle in that white dress, imagining that it's her riding my cock. Though if I was being honest with myself, I would never fuck Danielle here. She deserves a bed and soft lovemaking, not a hard fuck in my truck.

"Oh God, baby, I'm gonna come!" Blondie interrupts my thoughts and the sound of her voice almost makes me push her off of me in disgust, but once I feel her clench around my cock, the only thing on my mind is getting off. I pump into her three more times before I release myself into the condom.

She slides off my lap, but instead of fixing her clothes like I thought she would, she takes off the condom and leans down to start licking my cock clean. Holy shit, is this chick for real? I can already feel myself harden again.

"Let's go to your place, stud, and I'll take care of you all night long." Before I can reply, she latches on to my cock and sucks until I come again. Fuck, this chick is exactly what I need tonight. I pull her out of my truck and tell her she's driving. At least this way Danielle will have a way back to her dorm.

***

My phone would not stop ringing. As soon as it turned silent, I would get a notification that I got a voice mail and then a text message would come in. What the fuck? Can't they take a fucking hint? I don't even reach over to silence my phone; instead, I continue banging Blondie into my mattress.

After I finish and she finally passes out, I grab my phone to see what the fuck was so important. I have four voicemails and at least 10 text messages. The first one is from Danielle. Great, is she bitching at me for leaving? I open up the first three messages.

Danielle: Where are you? I need you!

Danielle: Zane, please, answer me. Where are you?

Danielle: Answer your fucking phone, please!

I don't read any more of the messages and don't even bother to listen to my voicemails. She has no idea what the fuck I'm going through and she says that she needs me? What, does she need me to hold her hand on the way to truck? Fuck. I don't need this shit right now! I have enough on my plate as it is.

I type out my message and then turn off my phone. I'm probably going to regret that in the morning, but she needs to understand that I'm not always going to be able to be there for her, even though I wish I could be. Fuck, this deployment is ruining everything. I toss my phone onto the end table and roll over to wake Blondie up so I can fuck her one more time before passing out.

***

It takes me longer than it should to get Blondie out of my bed, but finally I am able to call Danielle. It goes right to voicemail, but instead of leaving a message, I decide to drive over to her dorm. It's better to apologize in person for the way I acted last night anyway. Plus, I really need to tell her about my deployment. It's time she knows.

I walk outside and remember she has my truck. "Fuck!"

I call Liam and have him come pick me up to

give me a ride over to her dorm. It takes him a half an hour, but then we are on our way.

"So what the fuck happened to you last night, man?" he asks as we pull out of my parking lot.

"I hooked up with this chick. She fucked my cock till it about fell off, man!" I try to laugh, but it falls short. That shit isn't funny, but I don't need to explain to him about me and my feelings for Danielle.

He shakes his head and looks like he is pissed about something. Not sure what his problem is, I decide to ignore him. He'll get over it soon enough; he always does.

When we are almost to Danielle's dorm, he breaks the silence. "I can't believe you left your girl at that party last night to get your dick wet."

Who the fuck does he think he is? I feel like shit about doing it already, I don't need him to tell me how it is. "Listen, save the fuckin' lecture, I'm sure I'll get enough shit from her when I get to her place, all right?"

I know it was fucked up, but I'm sure Danielle understands and like I said before, she's used to this shit from me by now. And it's not like I left her there without a way home. I'm not a complete dick.

"Look, man, I didn't say anything to you before because I figured you wouldn't leave her there by herself, but if I were you, I'd make sure she is okay."

What the fuck does that mean? "Why wouldn't she be all right? I left my truck there for her and she's a big girl. She's fine. Pissed off maybe, but she'll get over it." I don't see how it's any of his fucking business, but if he doesn't shut the fuck up soon, I'm going to lay him out.

"Look, there was a guy at the party last night that has a bad reputation with the ladies. He takes what isn't his. All's I'm saying is, make sure she's all right."

He takes what isn't his? What the hell does that mean?

We pull up to her dorm and park by my truck, but I don't see her car.

"Where the hell is she?" I say more to myself than to Liam. I get out and look in my truck. Maybe she left a note, but I don't see one. My keys are still in the ignition, but what catches my eye is what looks like a blood stain on my seat. What the fuck? I know that wasn't there last night, so where the hell did it come from?

Liam comes up behind me and notices the same thing. "Like I said, you shouldn't have left her there."

Not only am I confused as to what the fuck he is talking about, now I'm really worried about Danielle. After hearing all this shit Liam is spouting and seeing this stain, I remember the text messages she sent me last night. Did something happen after I left?

"What did you mean that he has a bad reputation?" I ask, with anger radiating off of me in waves but needing to get this shit straight.

"Look, I should have told you when you showed up and I saw that your friend was a girl, and I'm sorry, but I thought you would be with her the whole time. He has a reputation for forcing himself

174

on women, but no one will turn his ass in. I'm not sure if it's true, but that's what people have said."

I instantly see red. If that motherfucker touched even one hair on Danielle's head, he is a dead man. "And you just *now* decide to fucking mention this!" I turn around and slam him against my truck. I have my forearm against his throat ready to kill this fucker for not telling me sooner.

"Whoa, dude, I don't even know if it's true!" he manages to get out.

I lift my arm from his neck and let him go. If something happened to her, it's my fault for leaving her. He should have told me, but I shouldn't have fucking left her. "*God fucking damn it!*" I yell.

I try to call her again but it goes to voicemail. She must have her phone off. She's not here, so that means she can only be one place. Home. I jump in my truck and peel out before Liam can say anything else.

I make it to her house in record time, but she's not there. I knock on the door but there are no lights on and when I look in the windows, I don't see anyone. Through the living room window I see a flash of white that catches my eye. It's a sheet thrown over the couch. Why would she have done that before she left for school? I thought she said that she wanted to come back here at least once a month, so why would she cover shit? Unless…fuck, unless she left! But where the fuck would she go? Think, Zane, think!

I head over to my parent's place to see if maybe they've seen her. When I walk inside, no one is home. Great. Just my fucking luck.

175

While I wait for my parents to get home, I go out back because I need fresh air and I don't want anyone to see me pacing like a crazed lunatic. Once I'm outside, I spot a box sitting on the grass by the fence. When I'm a few feet away, my name becomes visible. It's in Danielle's handwriting. What the fuck is this, and why would she leave it for me?

I tear open the top and find an envelope. I open it. Inside is a letter. I read it and the words drop me to my knees. She's gone. I don't know what happened, but I can guess. That fucker raped her, or tried to, and I wasn't there. She's right, I broke my promise. I reach into the box and pull out my brother's football. As I turn it over in my hands, I replay the words in her letter, each cutting me deeper than the last. *You really let me down. Not only did you break your promise to me. You broke me. I can't be here anymore. There is nothing here but pain for me. The thing that hurts the most is you. You have broken me down so far that I don't know if I can ever recover. Zeke's football. It was always meant to be yours. I hope it brings you peace. If you ever cared for me. Let me go. Always love you. I can never forgive you. I hope you are happy.*

I have ended up doing what I've always feared I would do if I ever told her how I really felt; she got hurt, she now hates me, and she's left for good. It doesn't matter if I was the one that physically hurt her or not. My actions played a part in her pain, and for that, I will never forgive myself.

I have no idea where she went, but I know her—

she will run far away and won't be back. And I don't have the time to look for her; I leave soon for my first deployment. Maybe she is right and I should let her go so she can move on with her life. She'll be better off without me. I'd only end up hurting her more in the long run.

There is one thing I can do to make it up to her, though, even if she never knows I did it. I will find that piece of shit that hurt her, and make him pay. He will regret the day he was born when I'm done with him.

CHAPTER 15

Four Years Later
Danielle

I wake up before my alarm clock goes off, rub my temples and stare up at the ceiling. I already have a headache, but I shouldn't have expected anything else since today is that day—the anniversary of the day my life changed forever.

Every year, it's the same thing: I wake up before the sun rises and I lie in bed with a headache from hell for an hour before can I drag myself out of bed. Then I put on my yoga pants, tank top, and tennis shoes and head out for a run. I don't keep track of how far I go. I just keep going until I can't feel my legs anymore. I don't know why I do it, but it makes me...feel, I guess. Then I come home, take a shower, and head into work. It doesn't matter what day of the week it is, I will always be in the shop when that day rolls around each year. Anything to keep myself busy.

I clip my iPod to my arm and head out the door.

I was never really a big fan of running when I was younger, but it has sort of become a release for me. Like working at the tattoo shop and drawing.

I start at a slow jog but soon move up to a nice steady pace and start thinking about my life and how far I've come since that day four years ago.

***

When I packed up the things I couldn't leave behind, I headed west, not sure where I would wind up. I figured I'd drive till I couldn't drive anymore. I ended up in a town named Dixon, about an hour from San Francisco.

Since I had been up since the morning I left home to meet Zane at college, the first thing I did was find a hotel and sleep for eighteen hours straight. I thought I would have trouble sleeping, or at least have nightmares, but I never did. I don't even think I moved an inch from the time I lay down to the time I got up the next day.

When I finally was able to wipe the sleep from my eyes, I took a long shower, then went to get some much needed food since I hadn't eaten anything substantial since the burger and fries at the bar before the party.

On my way back to my car from the diner, I see a sign that read *'Apartment for Rent'* on the door of a shop, a tattoo place named Sinners Ink. I decided to check it out.

When I walked into the shop, there was a mountain of a man standing behind the reception desk. He looked to be in his early fifties with his hair cut real short, a black sleeveless shirt that showed off muscular arms full of tattoos, and a black leather vest. As I could see that the vest indicated he was a part of a motorcycle club. There were a couple of patches on the front; one said **'President,'** another said **'Mack,'** and the last one read **'Forsaken Sinners MC.'**

He was staring at my face with a look of anger when I approached him, probably because of the bruise that is still healing on my cheek, but the expression was gone before I could think more about it.

"You lost, girl?" he said in a deep voice.

Even though I was shaking with fear, I spoke with more bravery than I thought possible. "I'm interested in the apartment for rent."

He seemed like he was going to turn me away, but must have decided I really needed it. "The rent is free, but you would have to work the desk here at the shop. Can you handle that?"

I was surprised that it was a work for rent deal, but happy that it would mean I'd have a job to keep me busy. I might not get paid actual money, but at least I'd be able to get out of that hotel room. I figured once I was settled, I could find another job to buy food and anything else I needed. I'd be fine for a while with the money I have in my bank account.

"What would I have to do?" I asked. I needed to make sure it was something I was capable of doing before agreeing. I'd never had a job before, so I didn't have any experience.

"Answering the phone, scheduling appointments,

and running the cash register. If you're wanting to work for more than rent, you could do the inventory, order supplies, clean, and make sure everything is stocked." It sounded too good to be true.

"I don't have any experience doing any of that. Would you train me?" I really wanted to take this deal, but I didn't want to lie to him either.

"Let me show you the apartment first. If you're still interested, we'll work out the rest later." Before I could answer, he was walking out from behind the desk toward what looked to be a back door. "Louie, watch the front."

I didn't look to see who he was talking to, instead followed him outside. In big letters, the back of his cut said **'Forsaken Sinners'** across the top and **'California'** at the bottom. In the middle, there was the MC emblem, which consisted of a skull, two guns crossing over and flames out the top. Two small patches on either side read *'MC'* and *'1%.'* From what I knew of motorcycle clubs, the *'1%'* meant they are an outlaw club. It's amazing what TV and books will teach you. Maybe that should have had me turning around and going back to my hotel, but it didn't. I actually felt safe around this man.

We walked out of the back of the shop and next to it there was another entrance that led upstairs. At the top of the stairs, there were two doors, one that said *'Stay Out'* and another that I assumed was to the apartment.

When he opened the apartment, my jaw practically hit the floor. It was bigger than I thought it would be, and way nicer than anything I could have hoped for. Plus, it was furnished, which pretty much sealed the deal all on its own since I didn't have anything but my clothes. All of this for putting in a couple hours downstairs? Shit, luck seemed to be on my side today. It was about fucking time something went right for me.

"I'll take it," I said without even walking further into the apartment. I turned to look at him and saw that he was staring at me. Not in a creepy way, but a deep in thought kind of way.

"You in some sort of trouble?" he asked.

Not wanting to tell him the full reason I was there, but knowing I had to give him something, I glanced away and said, "No trouble, but I had to leave." I hoped that would be enough.

I looked up and saw him nod his head. "All right, but if you are in trouble, you need to tell me. I can't help you if I don't know what's going on."

I believed him too. There was something about him that made me feel safe. "Let's go downstairs and I'll show you around the shop. You can move in tonight and start work tomorrow. Let me know if you need help moving anything or leaving where you are now."

I was smart enough to know he meant if I was leaving a bad place and needed someone there with me while I got my stuff out. It was nice of him, but I was alone at a hotel, so no help was needed.

I followed him out the door and down the stairs.

I started work the next day. It didn't take me long to learn how to do the inventory and stock the supply room. Everything else was really easy to do.

Mack paid me well for doing the extras, probably way more than I deserved, so I never had to find another job. Plus, I really liked working there. The guys I met were all nice.

***

During my first year at the shop, I was quiet and spent all my time either working or in my apartment. I met a few members of the Sinners when they would come in to talk with Mack or when they were getting tattoos done. Mack was the president of the club, and he was also the owner of the shop. At first I thought he only hung around, making sure everything was running smoothly, until one day I saw him tattoo a dragon that took up a guy's whole back.

Then there is Louie. He's a member of the club and works at the shop. He is a couple years older than me, tall, and solidly built. He isn't huge by any means, but I would bet on him to win a fight, that's for sure. He is also ruggedly handsome with short black hair, green eyes, and a smile that makes me break out in goose bumps. It is almost evil, sinister in a way, but sexy as hell.

Other members have come into the shop too, but I don't know them all that well: Skinner, who is the VP; Tom Tom, who is the secretary; and Toby, the Sergeant at Arms. Skinner and Tom Tom are both in their mid-thirties, with muscular builds. Toby is only about six years older than me, with dark brown hair in a crew cut, eyes the color of the sky, and a square jaw that is always sprinkled with stubble.

183

I learned a lot about the MC lifestyle while working at the tattoo shop. Sure, I'd read books about motorcycle clubs, but working at a tattoo shop owned by one and getting to know the members was something I thought I would never do.

I opened up to Mack a couple months after starting at the shop. I told him about my parents, how I lost Zeke and my grandmother, and finally about the night I left home. I left Zane out, though. It hurt too much to think about him, let alone talk about him. Mack became like a father to me, treated me like his own flesh and blood. And after everything that I had been through, it was nice to have someone like him care for me and make me feel protected.

Mack was pissed when I told him about what happened that night at the party, but then I asked if he would teach me how to defend myself, so it gave him something else to focus on and feel like he was able to help make it better—which he was. He called Toby, who was not only the Sergeant at Arms, but also a MMA fighter.

I started going to the gym with him every day to learn self-defense. After I had that down, we started messing around in the ring, boxing—him showing me how to throw a proper punch and how to block. When I was up there, I was able to let everything out; all the anger, all the pain, all my frustrations would melt off of me with my sweat. He also started taking me to the gun range to teach me how to fire a gun and hit a target. Even though I loved boxing and being in the ring, shooting made me feel powerful, like I had all the control. Mack even bought me my own handgun. I was finally starting to feel like myself again and becoming the person I wanted to be.

One day, I asked Mack about getting a tattoo and he insisted that he do it for me. He's an amazing artist. When he asked what I wanted, I told him I wanted a phoenix on my back, but I didn't have a picture to work from. I could have drawn something, but at that point, I hadn't drawn anything for a long time.

He designed the whole thing, and it turned out amazing. Most phoenix tattoos you see are full of color, but mine is black and gray. I wanted to show that when I rose up from the ashes, I was a different person—darker, and with the knowledge that life isn't always colorful, but full of pain. I couldn't have designed it better myself. That was the first of many tattoos I would get.

I started going to the Forsaken Sinners' clubhouse and bartending for them. I was able to meet the rest of the brothers and really start building a relationship with them. They considered me a sister since Mack had pretty much claimed me as his daughter. I loved the way I was around them and they way they filled my heart with love. Not the lovey-dovey type of love you get when you want to spend the rest of your life with someone, but the type you have for family. They make me feel sort of like a princess, their MC Princess.

Louie and Toby became my confidants. They grounded me. When I wasn't at the shop working or at the gym with Toby, I was hanging out with one or both of them. We'd go for rides on their bikes, shoot the shit at the clubhouse, or they'd teach me how to play pool and darts. While Toby was like a big brother to me, Louie became my best friend.

Around my second year there, I got so bored one day sitting at the reception desk I decided to draw to pass the time. So I started doodling on a blank page in the appointment book.

"You ever think about tattooing?"

Since I didn't realize Mack had come up behind me, when he spoke I about fell out of my chair. When I calmed down and righted myself, his words hit me. I never really thought about it till he mentioned it, but now that the thought was in my head, I wanted to learn. "Would you teach me?"

And so began my apprenticeship with Mack to become a tattoo artist. It took me a little less than a year to learn the craft, since I already knew how to draw. I worked side by side with Mack and Louie at the shop. I would still man the front when necessary though, which was fine by me.

A year ago, Mack signed ownership for the shop over to me because he wanted to spend more time at the club. Since I loved the shop as much as he did, he said he couldn't think of anyone better to take over for him—his daughter. He still comes in to help out when he's bored or we need the help, but mostly it's me and Louie.

I've come to love my new life. I have an amazing career, I bought my own house a few months ago, and I have a new family. I still harbor the pain and anger from what led me here, but I've been able to take all of those feelings and put them into my career as a tattoo artist or work them out at the gym or shooting range. Life is good. Except when August fifth rolls around.

***

After my shower, I head into the kitchen to grab a cup of coffee. What I'd really like is a shot of Jack, but I know that's a bad idea, at least until after I get back from the shop. Then I plan to drink a full bottle, listen to music, and design myself a new tattoo. My usual on this date.

As I'm walking out of the house, my phone rings. I don't even check the caller ID because there are only a handful of people with my number.

"Yeah?" I say as I unlock the truck door.

"Dani, where you at?" says Mack. Don't know why he's asking, since he should know after four years that I'm either in the shop or at least making my way there by now.

"Heading to the shop, why?" I start the truck and get a thrill when I hear the pipes cackle. Fuck, I love this thing! It was a birthday present from Mack last year, a hunter green 2013 Ford Raptor, extended cab. Did I mention that I love my truck?

Mack interrupts my thoughts. "You got a lot of appointments today?"

I wish. I only have one this morning, and it won't even take me an hour. Some college chick wants a small butterfly on her stomach—typical. "Nah, only one this morning. What ya got?" If I have to sit on my ass all day doing nothing I'm going to go crazy and probably end up breaking shit. I can't let my mind wander, not today. It will take me back to *that night*. I haven't had any problems the last couple of years forgetting what happened or at least moving on, but for some reason, whenever today rolls around, if I'm not doing something to keep myself busy or drunk and passed out, that's all I think about. Why that would happen to me, what did I do to deserve it, why Zane wasn't there, why he was such a dick, etc.

"Got a brother who wants a back piece. Can you work him in?" he asks.

A back piece will take a while, so I'll do it. "Yup. Who is it?" I love all the brothers, so it doesn't matter to me.

"Blaze. He transferred from another chapter this week."

That's news. "Yeah, I could fit him in. My morning appointment is at 11. He can come in any time after noon. Does he know what he wants?" I hope it will be something original that will last a while, hopefully all day.

"I don't know the specifics, but it's a big back piece from what he said."

Nice! That will take me at least six hours. "Does he have it drawn already or do I need to draw it out when he gets here?" That would use up even more time.

"No. He already has a sketch."

Shit, that sucks. Oh well, at least it's a big piece; it should still use up most of my day even without drawing it from scratch. Plus, I may have to change some things on it, depending on the quality of the drawing. "All right, tell him to come in around

188

noon."

"Thanks, darlin', I'll send him over. Be nice. He's a good brother, and we'd really like to keep him here." He knows I am sometimes a bitch to people I don't know, but I would never do anything to jeopardize the club; they are my family.

"Yeah, yeah." I hang up the phone as I'm pulling up to the shop. Louie isn't coming in today, so I'll have to set everything up.

I check the clock and see that I still have at least twenty minutes until my appointment comes in. That'll be enough time to set up my station, check my email, and grab a soda out of the fridge.

***

I'm just finishing the cleanup on the college girl when I hear the bell ring above the door. I assume it's Blaze, so I call over my shoulder without lifting my eyes from my work, "Almost done, Blaze. Have a seat, I'll be out in a minute."

I hear him mumble "Ah huh," and walk over to the couch.

"Okay, you're all done. Keep the covering on until you get home. Here are the directions for the aftercare. If there are any problems, my number's on the bottom," I tell my client, and start cleaning up my station. She already paid, so she gets up and walks out to the front.

When I'm almost done with my cleanup I say, "All right, Blaze, come on back."

As I'm sitting on my chair, I bend over to grab the supplies I'll need for the tattoo.

189

"Thanks for fitting me in, Dani. Mack said you were the best around." At the first word out of his mouth, I drop the bottle of antiseptic and the needle I was pulling out of my drawer—I know that voice. I hear it in my dreams.

I try to catch my breath, but I can't seem to get enough air. It can't be…

Out of the corner of my eye, I see him settle into my client chair. "You all right?" he asks, reaching out to touch me. I flinch away from him, but I don't look up. My heart feels like it's beating so fast and so hard it could break a rib.

It only takes a couple seconds for the shock and hurt to fade, and then there is nothing but anger. But anger is good. I need that to get through what happens next. "What the fuck are you doing here, Zane?"

CHAPTER 16

When I look up at him, what little breath I had is knocked out of me. Damn, the years have been good to him. Not a lot has changed, but at the same time, everything has. Holy fuck, look at that body! Zane was always buff, but I can tell he's been working out quite a bit. He has muscle on top of muscle now. I'm surprised that the shirt he is wearing isn't bursting at the seams. He's wearing his cut that says Forsaken Sinners and his road name, Blaze, but nothing else on the front to give me an idea where he is ranked in the club. But then again, he did transfer from another chapter, so he may not have rank here yet.

Then there is his face, which still seems to have stayed the same, except maybe he's even better-looking than before. His hair is still cropped short, but he seems harder, or rougher. Zane always had a look that said "Don't fuck with me," but now it's deadly.

When I reach his eyes, I have to turn away because looking into them brings back too many memories. I remember the first day we met in his back yard and seeing frustration in them. I remember the day we found out about Zeke and seeing the pain and anger sparking like a livewire. And then the look in them the last time I saw him— he was buzzed but had a look of lust mixed with anger when I saw him with that girl. The girl he left me for the night I was raped.

How dare he come here! This is my home. This is where I've rebuilt a life for myself after my old life was ripped away from me. He has no right to be here.

"Danielle…?" he whispers like he doesn't believe I'm really here, then reaches out to touch me.

I stand up so fast that I knock my chair over. I need to put space between us.

"Baby Girl…"

I hold my hand out in front of me, which causes him to recoil like I've slapped him. If he only knew how I felt. I want to do more than slap him. "Don't call me that," I seethe. I turn around and walk out of the room. I can't deal with this, not today.

I don't make it far before he rushes up behind me, grabbing my arm. "Danielle, wa—"

But before he can finish whatever it is he wants to say, I yank my arm out of his grasp, swing around, and punch him right in the face. It's a good shot too, has all my body weight behind it and the momentum from turning around so fast. Toby would be so proud.

"Don't you dare fucking touch me!"

He's holding his nose as blood gushes out of it.

192

Serves him right. I hope I broke it. It's the least he deserves after everything he put me through.

"Get the hell out," I say with a deadly calm, then go behind the desk to grab my phone. I want to call Mack and ask him what the fuck he was thinking sending Zane here, but then I realize he doesn't know. I'll have to explain if I call him now and I'm not sure if that's something I really want to do.

I look up from my phone and see that Zane hasn't moved a muscle. "You fuckin' deaf? I said get the fuck out! *Now*!" I yell. I can't deal with this; I don't *want* to deal with it. Not now, not ever.

When I left home, I told myself I would never see him again. I did everything I could to make sure that he would never find me. I sold my grandmother's house and left no trail of where I'd gone. I got rid of my phone and didn't get another one for almost a year, only using a burner Mack gave me when I needed one. I stopped using the name Danielle and now only answer to Dani. I was fine with the thought of never seeing him again, but looking at him now, I realize I feel more than anger. I feel like a part of me was missing and now its found its way back. I feel the love I felt for him all those years ago. And I feel guilty for leaving. I don't want to feel those things.

I sit down and whisper, because I don't have anything left in me, "Just go, Zane…" I don't look up, but after a couple of seconds, I hear him walk toward the door.

Before he leaves, though, he pauses. "Okay, Baby Girl, I'll leave…for now. But this ain't over. We are going to talk, and soon." With that, he leaves the shop.

I sit there, not moving for an hour. I can't believe Zane is back. Or should I say Blaze? And he's a part of the MC—my family. How messed up is that? Destiny doesn't know when to stop fucking with me. The bitch is still throwing me lemons, after all these years. Haven't I had enough?

Well, she can go jump off a cliff and hit every rock on the way down. "Thank you for the fucking blast from my past, bitch." Hope she heard me. I grab my keys and lock up. I hop in my truck to head home, but make one quick stop at the liquor store. Need to grab a bottle of Patron for that nice big lemon I've been served.

***

I have the bottle of tequila open before I make it through the door to my house, drinking it straight. I don't even notice the burn as it slides down my throat. It's barely five in the afternoon, but I don't care. I need to drown the thoughts from the past and forget. I don't want to feel what Zane awakened in me when he stepped back into my life. I hate that I long for him, that I've missed him and still love him. A small piece of me is happy he showed up today, but I need to bury that piece right now.

Walking into my bedroom, I strip off my jeans and shirt and head to the bathroom. Starting the bath water, I stare at my reflection in the mirror. "You will not fall apart. You can deal with this. It's been four fucking years, you'll be fine. This is nothing. You can handle this." I look myself in the eye and repeat this mantra, willing myself to believe it.

When the tub is full, I get in and lie back. I bring the bottle to my lips and take another big drink. Why did this have to happen today? If it had been any other day, would I have been able to stay in the same room as him and act like he was someone else?

I hear my phone ring in the bedroom, but I ignore it. It's probably Mack, asking what the hell happened. *Fuck*! I shouldn't have punched Zane, but it felt so good to let some of my anger out. I know deep down that what happened isn't entirely his fault, but I can't help but blame him. If he hadn't left me there, it never would have happened. If he would have helped me unpack like he said he would and not taken me to that stupid party, it never would have happened. If he had never showed up the day after Gram's funeral and said I should go to school with him, that he'd take care of me, it never would have happened. It *is* all his fault!

I hear my phone beep a message and then it starts ringing again. They can keep calling, though; I'm not answering. I don't want to talk to anyone. I don't want anyone to know that Zane and I have a past. I know it's not possible to keep it quiet for long; Mack will find out soon enough. Will he make Zane leave? And if he does, will I be able to watch him go again? I'm not sure I could.

The bottle of tequila calls to me, so while I lie back and try to relax in my bath, I continue to take greedy gulps of the burning liquid. I wish I could feel the burn, but unfortunately for me, it's going down easy. Today it's a good thing, though I know I will regret it in the morning. But I can't bring myself to care enough to stop.

After lying in the tub until the hot water turns cold, drinking half the bottle, and ignoring my phone, which goes off every couple of minutes, I finally drag myself out of the bathroom. I throw on my robe and walk slowly into the kitchen. I think it's time I start drinking out of a glass, though I'm not sure it matters now.

As I'm pulling a glass from the cabinet, someone starts banging on my door. It's so unexpected that I drop the glass and let out a scream.

"Dani! *Dani*! What's going on in there? *Let me in*!" Toby yells from outside.

"Dani, if you don't open this door in ten seconds I'm kicking it down!" Louie's voice booms with authority while Toby continues banging on the door. Shit! What the hell are they doing here?

I stumble to the door and try to unlock all the latches before I have to buy a new one. "Stand down, assholes, I'm coming!" I say loud enough they can hear me on the other side. I will end up hitting more than Zane if they kick my door in. This is really not the best day to mess with me. I'm the three deadly sins right now: dealing with the anniversary of the worst night of my life, Zane coming back into my life, and well on my way to being drunk. This is not a good time. Trust me, when I get drunk, I get mean. It must have to do with the fact that I have a lot of anger in me. Or it could be the fact that I spend all my time with bikers.

I finally get the last lock undone, but before I can

open the door for them, they are pushing it in. Toby is concerned and angry while Louie looks at me with complete and utter chaotic rage. What the fuck crawled up their asses?

"What the hell do you want?" I mumble as I walk back into the kitchen for another glass. Fuck! I have to clean up the broken glass too. I should fucking make them clean it since it's their fault it broke, but knowing the mood they are in right now, they'd probably end up causing more damage.

Toby starts going through all my rooms. I don't know what he expects to find, but I hope not finding whatever it is will calm his ass down and help me get him out of here faster. Louie is going to be the hardest.

"What do you want?" I whisper. I just want to be alone with my bottle and my hatred for everything and everyone. Is that too much to ask?

"What the fuck is going on with you?" Louie practically yells. It makes me take a step back. He's really pissed, like body shaking pissed.

"I'm fine, okay? Having a bad day is all." I don't want to get into anything with him right now, but I know he's going to push. Louie and I have a strange relationship. At first it was like we were best friends, but I know he has feelings for me, feelings I can't return.

I shouldn't have let it go that far, but one night I was having a really hard time getting rid of the memories of Nick and the way it felt when he stole my innocence. Louie was there for me and it just sort of happened. It helped me realize that what was done to me doesn't define who I am. Just because I had one bad experience with sex, doesn't mean that every experience will be like that. But afterwards, I knew we had gone too far and so I told him it couldn't happen again. Since then, things have been really strained between us. I love him, but I don't love him like that. Sometimes I wish I did. It would make things so much easier.

"You had a bad day? What the fuck happened? Does it have anything to do with Blaze showing back up at the clubhouse with a busted-up nose when he was supposed to be getting inked?" He knows something went down, but he doesn't know what. He also knows that he can only push me so far with certain things before I shut down.

"Leave it alone, Louie." I walk over to my couch, plop down, and take another swig from the bottle.

"Leave it alone? *Leave it alone*! You're here drowning yourself in a bottle of tequila and Blaze is back at the clubhouse saying it was all a misunderstanding! I'm going to ask you one more fucking time what the *fuck* is going on before I go back to Blaze and start beating the fucking answer out of him!" He's panting and shaking with anger. Well, he can kiss my ass. I don't owe him or anyone else any-fucking-thing. "Fuck. You," I say through clenched teeth, then get up and go to my room.

I pass Toby on my way there but don't stop to acknowledge him. Hopefully he will be smart and let it be. But of course, no such luck.

"Dani girl, did he hurt you?" Typical Toby, direct and right to the point. When Toby talks, you listen. He's the quiet type, always observing everything that goes on around him. And brooding and deadly when he needs to be. I hate it when he's like this. The way he looks at me with brotherly love makes me feel like no matter what, he will always have my back. I can never keep anything from him when he flat out asks me.

I sigh as I sit down on my bed. "He didn't hurt me, okay? Zane, or Blaze...I grew up with him, or at least mostly," I start. Toby squats down so he is eye level with me and takes hold of my hands, urging me to go on. I see Louie out of the corner of my eye, standing stock still by the door of my room. But if I want to continue telling the story, I can't look at him, so I focus on Toby because he truly is my rock.

"When I was thirteen, he and his brother Zeke moved next door to my grandmother." I see recognition cross his face. "Yeah, that Zeke. Anyway, after Zeke died, Zane and I became closer as friends. But then everything changed between us, at least for me." I take a sip of the tequila to help me go on.

"I started noticing things about him, but didn't know why. Then it hit me; I was falling in love with him." I feel a tear roll down my cheek, but when Toby goes to wipe it, I flinch away. If he touches me, I won't be able to continue.

"After he graduated, things went from bad to worse. I missed him like crazy, but he was distant. Then over Thanksgiving break it went too far. Zane came home unexpectedly, and one thing led to another. We didn't have sex, but it was close. I fell asleep in his arms, only to wake up to a letter from him telling me that it had all been a mistake. That he loved me, but only as a friend. That he couldn't lose me and that he was sorry." I heard Louie growl, but I ignored him. I wasn't done with my story, not even close.

"We barely talked during the next year-and-a-half. During my last year in high school, my birthday and graduation passed with nothing from him. But then my grandmother died, and I lost it. I was completely alone. My mom died, Dad left me, Zeke was killed, Zane wasn't around, and now my grandmother was gone. After the funeral, Zane showed up out of the blue. We fought and then he apologized over and over for not being there for me. He promised that we would fix things between us. I figured as long as I had him in my life, everything would be okay. I couldn't lose him, I just couldn't. He talked me into coming to school in Austin with him, so I packed up what I needed and left a month and a half later. The night I arrived at school, we ended up at a party. He started getting cozy with some girl, which was fine. But then when I got back from the bathroom, he was gone. I didn't think he'd leave me, so I sat and waited for him. But he never came back. I went looking for him and ran into this guy."

I stop there, not sure if I can go on. It's still raw to think about that night, especially today and knowing Zane is close. I glance up into Toby's eyes, looking for strength. He squeezes my hand and waits for me to continue.

"I asked him if he had seen Zane. I had a headache and wanted to leave. He said that he saw him a while ago, but would go look for him to let him know I wasn't feeling well. He told me to wait for him in one of the rooms since it was quiet in there. When he came back, he said that Zane had left with the girl a while ago, and that they were hooking up but Zane left his truck for me to drive home. He left me there, didn't even bother to tell me he was leaving. I think I started crying and the guy hugged me. At first, I was confused, but then it kind of felt nice to be comforted. I was so upset that I meant so little to Zane."

Shaking my head, I continue. "But then the guy started kissing me. I was so shocked at first that I didn't think to push him away, but finally I realized what was going on. I tried to make him stop, but he was too strong…I-I c-couldn't get him o-off of me…" A loud sob cuts me off. I start crying so hard, I'm not getting enough air. I can almost feel his hand over my mouth. I can feel him ripping my panties off, pushing inside me…

"Hey…hey, look at me," Toby says as he grabs my face, making me concentrate on him.

Finally, after a couple of minutes, I calm down enough to continue. "After he was done I ran out. I left in Zane's truck and went to the nearest store. I bought new clothes and the morning after pill since he never used a condom. I drove back to my dorm and tried calling Zane, but he wouldn't answer. I left voicemails and sent text messages, not telling him what happened, but that I needed him. But he didn't respond until about an hour later."

I harden my gaze and first glance at Louie, who is standing in my doorway with his hands balled into fists at his sides, then to Toby, who has a look of anguish mixed with anger on his face. I use my own anger and feed off of theirs to finish my story.

"He said he wasn't always going to be there for me and I needed to learn to take care of myself. That was it. He never even asked what had happened or if I was okay. So I drove to my grandmother's house, packed all my shit, and hit the road. I haven't spoken to or seen him since." Now they know everything that happened to me. I've bared all of my secrets, all of my scars.

The sound of someone punching the wall causes me to look up and into Louie's eyes. He has murder written all over his face. Before I can say anything, he turns and stalks through my living room. Then I hear something make a banging sound and glass breaking. I jump up and run into the room to see the front door hanging from its hinges and my grandmother's crystal angel lying broken on the floor. Louie's gone and there is only one place he could be going: to find Zane.

CHAPTER 17

I make it outside seconds after he does, but I'm still too late. I catch only a glimpse of Louie speeding down the road on his bike before he is gone. I run to my truck, fumbling with my keys to get it unlocked. I have to go after him.

"Dani, wait!" Toby is right behind me, but I don't have time to explain anything. I need to get to the clubhouse.

He grabs my keys and turns me around.

"Toby, I need to go after him!" I yell, trying to get the keys back.

Without answering, he takes my hand and pulls me over to his bike. I don't question him anymore, knowing we've wasted enough time already, and hop on behind him. The engine roars. I barely have time to wrap my arms around him before we are off, speeding down the road after Louie. *Please let us make it there in time.* I don't even know who I'm going there to stop—Louie or Zane. It doesn't really matter, as long as I get there before shit hits the fan. It's not Louie's fight, it's mine. And if anyone kicks

Zane's ass, it will be me.

We make it to the clubhouse faster than I thought possible, but not fast enough, because I can already see Louie's bike parked haphazardly by the door. Fuck! Maybe Zane isn't even here though, right? Yeah, and I'm best friends with that bitch Destiny.

Toby has barely stopped before I'm off his bike and running toward the door. I'll think about what I'm going to do once I get in there and can see what is going on. Then I can come up with a game plan.

I bust through the door in time to see Zane block a punch from Louie. I don't know if words were spoken first or if Louie just walked in swinging. All I know is that I need to stop this before it goes any further.

I run up and wedge myself between the two of them. "Stop it! Louie, back the fuck off!"

If he hears me, he doesn't show it, because he tries to go right through me to get to Zane. I push him back and get right in his face.

"Walk away, Louie, before I really get pissed off!" I've never been violent when it comes to Louie, but he is waging a war that isn't even his to fight.

Again, Louie is either so far gone in his rage that he doesn't hear me, or he chooses to dismiss me. Wrong fucking answer either way. I push him back a second time, but as my hands land on his chest, he surprises me by sweeping his arm and pushing me out of his way. The brush-off is so hard and completely unexpected that I fall into a nearby table.

I'm not sure if Zane was holding back because

he wasn't sure what Louie was pissed about or if he didn't think it was justified, but as soon as he sees me land on the table, he loses it. I've never seen him like this before—like he's possessed or something. He rushes Louie and throws a lightning fast left-handed punch to Louie's face, then follows up almost simultaneously with a right uppercut.

Louie flies backwards into Mack, who I didn't even see was there.

"If you *ever* fucking put your hands on her again, I'll kill you! I'll fucking *kill* you. Do you hear me?" Zane yells as he points a finger in Louie's direction.

Mack makes sure Louie is able to stand on his own before he walks over to me. "You all right, darlin'?"

Now that he mentions it, I think I hit my backbone on the edge of the table, but I won't tell anyone that. It will no doubt make Louie feel like shit because he caused it and seeing how Zane is giving him a look of death, it would be best to keep that information to myself. "Yeah, Mack, I'm good." I stand up and look at Zane, then back to Mack, not sure if he knows my history with Zane. He'll find out soon enough, though. I won't be able to keep this from him any longer. I can only hope he isn't upset with me for not telling him years ago.

Looking at the three of us, Mack first addresses Louie. "You—go get a drink and calm the fuck down. And if you ever lose your shit like that again around my little girl, I'll kill you myself." Not even waiting for a reply, he turns to Zane. "You—my office. Now." Zane hesitates for only a second before giving him a slight nod. He looks at me and

205

heads toward the back of the bar where Mack's office is located. Once he's out of sight, Mack turns to me.

"Look, I don't want to be telling you what to do, but it's about time you both clear the air." I open my mouth to tell him that it's a little more complicated than that, that he doesn't even know what happened, but he raises his hand to stop me. "I know that you both have some history. Blaze told me a little about what happened. I'm not saying that he was right to do what he did all those years ago, but you need to hear his side of the story. So you're going to go into my office, and you aren't going to come out until you two talk this shit out." He gives me a hard look that means I better not argue. Then he turns and walks to the bar.

Since I've pretty much lost any buzz I had going before Toby and Louie barged into my place tonight and I know I'm going to need some liquid courage to make it through talking things over with Zane, I step behind the bar for a bottle of Jack. Mack either doesn't notice what I'm doing, or he knows I need this. Either way, he doesn't say anything. Time to get this over with—for better or worse, this shit ends tonight.

***

I stop outside the door to Mack's office and take a deep breath, trying to prepare for whatever is about to happen. I honestly have no clue how this is going to turn out, but I do know I'm not looking forward to talking about that night. I've already had to go back in time once tonight, but I suppose it's better this way. With Zane back in my life, at least for a while it looks like, we need to hash this out. Otherwise it will get in the way of my family, and after everything they have given back to me, I won't do that to them.

Once inside, I close the door and look up into the eyes of the man who I loved more than anything. The man I would have walked through hell to have feel for me what I felt for him. But he's also the man who walked away from me when I needed him the most, who fed me to the wolves and broke me beyond repair.

"Baby Girl..." he whispers, surprised to see me instead of Mack.

I walk around the desk and sit down across from him. Without saying anything, I grab two glasses and fill them with Jack. I don't even wait for him to pick his up before I'm downing my first drink, then topping it off again.

Taking my time on my second glass, I sip slowly and set it down before looking at him. He still makes me feel like my heart will beat out of my chest. "Let's get a couple of things straight. The friendship that we had years ago is gone. I don't know you and I'm not sure if I want to, but the girl you used to know is dead. She died four years ago when you left her at a party to get your dick wet, so you can stop with all your 'Baby Girl' bullshit. I'm no one's baby girl, least of all yours."

I must have completely shocked him because he stares at me with his mouth hanging open—like a fish out of the water. I suppose when he knew me, I

207

only spoke up about certain things. Well, he'll have to get used to it if he plans on sticking around, because this is who I am now.

Finally, after a couple of minutes, he pulls himself together. Now when he looks at me, it's with possession, as if I'm his. It has me wanting to turn away, but I refuse to back down. "First off, you will always be Baby Girl to me. *Always*. Nothing you can say or do will ever change that."

I start to argue with him, to say that I don't want anything to do with him anymore, but he gives me a look I've never seen before. It has me snapping my mouth shut and waiting for him to continue. "Let me talk, then you can have your say."

He downs his drink in one swallow, then he begins to speak. "I know I fucked up a lot after I graduated, so let me clear up a couple of things." He drops his eyes to his lap, then looks at me head-on. "I've been in love with you since that first day you came over to play with me and Zeke, but I didn't think it was something I could act on or even tell you. At first I thought it was just puppy love, but after Zeke died, I knew that you were it for me."

He grabs the bottle of Jack and refills his glass, so I take the time to digest what he said. He's loved me since we first met? That can't be right. Before I can think about it further, he continues. "I wanted to tell you so many times—either sit you down and speak the words or kiss you so you would know how I felt, but I never believed you would return my feelings. I was sure that you only thought of me as a friend. Then, when my senior year hit, I realized that even if you did want to be with me,

208

you weren't ready. I needed to leave you be so you could experience life as a teenage girl and not drag you down with me, especially since I wanted to join the Marines."

I gasp out loud. He never once mentioned that he wanted to be a soldier.

"Yeah, I wanted to join like Zeke did, and I didn't tell you because I knew it would bring up bad memories. The day I left for school, I got into a huge argument with my parents. They didn't want me to join, afraid I would end up like Zeke, but I told them I would give school a shot, then decide later. Even though I was one hundred percent sure I was going to join, I figured I owed my parents that much, so I went off to college. I tried putting distance between you and me since you were dating that guy and I wanted to give you the opportunity to find someone that would deserve you. Though I didn't think he was it, I had to let you go to figure that out on your own." He looks away and is silent for a few moments.

"But then you told me that you broke up, and I couldn't reach you to see what happened. I swore to myself that if he hurt you, I was going to kill him. But you wouldn't answer your damn phone. That was also the day I had decided that I was going to quit school and join the Marines. I had so much to get done after I made that decision that I couldn't come home for the holidays, but I had to know that you were okay. So I came to find you and make sure you were okay, which led to that amazing night together. It was better than anything I ever fantasized about..." His eyes are on me, but it's like he is looking through me, back to that night. And what does he mean, it was amazing? The letter he left proves what he thought of that night.

"You mean the night you said was a mistake?" I almost growl at him. I can't believe the shit he is spouting right now. Does he really think that I would believe him after all this time and everything he did?

"I only said that because I was afraid I would lose you. I'm sorry I hurt you, but it was either that and at least have a hope of keeping you as a friend, or tell you I love you. But fuck, if I had told you that I loved you, and then told you about my decision to join the military, what would that have done to us? Huh? Yeah, you would have supported my decision and stood behind me every step of the way, but it would have ruined us too. You would have worried and been scared, and that would have led to you resenting me or even hating me. As much as I wanted to be selfish and keep you, I knew I couldn't. You have to understand, Danielle, I loved you more than anything and I was willing to sacrifice my happiness for you. For *you*!"

I stand up so fast my chair hits the wall, but I don't stop to look at it. I charge him. He stands up to ward me off, but I'm too pissed to be put off. "You did it for me? You arrogant piece of shit! You not telling me how you felt, keeping things from me, and making decisions on my behalf, is selfish, *not* the other way around! You should have fucking told me…" I stifle a sob, choosing to use the anger and pain to make me stronger. I try to hit him, but he sees it coming and grabs my arms, turning me around so my back is to his chest. Being pinned against him pisses me off even more. My body and heart are rejoicing in the fact that he is back in my life and holding me, but my head wants to override those feelings. I can't let myself be weak, not for him, not again.

"Let me go!" I yell and struggle against him, but it's no use. He's too strong and the way he is holding me doesn't leave room for me to do much.

"Calm down, Baby Girl, I'm not goi—"

"*Don't fucking call me that!*" I yell over him. I don't want him to use that name anymore. It's wrong. It signifies everything that we used to be, everything we could have been, it all hurts to think about.

When he finally releases me, I move to the other side of the room to put distance between us. I keep my back turned so he can't see how much this is effecting me.

"There's only one more thing we really need to talk about—that night at the party." I can hear anger in his voice, though I'm not sure if it's because I left after that night or because of something else. I keep quiet, waiting for him to continue. The sooner we get this over with, the sooner I can walk out of this room and go on with my life like he never came back.

"Before you got to Austin, I got a phone call from my superiors that we were getting deployed within the next couple of months. I was so pissed off. Now that you were finally going to be with me it was all getting taken away before I even had it. I was going to tell you that I had joined and was no longer in school, but there was never the right time. I wanted you close to me so I could take care of you and have you with me, but I knew I would need to tell you sooner than I wanted to and you were going to hate me." He lets out a long sigh, then continues.

"So when you got there, I took you to get some food because I figured you hadn't eaten much and I needed more time to think of how I was going to tell you. Then I got that phone call and I thought it was a sign. It gave me more time, with the added benefit of having some drinks in us for when I did tell you." He's quiet for so long that I turn around and see him staring at the floor. As much as I hate to admit it, he looks like he's suffering and that makes me happy. He deserves to suffer for what I went through because of him. I face him head-on, cross my arms, and wait for him to continue.

"I just wanted a distraction from wanting and needing you. That's what that girl was. I took her outside in my truck, but it wasn't enough to make me forget about you. She offered to go to my place and at that point, I was willing to do anything to get you out of my head. I thought you would be okay there if I left my truck for you to take home. You never had a problem being at a party by yourself before, but I should have known this was different; you didn't know anyone. I wasn't thinking straight, and for that I'm so sorry…"

Hearing him tell me he was sorry for leaving me there, even though he couldn't know what it led to, has a little bit of the ice in my heart melting. I hate that he is breaking down my walls, but I never could help it when it came to him.

"Zane…" What do I say to him? That I forgive him? I'm not even sure if I can forgive him yet. I need to let him know what happened after he left the party, so he will understand why I ran.

"Let me finish, please." He looks me in the eyes, waiting for me to let him continue. "When I got your text messages telling me that you needed me, the only thing I could think about was that I was going to have to leave soon and I wouldn't be there for you anymore. I was so pissed—at myself, at the world, and at you. I know I had no right to be angry with you, that it was all on me, but try to understand where I was coming from. I didn't even think when I sent that text message to you, I only knew that I was hurting and I lashed out." I can hear the anger in his voice and the self-hatred he must harbor.

"Then, the next morning, I had Liam drive me over to your place to apologize and to tell you about the Marines, but you were already gone. Liam was pissed that I had left you at the party, but I didn't know why. Until he told me about a guy that was there. Then I saw the blood on the seat…I knew something happened, and I could have killed myself for not being there for you. I broke every speed limit on the way to your house, but I was too late. You were already gone. I found the letter you wrote and that was the end for me. I had lost the only thing that mattered to me, and it was no one's fault but my own. And not only had I lost you, but I had played a part in physically hurting you, emotionally destroying you, and making you hate me." I so badly want to tell him I forgive him, but I can't. Not yet anyway.

"I will forever suffer for how I did things those last two years, but most of all, I will suffer for and regret the night I lost you for good. But I promise you this—that guy paid for what he did to you. He will never hurt you or anyone else again."

He already knew about what happened to me that night? A part of me is happy that I don't need to tell him, but another part feels shattered, knowing that he knows that I'm dirty, that I'm damaged goods. I never really thought about it before, but now that he knows, I wish he didn't. I don't want him to see me like that, as a victim, broken and used.

I have to get out of here and let all of this settle. He told me so much that it has my head spinning. I need some time. I turn toward the door and reach for the handle, but Zane puts his hand on my shoulder to stop me. It's not a gentle gesture, but it isn't hard either. Only enough to let me know that he doesn't want me to leave. But I have to.

"I know you can never forgive me for what happened that night, but I promise I will spend the rest of my life making it up to you. I'm not letting you go. You are mine, you always were. I'll give you space to think about what I said, but not for long. I love you, Baby Girl."

I open the door and walk out in a daze. I want this day to be over already.

I make it out of the clubhouse without noticing who is there or trying to talk to me. The only thing I keep hearing in my head are the words I longed for for so long—*I love you, Baby Girl.*

CHAPTER 18

It's been over a week since Zane explained what had been going on with him. He hasn't made an appearance at the shop since, but then again, it's not like he would randomly come here either after what happened the last time. And he doesn't know where I live. He hasn't sought me out and I haven't been to the clubhouse because I'm not ready to face him yet, though he hasn't been far from my mind.

I keep replaying what he said and piecing it into what I already knew. I think what hurts the most is that he kept something so important from me. I mean, joining the military is a big deal anyway, but since we lost Zeke, it made it even more important. I would have been upset and probably would have tried to talk him out of it, but I would have supported him with whatever he decided to do. I would have been proud of him, like I was with Zeke. Would it have been hard knowing he could get deployed and end up coming home the way Zeke did? Hell yes. I would have been terrified for him, but that's a part of life. But shit, he could have

215

just as easily been hit by a bus on the way to school too. If I've learned anything in this life, it's that our time here isn't a given. It's all a gamble, we never know when our time is up.

I would rather have known what was going on and why he was acting so strange than believe it was because he had forgotten about me or didn't care. I have lost so many people in my life, some because they made the choice to leave and some because they were taken, but I never thought Zane would be one who would have chosen to walk away from me. And not telling me how he felt about me and not giving me the chance to stand behind him, to me that feels like a copout. He didn't trust that I would be okay, that I would support him, that I would make the right decisions for us—for me. Yeah, that's what hurts the most.

As far as why he left me at the party that night— was it wrong? Yes! Do I understand? I'm starting to. But it all goes back to him not being honest and keeping things from me. If he would have been open with me from the beginning, I don't think that night would have happened. Would we have still wound up where we are today? I can't answer that. I can only tell you how the cards were actually dealt and what I did with my hand. I can only wish things had happened differently.

After thinking about what he told me and letting it all sink in, I find that I have a lot of questions for him. I have thought about getting his number from Mack or even going to the clubhouse, but every time I pick up the phone, or my keys to drive there, I stop myself. I can't bring myself to do it—maybe

I'm not ready or maybe I'm being stubborn. But in the back of my mind, I know the answer to why I'm holding back—I want him to come to me, to prove that I mean something to him. And each day that passes with nothing from him, a little piece of my heart ices back up and I build up my walls even taller and stronger. I can't let myself fall for him, because if I do and he is only acting out of pity or because he feels obligated, I don't think I'll be able to pick up the pieces once he leaves again.

I look up at the clock and see that I still have a couple of hours before I need to be in the shop, so I decide to go to the gym to work out some of my frustration. I usually go at night when there are fewer people there, but with the way I've been feeling this week, I need this now. I grab my gym bag and head out, looking forward to spending some one on one time with the punching bag.

***

I walk into the shop to find Louie sitting at the front desk.

"Where have you been?" He gets up and comes up to me. After that night at the clubhouse, he has either been super attentive and apologizing for pushing me into the table, or angry and possessive over me. It's really starting to piss me off. I know he has feelings for me, but I'm not his old lady or even his fuck buddy. I never should have had sex with him. I thought he understood that nothing would come of it, and he did, until Zane came back into the picture. Now he feels threatened that someone is going to take me away from him even though I'm not his in the first place.

"I was at the gym," I say with an edge in my voice. I'm not in the mood to deal with his shit today. Hopefully he lets it go and doesn't push me, because I'll push back.

I walk around him to check the appointment book. Looks like it is going to be a slow day. I only have two appointments and Louie doesn't have any. "You don't need to stay. It doesn't look like we'll be that busy, so there's no reason for both of us to be here," I tell him as I walk over to my station.

"So this is how it's going to be between us?" he practically yells from behind me. I guess I'm going to have to make it even more clear.

"What do you want from me, Louie?" I look up at him and cross my arms over my chest. Whatever is going on between us, we need to hash this out now before it gets worse. I don't want to lose him as a friend, but it seems to be a very real possibility.

"Fuck it, I don't need this shit!" He turns around and storms out of the shop.

That went well. I need to think of a way to fix this or things are going to be very uncomfortable around here. He needs to understand that what we shared is in the past and we aren't going to be together. I can't take it back now, so I'll have to deal with the fallout.

As I turn back to finish setting up my station, my phone buzzes in my pocket. "Yeah?" I answer without even looking to see who it is.

"You busy?" Mack asks.

I sigh into the phone and walk toward the back to

grab a soda. "Not at the moment. What's up?" I hope this is only a friendly call and he's not calling to ask how I am, or if I have sorted things out with Zane yet. Since that night at the clubhouse, Mack has been hounding me to talk with him. I know he's right, that we need to work this out, but I'm still digesting everything Zane told me.

"I wanted to let you know I'll be outta town for a couple of days. Got some club business that needs to be taken care of in Nevada."

I don't understand why he feels the need to inform me of what he is doing. It's great that he cares about me and wants to give me peace of mind, but it's really not necessary. "Okay, well, have a safe ride I guess…anything else?"

"Nah, just wanted to let you know I wouldn't be around, but if you need anything, give me a call. You got me?"

I have no idea what he thinks is going to happen or what I'd need him for, but if it makes him feel better, who am I do deny him that? "Will do. See you when you get back. Gotta go, my first appointment showed up," I lie. Not waiting for his reply, I head back out to the front of the shop. I pull out my sketch book to work on the tattoo I'm designing for myself. I haven't gotten inked in a while, so I'm overdue.

A couple minutes later, I hear the shop door open. A guy who looks to be in his mid-twenties walks in. "Can I help you with something?" I ask, putting away my sketch.

"Yeah, I wanted to see about getting a tattoo."

Well aren't you just Captain Fucking Obvious? I

219

push aside my irritation and smile. "Sure, what are you looking to get?"

He looks around for a minute before locking eyes with me again. "Uh, well…I'm not really sure. It's my first tattoo. What would you recommend?"

Is this guy for real? Who comes into a tattoo shop for their first tattoo without having anything in mind? It's not like going to a barber shop for a haircut and saying "just cut it." This shit is permanent.

"Well, that depends what you want and where you want it. Why don't you look through the display cases to see if anything pops out at you? Then we can go from there. Sound good?" I get up and show him over to the display cases of flash art. If there is one thing about tattooing that I hate, it's doing something generic. There's no challenge in it, no meaning. If you are going to ink your skin, it needs to mean something to you. But if that's what people want, that's what I'll give them.

After looking through the cases, he decides he wants to go with a skull on his right pectoral. He can't find one that he likes, so he gives me some ideas and tell me to roll with it. This, I can do.

"All right, why don't you have a seat on the couch and fill these out? I'll draw something up quick, and if you like it, we'll get started." I hand him the release forms and head over to my station to draw his design.

Thirty minutes later I'm done, and with his approval I start getting him prepped. Then I place the stencil to make sure it's where he wants it, and get to work. This piece should last me until my other appointment arrives, so I won't have to think about what I'm going to do about Zane.

***

I look up at the clock to see it's after five. I don't have any more appointments, but I want to stay open until at least nine. With it being Saturday, you can usually count on walk-ins later at night. They get an itch and decide they want a tattoo. They pick something off the wall or something small. I usually don't mind those type of last-minute clients, but tonight is different. I hope if anyone comes in, it will make it worth my being here.

I walk over to my station and grab my sketch pad to finish designing my tattoo. I really want to finish it soon so I can have Mack put it on me. All of my tattoos mean something, but this one is more personal than some of my others, kind of like my phoenix. It's a black panther, which will go on the side of my neck. It means death and rebirth, but also reclaiming your power in this life. It's a guardian of energy, and has the ability to know the dark. This is so I acknowledge that death is a part of life, but I have the ability to reclaim the power. It will watch over me and help me in my dark times.

My panther has a fierce expression and a paw up in the air, like he's defending me. I can't wait to have this finished and finally on my skin. I've been thinking about this idea for over a year, but it only started coming to life on paper a couple of months ago. I want it to be perfect, and with the last touches I'll put on tonight, it will be ready.

I've been working for a while when I hear the shop door open for the first time in hours. I'm putting the last bit of shading in my tattoo design, but don't want the person to think I'm ignoring them. "Be with you in a minute."

A moment later, I'm done and put my sketch pad away before heading out front. "What can I do—" I stop short when I see Zane standing by the front desk. I take a couple of breaths to stop my heart from going crazy, then move forward. "What do you want, Zane?" I ask in barely a whisper.

He pushes his hands in his pockets and looks at me sheepishly. "I wanted to see if you could fit me in for that tattoo we didn't get to do last time."

Of course he is here for a tattoo, Dani. Did you think he came here to see you? It scares me how much I was hoping that was the reason, but I know I shouldn't. My heart shouldn't be excited to see him, but knowing that he is here, within my grasp, makes me feel things that I never thought I'd feel again. Things I don't want to feel, especially for him.

Knowing I need to at least be civil and do my job, I walk around the desk to grab the release forms. "Why don't you fill these out and then we can take a look at what you're wanting?" Formal and to the point, that's the only way I can do this. It's business, and the faster I get that through to my heart, the better.

He walks up to the desk with a smile and grabs a pen. "It shouldn't be too difficult for you to manage. The person who drew it is the best there is," he says as he fills out the forms. The way he talks about the artist makes me pause. Knowing someone out there has captured his stamp of approval and drew something for him to permanently mark on his skin has me feeling angry and jealous. He used to think that about my drawings.

I don't reply. Instead, I wait for him to finish and lead him back to my station. "Where are you wanting to put it?" I ask as I set things up to get started.

"I want it on my back. I've made sure to leave it bare specifically for this tattoo," he tells me as he starts to take his shirt off. I quickly turn my back to him, needing a moment before I look. The last time I saw him shirtless was that night in my room when he gave me my first orgasm. I thought that was the turning point for us, and I was right, just not in the way I wanted.

Gathering all my strength, I turn around to face him, but even after preparing myself for this moment, I'm taken aback by seeing him half naked. This man is a god, with tanned skin, defined muscles, and mouthwatering tattoos on his chest and arms. I catch a glimmer by his nipple and raise my eyes to see what it is. Fuck me...he has his nipples pierced.

Taking him in, I feel my pussy pulse and my panties suddenly become wet. *Fuck, pull yourself together, Dani. Just do your job. Stop thinking about licking him all over and imagining the sounds he would make if you dropped to your knees and unbuckled his pants. Stop remembering how massive his cock was and how it felt in your mouth all those years ago. Fuck! Fuck! Fuck! Snap out of it!*

I look up and see him smirking, no doubt realizing what is going through my head. He always told me that I wear my emotions on my sleeve.

I harden my gaze and walk up to him. "Could you show me the design?" The faster I get this over with, the better. As long as I stay focused on the tattoo, I will be fine.

He reaches into a gym bag I hadn't even noticed he was carrying and pulls out a folder, handing it to me. I walk over to my desk and pull out the design. I gasp when I see what is inside. It's the sketch I drew for him when he graduated high school. He kept it all these years and now wants me to tattoo it on his back.

I look over my shoulder and see him watching me. Not wanting to show the effect this has on me, I clear my throat and stand. "I shouldn't need to alter much, unless you want to change anything before I copy this onto a stencil…" I trail off, waiting for him to tell me we are good to go.

"Nah, it's perfect the way it is," he says with a shy smile.

I walk over to the copy machine to make it into a stencil, and have him sit in the chair. I clean the area on his back, loving the feel of his skin beneath my fingertips. Working fast to get this part over with, I have the stencil placed and tell him to check it out in the mirror to make sure it's where he wants it. He only takes a couple of seconds to confirm it looks good, giving me a slight nod before sitting back down on the chair.

"If you could lie down on your stomach, it will

be easier for me to work and be more comfortable for you, since this will take a while." I sit down in my roller chair, put on my gloves, and get the ink ready.

"Do you want any color in this or do you want to keep it the way it was drawn?" I ask, acting like he is any other customer and the tattoo I'm inking on him isn't one that I drew years ago for my best friend.

"If you could just put color in the flag, that would be great," he says while he gets comfortable on the table.

When I have everything ready to go, I roll over to him and notice he has his face turned toward me, but his eyes are closed. I take only a second to enjoy the view in front of me before I start up my gun. "All right, here we go," I say and begin to ink the first line on the memorial for Zeke.

CHAPTER 19

I'm only about a fourth of the way through the tattoo when Zane starts talking. I'm actually surprised he didn't start in sooner. I don't comment on anything, only nod my head to acknowledge I am listening, or at least pretending to listen, when all I want to do is run away. I don't want to hear about his life and all that I have missed out on. It kills me to know that he went through two deployments and I never knew about it.

Halfway through the tattoo, he starts asking me about my life and what I've been up to. I keep my answers short and to the point, never getting too personal. I tell him that I moved here and met Mack on my first day, rented the apartment above the shop, and started hanging out with Louie and Toby. I never mention the nightmares or how I went back and forth on whether I did the right thing by leaving without saying anything to him. I don't tell him about working out with Toby or going to the shooting range. And I especially don't tell him about anything that happened between Louie and me.

When I have about an hour left on his tattoo, he starts reminiscing about all the good times we had with Zeke, the parties we went to before he left for college, and all the things he missed about my grandmother. I have to take a small break after he brings her into the conversation, but I pass it off as going to the bathroom.

When I get back to work, he is quiet for only a couple of minutes before he starts telling me how happy he is he decided to come here and that it was fate that brought us back together. That has me laughing—I agree that destiny had a hand in him coming back into my life, but we see it differently: he thinks it's the best thing in the world and I consider it a bitch, always trying to throw me for a loop.

"I've missed that," he whispers, so quietly I almost don't hear him.

I stop shading and look at him. "What do you miss?"

He looks at me for the longest time, and right before I can't take it anymore, he looks away. "Your laugh. It's the most beautiful sound I have ever heard. I dream about it sometimes…"

What shocks me the most is how open he is about his feelings for me. This new Zane is something I have never seen. We were always close, and he never shied away from telling me how much he cared about me, but I know now that he wasn't always being completely honest. So the fact that he is being so honest about his feelings is different—he's different.

I get back to the tattoo, and he's quiet for the rest of the time. It gives me a chance to really think about what has happened, the things he has told me, and where we go from here. I always thought that I would never be able to forgive him for leaving me at that party, but now that I know more of what he was dealing with...I don't know. It has me rethinking a lot of things. Do I miss my best friend? More than anything. Do I still get butterflies when he's around? Yes. Do I still love him? Maybe. And it's that maybe that decides it for me. I need to at least give this a shot. I owe myself that much.

We need to get to know each other again before going further though. I know I'm not the same person I used to be, and he doesn't seem to be either. We need to cover that ground first, then try to see what our feelings are. He says he loves me, but after he gets to know who I am now, he may not feel that way anymore. And that's okay, because I don't know how I'll feel when it's all said and done either. But I know I want him in my life. I've missed him.

I finish the tattoo, clean him up, and have him check it out in the mirror. It looks really good and makes me feel like even back then I had talent, which is something that I never really believed. And I have to admit, seeing him with my mark on him does something to me. I've never been the jealous or possessive type, but looking at him now, wearing my ink, gives me a high like I've never experienced before.

"Wow, Baby Girl, this is fucking amazing!" he says with a huge smile on his face.

I don't correct him for calling me Baby Girl, because it doesn't upset me as much as it did before. Plus, I need to get used to it if we are going to work on our friendship. "Happy to hear it. I'm actually really glad that you never got it done until now. It was neat being able to tattoo something that I designed for this purpose years before I got into this trade. And it's one that is close to my heart, so thank you." I give him a genuine smile, which seems to make him pause. I guess I haven't really smiled around him since he's gotten here.

I get started the clean-up. "So, um, do you want to go for a drink maybe?" I ask without turning around. If he says no I don't want him to see the disappointment on my face. I'm not even sure why I'm asking, but it seems right. We could sit down and have a couple drinks and catch up more. I should probably tell him that I forgive him and that I'm ready to move on from all that happened in the past. But maybe it's not the time to mention it— while having drinks that is. What if he takes it the wrong way? Will he think that I want to be with him? Shit, maybe I should tell him we should do lunch tomorrow instead. Yeah, lunch would keep it in the friend zone, right?

"You don't have to ask me twice, Baby Girl. There's a bar down the street that looks good. We could go there."

Shit, now what do I do? I can't really take it back now that he's agreed. Fuck. Well, I guess I'll have to go with it.

"Ah, yeah, the um, Double Down Saloon?" I've never been there before. I've actually heard bad things about it, but if that's where he wants to go, I guess we can go for one drink. Maybe after that we can go back to the clubhouse, or better yet, I have a bottle of Jack at home. Wait, no, that's a bad idea. That will definitely make him think we are more than friends. Fuck, why is this so hard?

"Yeah, that's the one. You been there?"

I shake my head and motion him over so I can cover his tattoo. With the number of them he has already, I'm sure he knows the drill about aftercare.

He puts his shirt on and we walk out front.

"So, how much do I owe ya?" He pulls his wallet out and looks up at me, waiting.

"Nothin'. Mack said this one is taken care of." It's not a total lie, since Mack usually doesn't make the brothers pay full price, but I don't want to take his money for this one. It was something close to home for both of us and it seems wrong to charge for it. Plus, this is my shop now so I don't need Mack's approval.

"You sure? We don't have to tell him I paid for it."

I laugh and grab my things. "Yeah, I'm sure."

He hesitates for only a moment before he puts his wallet away.

"I'm going to close things down quick, then run upstairs to change. I'll meet you there in say, twenty minutes?" Even though I no longer live in the upstairs apartment, I still keep some things there in case I don't want to drive home after a long day at work. It works out perfectly tonight, since I want to shower and change before having drinks with Zane. Not that it really matters since he's already seen me today, but it's one thing for him to come to my job, and another for me to willingly go out with him. I want to look good.

"I'll wait outside for you."

This is something we are going to have to discuss. I hate it when the guys treat me with kid gloves, like they need to watch over and protect me. I'm not as naive as I used to be, and since I've been working out with Toby, I think I can take care of myself. Shit, I've even managed to hand some of the brothers their ass a time or two. So yeah, I can handle walking down the street by myself.

"Zane, one thing you are going to have to get used to is that I'm not a little girl anymore. I am more than capable of taking care of myself. I'll meet you there." I don't wait for his reply, instead, I push him out the door and lock up.

***

I'm a little late, but I think it was time well spent. I re-did my hair, curled it and put it into a tight ponytail. Then I applied some dark eye shadow and eye liner, finishing off with some mascara and my red lipstick. When I looked in my closet for something to wear, I realized I didn't really have much to choose from. The best I could do was put on one my favorite pair of cut-off jean shorts that I left here a couple weeks ago and a white tank top. At least I have my leather jacket and black combat boots with me tonight. They will turn this casual outfit into something more than it is. I want to look sexy, but still me, and I don't want it to seem like I'm trying to impress him, because I'm not. I want to show him who I am now.

Leaving the apartment, I go back through the shop, lock up again, and head to the Double Down Saloon.

The first thing I notice as I walk in the door is that I'm the only woman here. Not like that's a first for me, but I don't know the men here, and this crowd looks rough. I don't mean biker rough; I mean rough in every sense of the word.

I look around for Zane and spot him in a booth, so I make my way toward him without stopping to get a drink first. I'll wait to see what Zane is drinking and go from there. Plus, I don't really want to deal with the men here. We may need to leave because they could cause trouble, and trouble is one thing I don't need tonight while Zane and I try to pick up where we left off.

As I make it to the table, he moves his eyes from his phone, eyeing me up and down. Knowing I look good and that he noticed makes me smile, but when I see his hard expression, I'm instantly on guard.

"Where the fuck have you been, and where are your fucking clothes?"

Whoa buddy, what the fuck? "Ah, I took a shower and changed. Is that all right with you, *Daddy*?" I say with as much sarcasm I can muster. "And I'm not even going to validate your other question with an answer."

He blows out a long breath and shakes his head. "I'm sorry, Baby Girl, I was just worried. I don't have your number and couldn't check to make sure you were okay. And you look too fucking sexy in those clothes to be legal, let alone in a bar with these fuckers looking at you."

I can tell that it's going to take him a while to see that I'm perfectly able to take care of myself and that he doesn't need to worry about me. Or maybe it's me who will have to get used to him being back in my life and caring. But he does have a valid point; having my number would probably calm him a little bit.

"Give me your phone," I say, reaching my hand across the table. Without questioning me, he hands it over. Well, at least it doesn't seem like he's worried I would see anything incriminating on there, so that's good.

I program my phone number under his contacts and then send a text message to myself so I can save his in mine, then hand it back to him. "There, now maybe you won't get your panties in a bunch."

That gets a smirk out of him and then we are back to an awkward silence. Great, this is not how I wanted tonight to go. Maybe we're not meant to be friends anymore.

"You want something to drink?" he asks, breaking the silence.

I look up at him with a grin. "Abso-fucking-lutely. I thought you'd never ask."

This time I get a full-on laugh out of him. "Well, I'm glad to see some things haven't changed," he says, as he gets up and walks over to the bar. He's not completely right, but I'll let him work out the details himself. He'll find out soon enough how much I've changed.

I make myself seem busy by looking at my

phone. I'm not really doing anything but staring at the text I sent myself from his phone, but people don't need to know that. I don't want anyone to come over and try talking to me.

Thankfully, it doesn't take him long to return with our drinks. The one time I did glance up to see if I could spot Zane, I noticed more than one set of eyes checking me out, and not in a way I like.

I take a drink as he's sitting down, and when the alcohol hits my taste buds, I have to smile. Jack is my favorite thing to drink, and I've missed sitting with him like this. We used to have some really good times, only him, me, and our good buddy Jack Daniels.

Twenty minutes later, his phone rings. "Yeah?" he barks into it, which makes me laugh because that's how I answer too. His eyes meet mine and I can tell that hearing me laugh makes him happy. It makes me happy too, because I feel like it's been forever since I've really laughed. Sure, I've chuckled and smiled, but nothing like I do with Zane.

"Yeah, she's with me." Knowing that he's talking about me to whoever is on the phone makes me quiet down and pay attention. I don't like not knowing who he's talking to and why they are bringing me up.

"On our way," he says, and hangs up. Without wasting a second, he tells me what's going on. "That was Mack, he wants us at the clubhouse."

I wonder what's going on. "Wait, he told me earlier that he was going out of town for a couple of days. Is he back already?" I ask when I remember my conversation with Mack this afternoon.

"I don't know what's going on or where he was going, but he's at the clubhouse now and wants us both there."

I nod as he starts sliding out of the booth. I do the same and follow him toward the door, but before we make it outside, someone grabs me by the elbow. I whip around to see who the fuck put their hands on me.

I look up into the cold, hard eyes of one of the guys who wouldn't stop staring at me while Zane and I were drinking.

"Take your hands off of me," I tell him calmly, pulling my arm free, then turn around to follow Zane outside. He hasn't even noticed yet that I'm not right behind him. But I don't make it even one step before the guy grabs me again, pulling me into him so my back is pushed up against him.

"Where you going, baby?" I struggle to move away, but he brings his arms around my chest, holding me in place.

"Last chance, asshole. Get your fucking hands off of me." If he doesn't release me in three seconds, he's going to regret ever touching me. I'm barely holding in my anger as it is. I flash back to the time when I wasn't able to stop someone's unwanted touch.

"I think the bikers can survive without their whore for one night. It's my turn for a ride," he says, then runs his filthy tongue from my ear down to my neck.

I'm getting ready to teach this fuckwit a lesson when Zane comes charging in, looking frantically around the bar. When his eyes find mine, his expression goes from worried to a pure rage. I can practically feel it rolling off of him from where I'm standing. It's fucking sexy as hell! *Shit, get your head in the game, Dani.*

If I don't do something now, before Zane makes his way over to us and takes things into his own hands, I'll miss my chance to beat this guy's ass and I can't let that happen. I need to do this.

I slam my boot down onto his foot, which loosens his hold enough to free me from his grasp. I throw my elbow into his nose, spin around to kick him in the nuts, and then grab him by his shoulders to deliver a knee in the gut. That should teach him not to call me a whore and put his hands on me again.

I look down at him sprawled out on the floor and decide he needs a little more incentive, so I kick him one more time. Leaning down, I make sure he sees me before I speak. "If you ever even *think* about touching me again, you're a fucking dead man. You hear me, you piece of shit? You're fucking dead," I tell him in a calm, but firm voice. Then I spit in his face and turn around to a stunned Zane.

"Let's get the fuck outta this shithole." Walking past him, I head straight for my truck. Thank fuck we are going to the clubhouse, because I need another drink or maybe even the whole bottle after dealing with that asshole.

Zane doesn't say anything as he follows me outside and watches me get into my truck, then rushes over to his bike that's parked on the other side of the street. I don't even wait for him before I turn onto the road and head toward the clubhouse. I want to get there and get myself a drink. I don't want to think about what could have happened had it not been for Toby teaching me self-defense, and I absolutely don't want to give my brain time to go back to the night I didn't know how to take care of myself.

I pull into the parking lot and see Zane come barreling in right behind me with a scowl on his face. Guess he doesn't like being left behind. He can get over it, though, because I don't wait for anyone. As I head inside, I hear him calling for me, but I ignore him and keep on going. My only objective is to get to the bar.

Mack looks over when I walk in, sees the expression on my face and immediately makes his way to Zane. I should go make sure Mack doesn't think he's the reason I'm so pissed off, but I figure he can handle himself.

"Give me a triple shot of Jack," I yell down to the prospect who's behind the bar. It doesn't take long till I feel two people standing behind me. I know they're Mack and Zane, but I wait until I've downed my first shot and demand another before I acknowledge them. I wait for the questions and the lecture, because I know both are coming my way from at least one of them.

"You wanna explain what the fuck that was back there, Baby Girl?" Zane asks with his arms crossed over his chest. I glance at Mack and see him in the same position and with the same look of irritation.

"What the fuck do you think? The guy put his

hands on me and called me a whore, so I taught him a lesson," I tell them in the same tone of voice I would use to tell you about the weather. They are both quiet for a while, only staring at me like I've lost my mind. Since neither of them is saying anything, I turn back to the bar and find a new shot in front of me. *Cheers to the fucking prospect.*

After a couple of minutes of silence, I turn to see if they need anything else. I have drinking to get back to.

They share a look of awe, mixed with anger and irritation with each other. Well, they can go fuck themselves. I don't need to explain my actions to anyone. They should be happy I didn't have my gun or knife with me, or they would have had a big mess to clean up.

I down my next shot and yell to the prospect to leave the bottle with me. It's going to be one of those nights. I'm going to regret it tomorrow, but right now, this is all I want: just me and my bottle of Jack.

CHAPTER 20

I wake up the next morning with a pounding headache and feeling way too warm under the heavy covers. It feels like someone has thrown every blanket within a ten-mile radius over me.

Opening my eyes, I realized that I'm not at home. But before I completely freak out, I notice a picture of my grandmother on the nightstand, like the one in my apartment. Why would I be at my apartment instead of my house?

When I throw the covers off so I can cool off and grab some Tylenol, my hand brushes against flesh. *What the fuck?* I turn my head to see who's behind me and come face to face with a sleeping Zane.

I practically fall out of my bed in my hurry to get away from him. I'm confused, and honestly a little freaked out as to why he is here, and more importantly, in bed with me.

As soon as I'm standing, I move quickly to the other side of the room.

"What the fuck?" I say louder than I intended, causing him to wake.

239

He sits up, wipes the sleep from his eyes, and looks over at me. "Baby, what's wrong?"

Baby? Since when does he call me baby?

"Ah, you mind telling me what the fuck you're doing in my bed?" What the fuck happened last night? Last thing I remember was challenging Toby to a game of pool while drinking out of the bottle of Jack. How did I get to my apartment? And why is Zane here with me? Fuck, I don't remember anything. Did we have sex?

Zane laughs quietly for a couple of seconds until he looks up and sees I'm not laughing with him. I don't find this shit funny at all! I've never drank so much that I couldn't remember what the hell happened. Or maybe I have, but I've never woken up to someone in my bed to make me question what I did the night before. If I find out we fucked, I'm going to kick his ass. He should know better than to mess around with a chick when she's three sheets to the wind.

"Well, after you finished that bottle of Jack, you were trying to pass out on the couch. I didn't think you'd want to stay at the clubhouse, so I asked Mack for the key to your apartment so I could put you to bed."

Okay, well that explains how I got to my apartment, but not why he stayed the night with me.

I don't say anything, only wait for him to continue, but he must think that's all I need to know because he doesn't say anything else. He sits there staring at me like I'm the one who fucked up.

"I'm going to ask you one more time before I lose my patience. What. The. Fuck. Are you doing here?" I cross my arms over my chest and wait for him to answer me.

"I figured I better stay to make sure you didn't throw up in the middle of the night and end up choking on your own vomit. What the hell do you think I'm doing, Danielle?" His voice turns hard. He's pissed, which only serves to pisses me off more. Does he really think it's acceptable to sleep in my bed? Okay, so it's sweet that he was trying to take care of me, but he could have slept on the couch or something.

"Well, I appreciate you wanting to make sure I was okay, but if I ever wake up with you in my bed without me inviting you there, you're going to be missing a certain part of your anatomy." I head into the bathroom. I need something for this headache from hell, and a nice hot shower.

When I step out of the shower, I realize that I forgot to bring in a change of clothes. I hope Zane is out of my bed, or better yet, out of the apartment all together.

I am almost to my bedroom door when I hear Zane coming up behind me. As I turn to ask what he's still doing here, he grabs me by the hips and pushes me into the wall, locking his lips on mine. Holy. Fucking. Christ. He tastes fucking amazing! It's everything I remember his kissing to be and more.

Without my permission, my arms come up around his neck, pulling him closer to me. My towel slips off of my body, but I don't even care. Zane growls and before I know it, he has lifted me up and wrapped my legs around him. Then I feel a dull pain in my back from the wall as he traps me between it and his body. I need to put a stop to this before it goes too far, but God damn it, this feels too fucking good to stop.

He breaks the kiss and lowers his lips to my neck. "Fuck! You are too fucking sexy for your own good." He groans and continues his assault, working his way back up to my mouth. Then he grinds himself against my bare pussy, which causes me to moan into his mouth.

I barely register that we are moving until I feel myself falling backwards onto my bed. Zane doesn't miss a beat as he breaks the connection with my mouth and starts trailing little kisses and licks down my stomach toward my pussy. Holy shit, the anticipation is almost too much.

When he makes his way all the way down, I feel his hot breath on my clit. "Oh God," I whimper. He's hardly done anything yet and I feel like I could come.

"You taste so fucking good, Baby Girl," he says. "I've dreamed of tasting you on my tongue for so long."

He sucks my clit into his mouth and I instantly come.

"Fuck!" I yell, but he doesn't stop. I can feel my pleasure rise again, which has never happened to me before.

"Zane...please..." I beg, not knowing what I'm begging for. All I know is that I don't want him to ever stop. He doesn't disappoint, alternating between nips and licks and sucking my clit hard. I'm breathing so fast that I fear I could pass out.

"Fuck…shit, don't stop." My second orgasm is right there, within my reach. I only need a little more pressure and I will fall over the edge again.

I feel him bite my clit, creating pleasure and pain so intense it has me contracting over and over, it's so intense I hope it never stops.

When I finally fall back down to reality, Zane is kissing his way up to my lips. "I can't wait anymore, Baby Girl, I need to be feel you squeezing my cock with your tight pussy." Nodding eagerly, I reach for his zipper and pull his cock out.

"I need that too! Please, Zane, fuck me." My words have him losing all control, but I wouldn't want it any other way. Spreading my legs wider, he hovers above me and stares deep into my eyes.

"Please," I beg, but it does the trick. Thrusting hard and fast, I feel him fill me up completely. He holds himself still, giving me time to adjust to his size. It's been almost a year since I last had sex, but I don't feel any pain, only intense pleasure.

"Fuck, you're so fucking tight." He still hasn't moved since his initial thrust, so I move my hips, trying to entice him to fuck me.

"Baby Girl, you need to stop that. I don't want to hurt you." He says, pained from holding back.

"If you don't fuck me right now, it will hurt me. Please, Zane. I need you." And that's all it takes for him to forget his worries and fuck me like we both want—like we both need.

He thrusts slowly at first while kissing me, then starts to pick up the pace.

Feeling him inside me, pounding into me at a fast rhythm, I feel like I've died and gone to heaven.

I've never felt this much pleasure from sex. Of course, I don't have much to go off of besides pleasuring myself, but it's more than I could have fantasied about. With Zane, my whole body feels alive with sensations I didn't even know existed.

Grabbing me behind my knee, he pulls my leg up over his shoulder, hitting a spot inside me no one but my vibrator has ever touched.

"Ahhhh! Fuck, right there!" I come on the next thrust, my pussy clamping down around his hard cock.

"Fuck, I'm gonna come, baby," he growls in my ear. He pumps himself inside me four more times, each so deep I know it'll leaving a lasting impression for weeks to come, before I feel him empty himself inside me.

Without pulling out of me, he rolls us over so I'm lying on his chest with him stroking my back.

After he's quiet for a few minutes, he lets out a long sigh, he says, "Shit, Baby Girl, I'm sorry. I didn't mean for that to happen."

I lift my head and glare at him. "Are you fucking kidding me? Your cum is still warm inside me and you're already apologizing and regretting it?" I yell at him, then get up to stomp into the bathroom.

I can't believe that fucking happened. What the fuck was I thinking, letting it go that far? But that's just it, I wasn't thinking. He surprised me when he kissed me and my brain shut off. Now he regrets it, like he did last time. *Fuck! I'm so stupid!*

Zane's knock on the bathroom door interrupts my thoughts. "Baby Girl, open the door."

I don't respond; instead I start the shower and

step inside. I need to wash his scent off of my body. I won't be able to stand smelling him on me when I face him.

"Danielle! Open this fucking door now, or I swear on all that is holy I will break it down," he yells through the door, but I don't answer him. I need to take a couple of minutes to think of the best way to deal with this. Can I still try and salvage our friendship now? Should I? God fucking dammit! Just when things were starting to look up, this had to happen.

"Baby Girl? Please…please open the door. I'm sorry, that's not how I meant that to come across. I fucking love you. Of course I don't regret what happened. I only meant that I didn't mean to *fuck* you like that, but I couldn't help myself when I saw you in that towel."

So he doesn't regret it? I could have sworn the way he said it that that was what he meant, but maybe I overreacted. Would he have clarified himself if I hadn't jumped to the worst possible conclusion?

I step out of the shower and unlock the door. He opens it immediately and starts to say something, but when he sees I'm naked, he stands there looking at me with his mouth hanging open. Hoping to get back to the way we were before I freaked out, I take his hand and lead him over to the shower. When I step in, he takes off his pants and joins me.

Turning me around so that I'm facing the wall, he grabs my body wash and starts washing my back. When he's done with that, he washes my front, spreading the lather onto my breasts. Giving them a small pinch, he then works his way down until he reaches my pussy.

"Open," he says, his voice husky with desire. I obey without question, anticipating his fingers touching me.

He rubs me softly, and grinds his hardening cock against my ass.

"I just had you, but I want you again," he says in my ear.

I moan, moving my hips with the same rhythm his fingers are fucking my pussy. "What's stopping you, then?"

Instantly, he pulls his fingers out of me and pushes on my lower back. Bending forward and placing my hands on the end of the tub, I feel his cock at my opening.

"Hang on, Baby Girl."

He slams into me in one hard thrust, and if I hadn't been holding myself up, my head would have hit the wall. He sets a fast pace right away, and doesn't slow until my first orgasm hits me.

"That's right, baby, clamp that tight pussy around my cock." His thrusts remain slow but deep until my orgasm has died down completely, then he picks up his pace again.

His hold on my hips is hard, but it only adds to my pleasure. I start meeting him thrust for thrust, wanting to make him to lose control.

"Fuck me harder, Zane," I say. I am instantly rewarded with him pulling almost all the way out and slamming back into me.

"Is this what you like? You want me to fuck you so you won't be able to walk?" I don't answer him, but he already knows the answer. My pussy clamps down around him again at his words and this time when I come, he follows me into oblivion.

***

A couple hours after our shower, we are still lying in bed. We haven't spoken much, only holding each other and exploring each other's bodies.

Zane is the first to break the silence. "What are you thinking?" he asks in a quiet voice.

Knowing we need to get this talk over with, I don't hesitate for long. "I was thinking about where we go from here." I continue running my hands across his chest with my head on his shoulder. I love lying with him like this. It's like we were made to fit together.

He reaches up and lifts my chin so I'm looking into his eyes. "I don't know what you think is going on here, Baby Girl, but you are mine. I'm not letting you go. I just got you back and nothing will take you away from me again, not even you," he says with conviction and maybe even a hint of anger, though I don't think it's directed at me.

Maybe he's right. We've lost so much time and even though I don't want to admit I still love him, I know I do. Instead of answering him with words, I let my kiss show him how I feel.

This time when he enters me, it's slow and with purpose. This isn't about our pleasure, it's lovemaking in its purest form. When we come together, I call out his name while he calls out mine.

We fall asleep still connected, then wake and make love again before we finally get out of bed.

When he walks into the kitchen after his shower, he comes up behind me, wrapping his arms around my waist. "Mack called, said he wants us to stop by the clubhouse."

I completely forgot Mack wanted us there last night for a reason; we never got around to finding out why. Or at least I didn't.

"Did he ever tell you what's going on?" I'm hoping Zane at least has an idea what to expect. It must not be club business if they want me there too.

"No. Let's go find out." He smacks my ass and walks over to the couch to put on his boots.

I head into my room to get dressed. Then we are out the door and on our way to the clubhouse.

As we walk inside, I notice that most of the brothers are sitting around a couple of tables in the corner of the bar area. When Mack sees us enter, he stands and heads our way.

"Let's go into my office." Without waiting for either of us to reply, he walks away and we follow silently.

When the door is closed, Mack lets out a long sigh and looks up at us as we each take a chair across from him.

"What's goin' on?" I ask, wondering what is so important that he wants me here to listen.

"I normally wouldn't bring you into this, but you are like a daughter to me." He pauses only briefly before continuing. "We have some problems with a rival gang a couple of hours north of here, the Rebels. A couple of them were spotted outside of

248

town while I was on my way to Nevada. Things are going to heat up soon and I want you prepared. Blaze, if you aren't out on club business, I want you with Dani."

Zane nods, then Mack continues, looking over at me. "Dani, I don't think anyone would come after you to get to the club, but I want you to start carrying in case. I'm going to try to have someone on you at all times, but if things get bad or something happens, I want you to be prepared."

Shocked, I stare at him.

In all the time I've been here, the club has never had any problems with anyone—civilian or rivals. Why now? "What's going on? Why are they here?" I ask, trying to make sense of this.

Mack shakes his head slightly. "I can't give you all of the details, but they think we caused problems for their business. It's not true, but until we can prove to them we have nothing to do with it, we are going to take precautions."

Even though I want to ask for more, I know he won't tell me, so I'll take what I can get. "All right, I'll be prepared." I glance over at Zane and see him staring at me with a look of worry.

"Prez, we can do better than having one man on her and making sure she's carryin', can't we? If the Rebels have done any recon on the club, they will know that she is important to us. We can't risk her."

I get what he's saying, but I don't want to pull any more brothers away from something they could be doing to help the club. "Zane, I'll be fine. I'm a good shot and know how to protect myself. I'll be fine, promise."

He doesn't look convinced or happy about it, but he nods. "Fine, but I'm going to be with you as much as I can. I don't know what I would do if anything happened to you."

I see confusion on Mack's face, but he covers it quickly. I guess I should tell him soon about Zane and me, but today isn't the day. I'm sure he knows something is going on, just not the specifics.

"Dani, why don't you go on to the shop? But stop by here when you're done tonight. Zane, church in a half hour." Mack gets up and leaves the office, closing the door behind him.

Zane looks at me, deadly serious. "If you see anything out of the ordinary, you let me know. Don't take any risks and make sure you have your gun on you and within reach. Not in your purse or where ever else you keep it."

I roll my eyes at him and stand up. "Zane, I'll be fine." I'm irritated that he's treating me like I'm glass, like I will break with the slightest touch.

"I know you will, Baby Girl, but I can't stand the thought of someone coming after you. I can't lose you again." He stands up and comes up to me, kissing me lightly on the lips. "I'll see you later tonight, okay? Call me if you need anything."

I nod and then head out of the office. I wave to Mack and walk outside to my truck.

On the way to the shop, I try and come up with a reason why a rival club would be hours away from home and scoping us out. Mack said they think we fucked with their business, but why would they think it's the Sinners? Did they have beef with us years ago and are blaming us now because it is easy? Whatever the reason is, I hope this shit blows over soon, because I don't know how long I'll be able to tolerate all the brothers being on high alert. Shit's going to get nasty fast, and I don't want to deal with a bunch of overprotective bikers.

CHAPTER 21

It's been almost a month since the meeting with Mack at the clubhouse. I've been cautious, always looking at my surroundings and anyone who comes into my shop. But there has been nothing and nobody out of the ordinary. A part of me agrees with Zane when he said that if they did any amount of research on the Sinners, they would know I'm connected to them. But that would also mean that they put a tail on me, and if they did that, they would know I'm one bitch they don't want to fuck with.

Not only would I make sure to give whoever is trying to use me to send as a message an ass-kicking they wouldn't forget, but they would also have a bunch of angry bikers on their hands. It's one thing to go after an MC and maybe fuck with their brothers and business, but it's a whole other deal to fuck with a woman who is protected by them. And I don't mean to be arrogant or anything, but I'm pretty damn special to that club—not only to Mack, but to all of them. They took me in and now I'm like a sister to most of them. So if you fuck with me, well, let's just say you'll wish you were never born.

All the brothers have been busy keeping an eye out for the rival club, making sure they aren't venturing into town and causing problems. I've had a prospect following me around whenever I leave the shop, go home, or even work at the shop. It's really grating on my nerves, but I don't fuss because I know tensions are high right now. If this is what will give them a little peace of mind, I'll deal with it.

Zane and I have barely had any time to talk, let alone see each other, since the meeting with Mack. I've only seen him in passing when I've stopped by the club to check in. I really want to call him up and tell him to come to my house, but I can't pull him away from club business right now; it wouldn't be right. He has a job to do and I won't stand in the way. I've learned over the years that whether you are an old lady or family member, you don't come between the brothers and what they have to do.

Tonight, I'll go to the clubhouse and sit down with Mack and Toby. I've been on guard, but haven't seen anything that would cause worry—no encounters with the Rebels or anything suspicious around the shop or clubhouse. I think it would be all right to at least get rid of my bodyguard. I'll still carry my gun, but there is no need to be followed around.

On my way to Sinners Ink, I decide to give Mack a call to let him know I want to talk to him tonight. I don't want to run the risk of him being out and not getting this taken care of.

As I'm pulling up to the shop and getting ready to dial, my phone rings. It's Mack.

"Where are you?" he yells in my ear, but I barely hear it because I can see the prospect outside, looking at the broken front window. What the fuck happened and who the hell did this?

Mack pulls me out of my thoughts by yelling into the phone again, which causes me to flinch and pull it away from my face. "Dani!"

Bring it back to my ear again, I yell back at him, "What the fuck happened to my shop?"

He must already know what is going on because the prospect would have called him, which is probably why he called me in the first place. This couldn't have been the rival club; they don't do petty shit like this. Someone else did this, and mark my words, when I find out who it was, they are going to wish I'd called the cops on their ass. But I won't—no, I'm going to take pleasure in teaching them not to fuck with me or my shop.

"I'm on my way right now. We'll figure it out when I get there. Do *not* go inside, do you hear me?"

Like I'm going to stand outside waiting for him to come and "clear the scene." Does he even know who he's talking to? "Yeah, sure," I reply, then hang up before he can say anything else.

Walking up to the prospect, I see he's on his phone, so I decide to go inside without him. I want to make sure nothing was stolen and see how much damage I'm looking at. I really hope it's only the window. If it's more than that, I'm going to have to

254

close down for who knows how long to get everything fixed and replace whatever is missing. Fuck, I can't believe this happened!

Drawing my gun, I cautiously walk inside, aware of everything around me in case someone is still inside. After briefly checking out the busted window, I walk slowly toward the front desk. I take the money out of the till every night before I leave, so I don't have to worry about that being stolen, but I want to check on the computer.

Stepping around the desk, I see it's a little on the messy side, but the computer sits untouched. Then I make my way toward the back where our stations are set up. I check Louie's station first, but there's nothing out of place, so I move on to mine. I instantly regret walking back here because all of my supplies are thrown around the room, my tattoo gun lies broken on the floor and on the wall where I have a huge canvas with my name written in graffiti, someone took red spray paint and wrote *'WHORE'* over it. This wasn't random, this shit is personal. I've been targeted.

I'm still standing in front of the wall looking at the red spray paint when I hear motorcycles pulling up to the front of the shop. Seconds later, I hear shouted curses. Not even bothering to try and figure out what is going on outside, I walk toward the canvas and reach up to take it down. But before I even touch it, Zane is yelling my name from the front.

My hands pause in the air and in less time than you would think it would take someone to get from the front of my shop back here, Zane is pulling me away from the wall and into his arms.

"You okay, Baby Girl?"

I scoff and step out of his embrace. "Does it fucking look like I'm okay? Look at my fucking shop, Zane!" I turn around angrily, rip the canvas off of the wall, and throw it toward him. I know I should stop right now and not take this out on him, but I'm too fucking angry to be thinking rationally.

"No! I'm not okay! Some motherfucker broke into my shop and destroyed my work station. And not only do I have to deal with the busted window and broken tools, they wrote *that* over my fucking name!" I yell, pointing at the picture I threw at him. "So no, I'm not okay! I'm fucking pissed!"

He doesn't say anything, he only stares at me, in shock and maybe a little angry himself.

I turn my back to him and look around the room. It's going to set me back a couple grand to replace all of this and fix that window. It's not like I'm hurting for money, but it's money I shouldn't have to fucking spend. When I find the person who did this, I'm going to string him up from the ceiling and tattoo the words "Needle Dick" across his forehead. Then I'm going to have a little fun by making long, narrow slices with my buck knife across his chest and stomach. I might even see how much I can cut him before he passes out from either blood loss or pain.

I walk into the back room and grab the broom, dust pan, and a couple of boxes and start picking up the mess. Zane is still standing there, silently watching me. I don't even acknowledge him. I want to get this shit cleaned up, call someone to come in and fix my window today and then go home and order new equipment. Since it's a Monday, it shouldn't be too much of a problem to close down for a couple of days. I'll make sure to rush my new supplies so I have them in by Wednesday, then I can spend Thursday cleaning up and making sure everything is back in place.

After a couple of minutes pass of Zane not moving or saying anything and me flying around the room, throwing everything into the boxes to get rid of, he goes back out to the front of the shop. I don't waste time checking to make sure if anything is salvageable, it's all trashed. I also don't even bother to watch him walk away, nor do I take a moment to feel like shit for using him as my metaphorical punching bag.

When I finish picking everything up off the floor, I sweep to make sure I got all the tiny bits and pieces, then head out back with the boxes to throw them in the dumpster. At least my tattoo gun wasn't new; I was wanting to buy new equipment anyway, I just wasn't banking on doing it this soon. I could have gotten at least another year out of it.

As I walk back into the shop, I hear Zane and Mack arguing with each other. Since I don't feel like breaking up their hissy fit, I bypass them and head out to my truck.

I don't make it far before Mack is running to catch up. He steps in front of me. "Where the fuck are you going?"

Trying to calm myself by taking a couple of deep breaths, I cross my arms over my chest and glare up at him. "Well, I'm going home to put on some sweats and then I'm going to order new equipment. Then I'm going to come back down here and make sure someone comes in to fix my window." I move around him and continue on toward my truck.

After I jump in and close the door, I notice Mack glaring at me through the windshield and Zane approaching behind him.

Not giving either of them time to stop me, I pull out of my parking space and drive to my house. I want to get everything ordered so I have one less thing to worry about. I also need to get a sign to put on the door to let people know we will be closed for repairs, so I decide to stop at a store to pick up supplies to make one.

In the store parking lot, I give Louie a call to let him know what happened.

"Dani, are you okay? What the hell happened?" I completely forgot that one of the brothers would have called him to let him know about the break-in. Now that I think of it, I'm actually surprised he wasn't there to check it out for himself.

"I'm fine, Louie, just wanted to let you know I'm going to close down until Friday, so don't worry about coming in." I get out of the truck and head into the store.

"Yeah, okay, that's probably a good idea. That will give us some time to figure out what we are dealing with," Louie says with irritation evident in his tone.

I blow out a long breath, but the tension in my body isn't going away. I doubt I'll be able to calm down until we find out who did this.

"Where are you at?" I ask. "I thought you would

have been there, checking everything out."

Picking up a blank sign, I head to the check out.

"I would have, but I'm out of town till tomorrow." Wow, I've really been out of it lately. I didn't even know he was gone.

"All right, well, I was going to ask if you could call all of our appointments to reschedule, but I'll do it when I get back to the shop tonight. I'll call you Thursday to let you know if you should come in Friday or not."

Hanging up the phone, I make my way out to my truck and turn toward home. Hopefully the brothers will have something by the time I get back to the shop. It shouldn't take long for the guys to figure out who did this or at least find someone who might have some information. Once I find out who did it, I can decide what I'm going to do about it. I don't care what the brothers think, I'm going with them to confront the person. I could have gotten over the broken window and even my trashed equipment, but writing *'WHORE'* on that canvas is something I can't let go.

***

By Thursday I'm open for business again. My equipment was delivered last night and the window was fixed right away Monday, so there was no reason to wait till Friday. I had called Louie last night to let him know he didn't have to come in today, but he should plan on being here tomorrow.

I was able to reschedule most of the appointments we had this week, and thankfully, our

259

clients were all understanding. I was able to work a few in today, but most are due in tomorrow. It'll be busy, but Mack offered to come in too to help us catch up.

Things with Zane have been a little sketchy since that day at the shop. Even though I feel bad about the way I left him there Monday, I haven't apologized for it. I called him that night after I got home from making sure the window was fixed, but we never brought it up. I figure if he hasn't made a big deal out of it, then I'm not going to either.

My first client comes in as my phone starts ringing. It's Zane. Since I need to get going on this tattoo, I let it go to voicemail. Leaving my phone on the front desk, I lead Marlee back to my station to get started.

"So, what are we doing today?" I ask as I sit down, and wait for her to tell me what she wants. I don't have anything drawn up for her since I was busy with getting everything fixed here, but she doesn't seem to mind.

"I want to do a cherry blossom tree, starting on my lower back and working up over my shoulder."

Sweet, I've done a couple of those and it's something I don't really need a stencil for. I only make a few marks as guidelines, and I'm good to go.

"All right, cool. Since it's so big, I suggest we start at the bottom and work our way up. I can probably have it done in two sittings. You okay with that?" Some people don't want to deal with unfinished tattoos, even if they only have to wait a couple of days, but hopefully she'll agree with me

260

because there is no way I can fit the whole thing in today.

"Yeah, sounds good," she says and sits down on the chair.

I have her take her shirt off and start marking where I want the tattoo to be. She won't be able to see what it will look like since I'm going to freehand most of it, but at least she'll be able to get an idea of how it will flow, from her back and up around her shoulder.

As I finish and ask her to go look in the mirror to make sure she likes the placement, my phone rings again. I never answer when I'm with a client so I ignore it and have her sit down so we can get started.

Two and a half hours later, I'm done with most of the back and have a good start working around her shoulder. I clean her up and hear my phone ringing in the front. Ignoring it, I put some Vaseline on her new ink and cover it with a bandage. "All right, you're good to go. Let's go up front and get you scheduled for a time to come in and finish this."

I'm really happy with how the tattoo is turning out and can't wait to see it finished. I may have to take pictures to post on the website and in my portfolio if she is okay with it. I don't do that often, but every once in a while I have someone come in and ask for a cool design. I don't have any cherry blossom trees, so it will make a great addition to show off.

We set her up to come in on Monday, she pays and turns to leave. As she reaches the door, it bursts open, causing her to jump back in alarm.

Zane comes barging in, almost knocking Marlee over in the process.

"Why the fuck aren't you answering your fucking phone?" Zane yells, rage evident on his face.

I spare a glance behind him to make sure Marlee gets out okay. She stands there in shock for a couple of seconds, then hightails it out. I turn a heated gaze back to Zane and cross my arms. "What the fuck? Who the hell do you think you are, barging in here and nearly knocking my customer over, huh?" I'm so pissed that red tinges the side of my vision. So what if I didn't answer my phone? He needs to realize that I'm not going to drop everything every time he calls me.

Charging right into my space, he backs me up against the wall beside the desk. With barely an inch between us, he stares down at me with irritation. "Why. The. Fuck. Didn't. You. Answer. Your. Phone?" He bites out every word separately. I see his nostrils flare and his eyes look black with rage. If he was anyone else, I might have flinched from the venom in his tone, but this is Zane, so I push him back and get into his face.

"I was fucking working, jackass! You can't come in here and scold me like a child for not picking up my phone. Even if I wasn't working, if I don't want to talk to you, I fucking won't!" I stand my ground and level him with a seething glare that rivals the one he is giving me. He needs to get it through his thick fucking skull that I'm not his property and I will not stand for him bossing me around. Just because we've fucked a couple of

262

times doesn't mean I have to bend to his will.

Neither of us looks away from the other for a good two minutes before he lets out a breath and relaxes his stance, but only slightly. "Look, things have been tense lately, and I got word this morning that we haven't been able to get eyes on our little visitors. When you didn't answer your phone, I didn't know if they fucking got to you or where you were. And since I was out of town, I couldn't just come here and check on you right away. You need to answer when I call so I know you are okay, at least while we are on guard."

Knowing he means well doesn't cool my temper at all. How many times to do I need to fucking tell him that I can take care of myself?

Turning around on my heel, I walk behind the desk. "You don't have to worry about me. I don't fucking need you to protect me. So, now that you know I'm still breathing, you can leave." I look down at my schedule, pretending to be busy so he'll get the hint and leave.

"Baby Girl..."

I'm done listening to his shit. I want him to get the fuck out so I can get on with my day.

"I said leave. Now, Blaze." I've never used his road name before when talking to him. He's always been Zane to me, but I'm too pissed off to say his given name.

When, after a couple of moments he still has not moved, I look up at him and cock my head to the side. I give him a hard stare until he turns to walk out the door.

"Fine. Have it your way. I'm done with this

shit."

I don't reply; it's not like he wants one anyway. He can go fuck himself. I've been doing fine without him for four fucking years, so I don't need him now. I doubt those fuckers in the rival club will come after me anyway, but if they do, I'll be ready, if only to prove to him that I can handle anything life throws at me.

The rest of the night goes slowly with four other appointments and one walk-in. It's late by the time I lock the doors. I clean up the shop, thinking about what happened with Zane earlier. Maybe I should go and apologize. I've been a bitch to him a lot since he's come back into my life, but sometimes it's hard to bring someone else in and let them take care of you after looking out for yourself for so long. I mean, yeah, Mack and the brothers watch out for me, but it's different with Zane.

I decide to stop by the club to talk with him and see if we can move past all of this and start over. Heading to my truck with the money from the till, I pull my phone out to call Zane when suddenly I feel a sharp pain in my head and everything goes black.

CHAPTER 22

Zane

I can't seem to get over the way Dani acted this afternoon. You'd think that after everything that has happened to her in the past, she'd be thankful to have someone care about her and want to look out for her.

After our fight, I walked out of the shop earlier. I took the scenic route back to the clubhouse because I needed time to think. Maybe coming here was a bad idea. As much as I'm glad I found her after all this time and I can see that she is okay and she's made a good life for herself with people to stand behind her, maybe things would have been better if I didn't push.

I never thought I'd say this, but she could be right—we've both changed over the years, maybe too much to finally be together. I'm not sure we even have a friendship anymore. Everything is strained and not the way it used to be. It's probably my fault, the way I treated her before I left and what happened when she left, but fuck! I'm trying here. The least she could fucking do is understand where I'm coming from and give me a break.

Walking into the clubhouse, I realize I was driving around for longer than I thought. By the looks of the party already started, it's past eight. I make my way toward the bar and catch Louie glaring at me. I clench my fist, wanting to change direction and go put him on his ass again. I know there was something between him and Dani. I may not have the details, but I know it was more than friendship. The way he defended her proves it. Maybe he's the man who deserves her, not me. At least he never did anything to hurt her like I have.

I shake my head and walk to the bar, not wanting to think about her with someone else. Sitting on the stool, I don't even have to ask for the bottle of Jack to appear, they know.

Downing my first glass straight, I motion for the prospect to bring me a beer too. I don't want to get completely wasted and not be able to think about what I'm going to do about me and Dani. Something needs to happen and soon.

Mack taps me on the shoulder and sits down beside me at the bar. "Did you find Dani?" he asks, but the look on his face shows that he knows I did, I just didn't like what happened when I found her.

"Yeah, I found her all right." I fill my glass with Jack again and take a good drink before turning back to Mack. He had to have come over for more than asking me about Dani. "We got anything new about our visitors?" I want this threat gone so I can sit my girl down and figure out where we go from here.

"Let's go into the chapel." He doesn't even wait for me to answer before he is up and heading toward the room where we hold church. They must have more information to help us figure out what to do about our problem with the Rebels. We have to be very careful in a situation like this. Not knowing exactly why they are here means we can't make the first move, so we have been waiting and watching.

Following Mack into the chapel, I take a seat and set the bottle of Jack and two glasses down on the table. I don't miss that it's only him and me here, but maybe he's already briefed the rest of the brothers while I was with Dani. Or maybe this has nothing to do with the Rebels and it's about me switching chapters. Has Dani told him she doesn't want me here? "What's going on?" I ask, wanting to get whatever it is he wants to tell me over with. I'm tired of all the guessing.

"Look, I understand it ain't none of my business, but I know what happened between you and Dani all those years ago."

Not sure where he's going with this, I take a drink and nod for him to continue. Doesn't matter who he heard it from or what was said, Mack is the type of man to always give the benefit of the doubt if you are worthy, and I haven't given him any cause not to trust me or my word.

"Have you asked her how she has gotten over what happened or the struggle she went through?"

What is he getting at? Of course I've talked to her about it. That night he made us go back into his office we discussed everything there was about that time in our lives. Or wait, did we actually go over any of *that*? Now that I think about it, I'm not sure if we did. She mentioned that the person I knew all those years ago is gone, but she never said why or how. And I never asked what she went through in the years after what happened to her; I only told her what I had gone through, and that now that I had her back in my life, I wasn't going to let her go. Shit! How could I not ask her all the important questions?

Mack must have gotten his answer from the look on my face because he nods his head and continues. "I'm not going to tell you everything because that's her story to tell, but I will say this."

He pauses for a couple seconds and lets out a long sigh. "She wasn't as bad as you would think in the way of being jumpy and afraid of men after what happened to her. Instead, I saw a spark in her the first time I met her. It's what told me that I wanted to be there for her any way she needed. She picked up the pieces herself and didn't ask for help or pity, she only wanted us to stand behind her. Some may think that we've held her up and showed her the way, but the truth is, she did that all on her own."

He stands up and heads toward the door, but turns around before walking out. "Maybe that will help you understand a little bit about who she is now." Without saying anything else, he leaves.

Staring at the wall, I replay what Mack told me and run it against what I knew about Dani when we were younger and what I've seen since I've been back in her life. I can see what he means because I've seen that spark of strength, but I mistook it for

268

arrogance and thinking she is invincible because she has the club. But that's not it at all. No, it's the knowledge that she can take care of herself and will be okay. She won't let anything break her.

I stand up and rush out of the chapel. I race back to the shop, hoping I don't miss her. I want to tell her that I'm sorry, not only for what happened years ago, but for not understanding.

A block away from the shop, I can see that it's dark, so she must have closed already. I drive past so I can turn around to head to her house, but what I see stops me in my tracks.

The first thing I notice is her truck parked on the side of the street. As I slow down further, I take in the scene in front on the shop door. Jumping off my bike, I race over and see Dani's keys and a cash box lying—with money sticking out—haphazardly on the sidewalk. Knowing the person who jumped her only wanted her, not the money, makes my blood run cold. But the thing that really chills me to the bone and has me so pissed I see red is fresh blood splattered on the sidewalk.

Someone took Dani. Someone took my baby girl and made her bleed.

I pull out my phone and call Mack to fill him in on what I found. Then I grab her keys from the ground to check around inside the shop for any clues as to who took her.

By the time Mack and the rest of my brothers show up, I still have jack shit to go on. Nothing adds up; the break-in at the shop and now this. It has nothing to do with the club, but everything to do with Dani. I don't know why or who, but when I find out, heads are going to fucking roll. I can promise you that much.

I walk back outside to talk to Mack and see if he has any ideas who would have done this to her, if anyone over the years has ever had a problem with her for any reason. When I'm out on the sidewalk again, I take a breath and glance around for anything I can use.

Hearing people shout and laugh down the street, I look toward them to see if it would be any use asking if they saw anything. Then it occurs to me who might have done this; who would have a personal vendetta against her. He's probably watched her for a while, checked out her routine, and when she was alone, he struck. Fucker is going to pay.

Not even caring who I run into, I charge down the sidewalk to the Double Down. I make it there without being called out, which is good for them because I would kill any motherfucker for keeping me from finding Dani.

Once inside, I see the same group of guys that were here that night Dani and I were here. Walking over to the guy closest to me, I grab him by his shirt collar and pull him up so he is standing in front of me. "Where the fuck is he?" I growl.

The piece of shit tries to swing around and take a shot at me, but I don't give him that chance before I'm slamming his head onto the bar. "I said, where the fuck is he?" If he doesn't start giving me answers, I'm going to knock him out and move on to the next. I hope it won't come to that, not because I don't want to hurt this fucker, but because

I need to find out where the hell Dani is before it's too late.

Groaning, he tries to break my grip, but I hold on to the back of his shirt to keep him within my grasp. "I don't know what the fuck you're talkin' about, man!" he whimpers. *Fucking pussy.*

"Wrong answer," I say and slam his head into the bar again, watching him slide to the floor.

Without checking to make sure fuckwit number one is out, I move on to the next closest guy. I use the momentum from pulling him toward me to my favor, lifting my leg and slamming it into his stomach, knocking the wind out of him. "I'm only going to ask you once before you wind up just like your buddy—where the fuck is he?"

He gasps for air and I give him a couple of seconds to recover so he can talk. This requires more patience than I feel, but I know he's going to answer me. I can see it in his eyes; he doesn't want to end up like his friend on the floor.

"He's got a cabin a couple miles outta town." Still trying to get air into his lungs, he stands up to face me.

Stepping up to him, I see him flinch, which has me laughing inside. These fuckers act like they are tough shit, but when faced with someone who uses force to get what he wants, they turn into scared little bitches.

I reach around him to grab a napkin and steal a pen from a waitress walking by. I hand it to him without saying a word. He scrawls an address and I grab the paper from his hand.

Walking out the door, I don't even call Mack to

let him know what is going on. I'm going to take care of this fucker myself and take great pleasure in it. I only hope I'm not too late to save Dani…again.

***

Danielle

As I come to, the first thing I notice is that my head is pounding so hard I feel it could pop a blood vessel. The second thing I notice is that I'm lying down and cold. I try to reach for the covers, wondering why I'm so cold and my head hurts, but my hands won't move. *What the hell?* My hands are tied above my head.

When I open my eyes, the light shines so bright it hurts. I have to close them again for a second and slowly open them to adjust to the light. I glance around the room I'm in. I have no idea where I am. Looking down, I notice my clothes have been taken off; the only thing left on my body is my underwear and bra. It's a small mercy, and I'm thankful for it. But the fact that I have been knocked unconscious and tied half-naked to a bed tells me that whoever took me is not done, not by a long shot. As I lie there trying to think about the last thing I remember so I can begin to figure a way out of this, I'm interrupted by the door opening. The guy has a mask over his head so I can't tell what he looks like, but there's something about him that seems familiar.

"What do you want?" I whisper, trying to buy time to come up with a plan to get myself out of this mess. I'm sure no one else will be coming. Zane is done with me and everyone else won't be looking for me, at least not until tomorrow when I don't show up to work. They may not even notice I'm missing for a few days, thinking I'm pissed off and ignoring everyone. *Fuck, why do I have to be a bitch to the people around me? Why couldn't I let Zane in and let him care for me?*

The man comes closer and stops beside the bed I'm tied to. He pulls a chair around and sits close to me on the bed. Reaching out his hand, he runs his finger down my cheek toward my breasts. Oh my God, please don't let this happen to me again. Fuck, I don't know if I'll be able to come back if it does.

"Please...j-just tell me what y-you w-w-want." I've completely lost it. Knowing what is about to come, I can't take it.

He starts to laugh at how weak I am as his finger travels further down. He slowly runs it over one breast and up the other before coming down again between them. When he gets to my belly button, he pulls his hand back. I almost sigh in relief but then he reaches up to take the mask off. I know I've seen him before, but I can't place him for the life of me. Maybe it was the knock on the head, but I don't know how I know this man.

"There's no reason to cry, doll. You're going to like everything I do to you because you're nothing but a whore." He sneers at me. Suddenly, it all comes back to me, where I've seen him and what happened the last time I was in his company.

The guy from the bar. The one who grabbed me when I was walking out behind Zane. The guy whose ass I beat for touching me. The guy who probably broke into my shop and wrote *'whore'* on my wall.

Instantly, my fight comes back and I stare him straight in the eye. "You're a fucking dead man. I'm going to take great pleasure in torturing you until you take your last vile breath."

He stands up and begins to laugh, but cuts it off abruptly.

Reaching down, he tears off my bra, then reaches for my panties. Once I'm completely naked, he leers at me. "You're going to take great pleasure in me shoving my dick so far up that pussy of yours that it will come out of your mouth. And you know why you're going to do that? Because you're nothing but a fucking whore." He ends his rant by spitting in my face like I did that night I left him on the floor of the bar.

He reaches down and starts to unbuckle his pants. I don't turn away or shed another tear. If this is going to happen, I won't give him the thrill of hearing me cry or scream. And when it's all done, I'll pick myself up again and make him pay.

Suddenly, the door flies open and Zane is standing in the doorway. He came for me. Even after everything I've put him through, he still came. I'm so happy I can't help the grin that takes over my face.

It takes only seconds for Zane to have the bar guy on the floor. He stands over him with a gun, ready to kill for me.

"Wait," I say. Zane must see the pleading in my eyes, because he puts his gun away. He ties the guy's hands and feet with zip ties. *Where did he get those?* Then he comes over to me to make sure I'm okay.

Untying me, he runs his hands over every inch of my skin. "Are you hurt, Baby Girl?"

I reach up and take his face in my hands. "I'm fine, Zane. Thanks to you." I lean in and give him a kiss. I catch a brief look of surprise before he clears his face of all emotion. I know that is his way of putting everything aside so he can get the job done.

"Here, put this on." He takes his shirt off, and hands it to me. Thank God, because I don't want to have to kill this guy while I'm naked. He doesn't deserve a show before going to hell.

Once I have his shirt on, I walk up to Zane, who is standing in front of the bar guy. If looks could kill, the guy would already be dead, but luckily for me they don't, because I want to be the one to make him pay.

I reach for Zane's gun, but his hand stops me. I don't argue or even pull my hand back, I only look into his eyes and let him see how much I need this. Zane finally releases my hand and allows me to take the gun.

Not sparing any time to think about what I'm going to do, I turn toward the sick fuck cowering on the floor. I aim at his left leg and shoot without hesitation. He screams, and it is music to my ears.

I move to the other leg and shoot. Then I point the gun at his dick. I let him think about where I'm going to shoot him next and it doesn't take him long before he's a blubbering mess, begging me to let him go. But I do to him as was done to me—once by the college guy four years ago and now with this guy—I don't have mercy for him. I shoot, then turn around to head out the door. "Let him bleed out."

Zane doesn't argue. He closes the door and makes sure the guy can't get away. We must be somewhere secluded, but he still doesn't take any chances.

He makes a call to have someone come clean up the mess and walks over to me, taking my hand. With a soft kiss to my lips, he pulls me toward his bike. "Let's get you home, Baby Girl."

CHAPTER 23

When I walk into my house, I'm still wearing nothing but Zane's shirt. It was a little awkward riding on his bike with no panties or pants, but I managed.

I strip and head right into the bathroom. I need to wash this day off my skin so I can be done with it all.

I try not to think of the events from the last couple of hours, but when I'm under the spray, memories from years ago, mixed in with what happened tonight, hit me with full force. First the guy from the bar walking in and running his hands over my body, then Nick from years ago holding me down and forcing himself inside me. Then it goes back to the bar guy calling me a whore, then to Nick saying that I wanted what he did to me—that I asked for what he did. That I liked it.

My head starts to spin from all the memories. I drop to the floor of the shower, pull my knees up to my chest, and start rocking back and forth. I need to get these thoughts out of my head, build up my

277

walls again so I don't have to relive those moments. I feel weak right now and I can't let that happen— I've worked too hard to get to where I am. Weak girls get hurt because they can't handle what destiny throws at them. I need to be strong, powerful, and unbreakable. Destiny can kiss my ass—I'm taking over, writing my own story.

Suddenly the shower curtain is pushed aside and before I can even blink, Zane is sitting behind me, holding me close to him. He didn't take his clothes off before getting in with me, but he either doesn't notice or doesn't care. "Shh, it's okay, Baby Girl. I got you. I'm here. I won't let anything happen to you, I promise."

And I break; I can't hold on any longer. Tears from years of being too strong and hurting release and mix with the water of the shower.

"Let it out, I'm right here. I'll never leave you again, Baby Girl. I love you."

I don't know how long we stay like that—him holding me while I cry years' worth of tears—until he stands me up and tenderly washes my hair and body. There is nothing sexual about it; I've never had anyone take care of me this way.

We step out of the shower and he wordlessly rubs the towel over me, then carries me to my room, lays me on the bed, and pulls the covers over me. Then, he quickly takes off his wet clothes, dries himself off, and slides in beside me. We stare at each other, not saying anything, but speaking with our eyes. I'm telling him that I love him and showing him what it means that he was there for me when I needed him. He's telling me that he's here to stay, that he loves me and will do anything to protect me. I think this is the most important conversation in my life, and there are no words spoken.

Leaning over, he kisses me softly, barely brushing his lips against mine. Before long, I deepen the kiss, which has him rolling us over so that he is cradled between my legs. Without breaking the connection our lips share, he enters me slowly. He's now *showing* me how he feels by making sweet, slow love to me.

Arching into him, I break the kiss, tipping my head back on a moan. It feels so good to have him inside me again, like he was made for me. Speeding up only slightly, he kisses down my neck to my breasts. I can feel my orgasm coming up fast and there is nothing I can do to slow it down. "Oh fuck, Zane, I'm gonna come," I groan.

Releasing my nipple, he kisses his way back up to my lips. He looks into my eyes while he continues thrusting in and out of my pussy, bringing me right to the edge. "I love you, Baby Girl...forever," he whispers, and that's all it takes to make me fall over the edge and scream out his name.

Zane silences my screams with his mouth, moving faster, and comes inside me after a few more thrusts. Feeling his hot come hitting my cervix causes another mini-orgasm to tear through me. With my pussy milking his cock from the aftershocks of my orgasm, he moans into my mouth.

He pulls out of me, walks into the bathroom, and

returns with a warm wash cloth. After cleaning me up gently, he tosses it to the floor and slides back under the covers. Rolling us over so my back is to his front, he strokes my arm and holds me tight against him.

I don't know how long we lay like this, not talking, but as I'm almost asleep, Zane whispers, "Will you tell me about what happened to you four years ago?"

His question surprises me and has me quiet for so long he reaches up to my shoulder and turns me to face him.

Staring into his eyes, I know this is something we need to talk about; it's something he needs to know. Hopefully after I tell him, we can both move on and together we can help each other heal. "After I left that party you took me to, I drove to the dorm and tried to get ahold of you. I was so scared and didn't know what to do. I don't want to go into detail about what he did, but let's just say that he hurt me in more ways than one. I think the things he said afterwards were the worst part of it all." I look away, thinking back to that night.

Zane waits patiently until I'm ready to continue, knowing that this is something he can't push me on. "When he was done and I curled up into a ball crying, he stood over me and told me that I wanted it, that I had asked for it." Zane growls, but I don't stop. "I knew he was wrong and that what happened was something that he did to me, not that I was 'asking' for it. But after I got your message, I was hurt and all alone, and before I knew it, I was back at my grandmother's house. When I got there, I went right to her room and lay on her bed with her picture. I think I just wanted to be close to someone who would understand. But I got no answers, only pain. I don't know what I thought I would get, I mean, I knew she was gone, but I don't know—I had to be there, I guess."

I roll over onto my back, needing a little distance before I can continue.

"After laying there for a couple of hours, I knew I couldn't stay there. The only way for me to get past everything was to leave. I had no one, but I was angry, and determined that I would make it without anyone, especially you. But the most important thing of all—I wasn't going to let what happened to me dictate how I lived. So I packed up what little I couldn't leave behind and I drove." I take a deep breath before continuing. The hard part was pretty much over now I had to tell him the rest.

"I didn't even know where I was going, I just kept driving until I couldn't drive anymore. I wound up here and figured this was a good as spot as any to start my life over. I found Sinners Ink and met Mack and Louie, rented the apartment and started working for them. I stopped using the name Danielle and only answered to Dani because I didn't want anything to do with that weak girl who lost everything and everyone that ever mattered to her."

Zane tries to speak, but I know what he is going to say, so I stop him. "I know that I didn't have anything to do with most of the people leaving me and what happened to me that night, but that's how I felt. My mother died, my father left me because he didn't want me. Zeke died, then Gram, and then I

281

felt like I was a burden to you too, and that's why you said what you did that night and ultimately, I lost you. So yeah, I didn't want to be weak…I couldn't."

Turning back over so I can look at him again, I continue. "That's how I got on with my life—I built walls. I made myself into a person who did everything herself and only depended on certain people, and even then, not to a point where I wouldn't be able to go on if they left me too— because I thought eventually they would; everyone else had," I say quietly.

"I started training with Toby, thinking that if I were stronger, I would be able to protect myself from bad things happening. I worked hard and lived my life the way I wanted. Everything I have today isn't because of luck or something that 'destiny' threw my way. I worked hard for what I have— through blood, sweat, tears, and changing myself. I have what I have because of what I did back then, and what I continue to do now." I say this with pride, happy with the way I turned out.

"It's who I am, Zane. It may not have been the right thing, but it's what I had to do at that time to get past what happened. I hope that you can still love me for who I am now and not who I was, because that girl is gone and I don't think I can, or even want to get her back."

I close my eyes, letting him digest everything I've said. I know I need to tell him how I feel about him, but I'm too vulnerable right now. I will tell him, but I need to get back to my center first. Everything is still too raw.

REWRITING DESTINY

After what feels like hours, he takes me in his arms, waiting until I open my eyes and look at him. "Baby Girl, I love you for who you were when we were growing up, how you overcame the trials life put in your way, and who you are today. There is nothing that you could have done or could do now that will ever change the way I feel for you. You are it for me—you're my Baby Girl. You're mine and always will be." Without letting me say anything, he presses his lips to mine in a hard, passionate kiss. It's exactly what I needed in this moment.

Feeling like I need to get a little control back, I take the kiss to the next level. I push against his shoulders to make him lie back on the bed so I can straddle him. I want to show him how I feel and how much I love that he loves me and takes me for who I am.

I don't give him any time to think before I'm sinking down onto his hard cock. *Fuck, I love the way he feels inside me.*

"Oh fuck, Baby Girl. So fucking tight and wet for me." He groans as he grabs my hips to take control, but I don't let him. Grabbing his hands, I pull them over his head and hold them there. Of course I know that if he didn't really want me to, I wouldn't be able to, but it makes me feel strong to feel I have the upper hand.

"Do you like that, Zane?" I ask, swiveling my hips around his cock. He closes his eyes and growls, which has me laughing quietly for torturing him. But it's such sweet torture, and if his moans and groans are anything to go by, he is loving every second of it.

When he opens his eyes, I can see that he is close to losing it, so I don't have long with him like this. Lifting myself up so only the tip of his cock is inside me, I stop and look into his eyes. I hold his gaze and then slam myself down on him as hard as I can. The power behind it and the pleasure it brings has us both gasping through a moan.

Without giving him time to recover, I lift up again and hold once more. When his eyes lock with mine, I repeat the action of slamming myself onto his cock. The grip I have on his hands is getting harder to hold since he is starting to fight me, but I slide back up once more and thrust myself onto his cock.

He rips his hands away and places them on my hips. He doesn't make a move to control my movements, but lets me know that he is done with the teasing. But I'm not. Not quite yet. There is one more thing I want to do before I give complete control over to him.

Rising up, I slowly slide down until he is completely buried inside me. I swivel my hips once before pushing myself up one more time. I wait until he is looking at me and finally I say the words I've wanted to say for so long. "I love you, Zane."

Hearing me finally say I love him must take the last thread of self-control he has, because he grabs my hips and flips me over so I'm on my back looking up at him.

He pounds into me relentlessly and I feel my orgasm rise. "I. Fucking. Love. You. Baby. Girl," he all but growls with each thrust, and I can't take it anymore. "Come with me, now!" he shouts as I release, coming all over his cock. My orgasm sets him off and I can feel him come inside me.

Thrusting once more before holding himself still, he looks down at me and kisses my lips tenderly. "I love you," he whispers again.

Rolling us over so he's still inside me, but I'm lying on his chest, he strokes my back while we catch our breath. Before I fall asleep, I hear him say, "You're mine, Baby Girl. Forever."

***

The next morning, Zane and I take a shower and head to the clubhouse. I know Mack will be worried about what happened yesterday so I want to show him I'm okay. That man has really become a father to me. He is always looking out for me, protecting me, helping me stand on my own two feet, but will also carry me if I admit I can't do it alone. I really do love him and no matter what our blood says, he will always be my dad.

Before I've even taken two steps through the door, I have brothers coming up to ask me what happened.

"Dani, you okay, girl?"

"Princess, you scared us!"

Everyone is speaking at once, but I wouldn't want it any other way. I smile at them all and hold up my hands to quiet them down. "I'm good guys, I'm good."

I look up to see Zane watching me. I give him a big smile and turn to the brothers once more. "The sick fuck won't be bothering me or anyone else ever again." I catch Toby's eye, and he gives me a look of pride. Damn right that fucker should be proud; he taught me everything I know.

With that, everyone cheers and they usher me to the bar. Prospect Tyler, I think his name is, walks over to us with a bottle of Jack and starts lining up shot glasses. Fuck, it's like ten in the morning! But we are at a motorcycle clubhouse. I guess if they are awake, they are drinking.

Once all the shot glasses are filled and everyone has theirs, they raise them high in the air. "To Dani—Princess Sinner!" Tom Tom yells. After downing the shots, most of the brothers head back to where they were when we arrived. Only a few stay with us.

"You sure you're okay, princess?" Tom Tom asks, concern in his voice.

I give him a smile and move my eyes over to Zane. "Yeah, I'm going to be just fine."

Tom Tom glances between Zane and me. I can tell he's confused.

Zane notices the change and addresses Tom Tom. "You good brother?" he asks.

Tom Tom stares levels him with a glare for a couple of seconds before walking up to him and clasping him on the back. "Yeah, I'm good, brother. Just don't fucking hurt our princess here or I'll bury you alive." With those parting words, he walks off and leaves me watching after him.

Zane laughs his words off and takes me by the hand, pulling me off my stool. "Come on, baby, let's go find Mack."

I follow him into the hallway and then stop

outside Mack's office door. I'm suddenly nervous, feeling like I'm bringing a boy over to meet my dad for the first time. I guess in a way, I am. Even though Mack already knows who Zane is, and I'm no little girl anymore, I still want his approval and for the two of them to get along after he learns we are together.

I look up at Zane one last time before opening the door. Mack sits behind his desk with his head in his hands, bent over like he is exhausted. When Zane closes the door behind us, Mack lifts his head. He is instantly out of his chair and storming toward me. Before I can even guess what he is doing, I'm picked up off my feet, surrounded in his arms. I laugh but let him have this. I can't even imagine what he must have felt knowing that I was missing last night.

What feels like hours later, he finally puts me down but doesn't let me go. "You had me worried, darlin'." If I didn't know better, I would say that those were tears in his eyes.

I step into him and give him another hug. "I'm sorry, but I'm fine. Zane found me before anything could happen."

When I release him, he puts his arm around my shoulders and faces Zane. "Thank you for finding my girl, Blaze. I don't know what I would have done if something happened to her." Looking down at me for a brief moment, he reaches out his hand.

Without hesitation, Zane shakes it. "I would walk through hell for Dani. I love her, Prez, and I plan on spending the rest of my life making sure no harm ever comes her way again."

Oh shit, way to throw it out there! Fuck, I wanted to sit down with Mack and tell him myself.

Before I can worry too much, though, Mack lets me go and pulls Zane in for a hug. "It's 'bout fucking time you kids took your heads outta your asses." Turning to me, he lifts me up and whispers in my ear. "He's a good man, darlin', and I'm happy for you."

I can feel tears filling my eyes, but for once, I don't do anything to hold them in. I'm so happy that everything I've ever wanted has finally come true. I have a family, a job I love, friends that mean the world to me, and the man I love back by my side. Life is good.

EPILOGUE

Three Months Later

Waking up before my alarm goes off, I make my way into the bathroom. Zane had some club business to attend to for the past two days, which means I've had sleepless nights worrying about him and missing him lying next to me.

I look in the mirror and notice that my face is a little on the pale side and I have dark circles under my eyes. On top of not sleeping, I haven't been feeling well either. But when you own your own business, you don't really have the luxury of calling in sick, though I doubt Louie would mind. He'd be okay with anything if it meant he didn't have to be in the same building with me.

Things between us have been tense on the best of days and really awkward on the worst. I wish we could go back to the way we were even a couple of months ago, but I know that can't happen. Sleeping with him was probably not the best thing to do, but I hope he knows what he did for me back then. He helped me move on, and for that, I will always be grateful. I only wish it didn't come at a cost.

After a quick shower, I dress in my favorite sweats and off the shoulder t-shirt. I don't bother putting makeup on because I'm sure I will either be sweating this flu away or puking in the employee bathroom at some point today. Oh, the joys of being sick.

Twenty minutes later I walk into the shop and notice that Louie isn't in yet. We hired a girl named Harlow a couple of weeks ago to work the reception desk and she has been amazing to have. She's a little spitfire. I love it. I especially love how she gives as good as she gets when the brothers are around. You have to around those guys. But what I think is really funny is the way she is with Louie. She doesn't take any of his shit and is always hard on him. I think we are going to be really good friends.

"Hey, Low, what we got today?" I ask as I stash my purse under the desk.

She gives me a smile and flips through our appointment book—yes, we still do it old school. "You only have two today. One in about an hour, and the last one not until six tonight."

I nod and head over to my station. "You heard anything from Louie?" Usually he is here by now.

Harlow scoffs at my question and whispers, "Asshole" under her breath. I laugh. "He called and said he was going to be late," is all she says.

Okay then, guess I'll leave that one alone for right now, but Louie and I need to sit down and have a talk. Not just about us, but about punctuality, it seems. "All right. Do we know what my first appointment wants? I'd like to get it drawn out before they get here." I want to get this day over as soon as possible. I can't wait to curl up in my bed and sleep until this cold goes away. Or at least until tomorrow afternoon when Zane will be back.

"Yeah, he said he wants a tribal cross on his shoulder. Not sure if he wants anything particular, though."

Well, I can at least get started on it to give him an idea, and if he wants to change it, we can go from there. "All right, thanks, Low." I sit down on my stool and start to sketch.

***

By nine o'clock, I'm completely drained. I finished my two appointments, along with three other walk-ins.

Louie showed up two hours after I got in and he smelled like a whorehouse. I know better than to say anything to him when he's like that—it makes him feel backed into a corner—but I did tell him we needed to talk. He gave me a slight nod to at least let me know he heard me, but then went to his station and I didn't see him the rest of the day. Until now, that is.

"I'm headin' out," he says as he walks past my station.

Even though I feel like shit and want to pass out, we need to talk this shit out now. "Louie, could you come over to the house for a bit? I need your help with something." I don't need any help, but I figure it's the only way that he'll come over.

He hesitates at the front desk but turns around after a couple of seconds. "Uh, yeah. Give me thirty minutes?"

I nod and watch him leave. I have no idea how this is going to go down, but I hope we come out the other side with our friendship intact.

I'm sitting at the kitchen table with a cup of coffee when he knocks. I open the door and walk back to the table, knowing he'll follow.

"So what do ya need, Dani?" He doesn't sit, instead leans against the doorframe with his arms crossed. I give him my best *take no prisoners* stare. When he sees it, his arms fall with a heavy sigh. "I guess I'm here for a talk then, huh?" He walks over to the coffee pot to pour himself a cup, then takes a seat across from me.

"Look, Louie, I know things have been different for us these last couple of months, but I want my best friend back." I leave it at that and wait for him to speak. I know he's choosing his words carefully from the look on his face. He's always careful with his words when he needs to be. It's one of the things I love about him—he doesn't speak out of anger and only says what he means. You always know that he will say what's on his mind, and he doesn't sugarcoat anything. But he makes sure he knows what he wants to say before it comes out.

"I miss you, Louie," I whisper, trying to get him to understand how much I need him back in my life, the way it used to be.

Finally he looks up at me with a slight smile. "Listen, I know I haven't been there for you and

I've been a dick, but I needed to get my head around you and Blaze. I've had you and me in my heart for so long that it's taken me a long time to see that you and him are made for each other. I'm sorry I've let you down, Dani, I really am. I wasn't there for you to lean on when you needed a shoulder and I wasn't there when that piece of shit took you. Can you ever forgive me?"

I don't say anything as I get up and walk over and wrap my arms around him. "There's nothing to forgive. I love you, Louie, you know that, right? Just not the way you want, and I'm sorry. But you deserve someone better than me—someone who will love you like you deserved to be loved." I kiss his cheek and hug him tight against me.

"Yeah, well, we'll see about that I guess."

I know someone will come along and be worthy of his love. She will be amazing, loving, and have enough wit and sass to keep up with him. Though she is going to have to prove herself before I give my approval, and if she ever hurts him, I will hunt her down and make her wish she were never born.

***

Zane called and said that he was going to be gone another day, so since I'm feeling better this morning and don't have to be at the shop, I decide to go down to the gym and work out with Toby. I haven't seen him around much lately.

As I walk into the gym, I see him in the ring sparring with Dean. He looks up when he hears me enter, then goes back to sparring.

"Yo, Toby! You in the mood to get your ass kicked today?" I yell up at him, knowing it will earn me a rare smile. Toby is a unique soul. He is very quiet and is always watching. I bet he knows everything that goes on around him without even trying or talking to anyone, that's how perceptive he is. But you can bet that when he needs to be heard, he is the only one you will hear. He has a voice of authority and you can't help but listen and do as he says. He is also very intimidating without even trying. It's a combination of his stance, his deep blue eyes that seem like they can look right into your soul, and all his muscles and tattoos. And now that he shaved his head, he's even scarier looking. You don't want to fuck with him, that's for sure.

He laughs and finishes up with Dean before jumping down and lifting me up into a bear hug. "You sure you want some of this, Dani?" he asks with a smirk.

Damn, this man is fine! "The question, is Toby, do you want some of *this*?" I say, motioning to my whole body. I know I can't take him, but I can give him a run for his money at least. What can I say? I learned from the best.

Once we are both in the ring and tapped up, we both start bouncing around, looking for an opening. I find mine a minute later when someone walks and Toby drops his guard long enough for me to strike. My right cross brings him back into the ring and by the look on his face, he isn't going to go easy on me. Fine by me.

"Little distracted, are we, Toby?" I laugh as I bounce back after the hit I landed. He doesn't say anything, which only eggs me on. "Waiting for someone?" I prod, knowing it will wind him up more.

He shakes his head at me and gives me an evil smirk. "Why don't you worry about the fact that I'm going to drop you on your ass in about five seconds?" With that said, he leaps toward me, faking a swing. When I block, he sweeps his leg out and drops me just like he said. I shake my head and stand up to get him back.

After our first round in the ring, we jump down to get some water. I love working out with Toby; it's always a great way for me to work off excess energy, plus he really is a great teacher when I want to learn anything new.

"So, Toby, you expecting someone?" I ask after I put down my water bottle. Every time someone has walked into the gym, I've seen his eyes go toward the door. He doesn't turn his head completely like he did that first time, but still, I noticed.

He shakes his head, but I know he isn't angry with my questioning from the small tilt of his lips. "You're a nosy little girl, aren't you?" he says as he returns to the ring. I follow suit, but I don't jump up after him. I stand with my hands on my hips and wait for him to answer me. I know there is something there, and I will find out.

When he turns around he notices my stance and lets out a long sigh, then leans over the ropes with his hands dangling down. "You aren't going to let this go, are you?"

I shake my head because he knows me well. I'm like a dog with a bone when I want information. I don't push often, but when I do, you better just give it to me.

"No, I'm not expecting anyone, but I'm waiting. Let's leave it at that."

He looks down at me, but I don't move. *I need a little bit more than that, buddy.* Reading my message loud and clear, he sits down on the edge of the ring and hangs on to the last rope for support.

"A couple of weeks ago, a girl came in for a class I was teaching. I've never seen her around here, but I got this vibe off her that she wasn't taking the class for shits and giggles like some that come in. I don't know, I guess she stuck with me. I keep thinking about her—wondering what her story is and if she is okay." He trails off, thinking back to that day, so I remain quiet until he is ready to continue. When he looks up at me, I notice a look in his eyes that I've never seen before—pain and longing. "I guess I'm hoping she comes back. There's something about her, Dani. I can't put my finger on it, but I want to do everything in my power to protect her—make sure she is okay."

I jump up next to him and lay my head on his shoulder. "She'll be back, Toby. If not because you're the best teacher around, because she felt how genuine your concern is for her. Just give it time." After sitting like that for a couple of minutes, we both stand up and go for round two.

Not long after we start, I begin to feel dizzy. It's probably because I haven't been to the gym much the last couple of weeks; I need to get my body back into this routine. But as the minutes pass, I start to feel worse, to the point where the whole room starts to spin.

I drop my hands to my knees and bend over, trying to catch my breath and get myself together.

"Dani? You okay?" I can barely hear him, and when I look up, everything around me starts to fade.

"I...I...Toby...?" I feel myself fall and hit the mat. Toby comes up beside me and touches my face.

"Dani! Dani, open your eyes, babe! *Dani!*" I hear him yell, but I can't answer him. I feel him lift me up into his strong arms, and before everything goes black, I think of Zane.

***

Zane

We are finishing up talking with the Rebels, working out a better truce. We now know why they have been in our territory and why they thought we were messing with their business. Turns out, they had a traitor among them who wanted to steer the suspicion toward us to cover his own ass.

I check my phone as we walk outside to our bikes and see that I have ten missed calls from Toby, three missed calls from Louie, and about twenty text messages. What the hell is going on? Instead of looking through the messages, I decide to call Toby first to see what the problem is.

He picks up after the second ring but I barely get one word out before he starts yelling. "Where the fuck have you been, brother? Dani needs you!"

What the hell? "Slow the fuck down, Toby.

What do you mean, she needs me?" I'm now running toward my bike, my adrenaline pumping. I need to get back now! I don't know what is going on, but whatever it is, it has Toby freaking out.

"Dani, she was at the gym with me when she passed out. I drove her to the hospital, but they won't tell me anything!"

I hang up the phone and don't even wait for the rest of my brothers to get on their rides, I peel out of the parking lot. I've got to get to my girl.

I make the hour drive in under thirty minutes, going at least ninety the whole way. I park my bike in front of the hospital and run inside.

When I reach the reception desk, the nurse looks up at me in fear.

"I'm here for Danielle DeChenne," I say, trying to catch my breath.

"One moment, sir," she says as she starts typing. I don't have fucking time for this!

"Tell me where the fuck she is!" I yell, but before she can answer, someone comes up behind me and puts their hand on my shoulder. I turn around, intent on dropping the motherfucker who is keeping me from my girl, when Toby restrains me.

"It's me, brother. You need to calm down before they kick you out. You won't do her any good in jail, okay?"

I take a deep breath and turn back to the nurse behind the desk. "Can you tell me which room she is in and what is going on?" I say, my voice calmer, but still laced with anger. I need to get to her; she needs me.

"Sir, she's still in the ER being checked out. If

you could wait over there in the waiting room, the doctor will be out shortly to talk with you." She points to a room with a TV and chairs. Even though I don't want to sit back and wait, I know Toby is right. Heading in that direction, I notice for the first time that Louie is already there, along with Harlow.

After five minutes of sitting, I can't take it anymore. Instead of going back up to the front desk, I pace the room. I need to get rid of this nervous energy somehow.

Ten minutes later, Mack and a couple of the other brothers come in. They see us waiting and bypass the nurse at the desk and come straight over.

"Do we know anything yet?" Mack asks, worry lining his face.

Toby answers for me, knowing if I stop pacing I'll lose it again. "Nah, they haven't said anything besides the doctor is still with her."

Mack comes up to me and places his hand on my shoulder, stopping me in my tracks. "She'll be all right, son, she's a fighter. Whatever it is, we'll handle it."

I nod my head and go back to pacing.

An hour later, a doctor finally walks into the waiting room. "The family of Danielle DeChenne?" he asks the room. His eyes widen a bit when Mack, Louie, Toby and I all walk up to him.

"We're her family. I'm her father, these are her brothers, and this is her fiancé", says Mack, pointing to each of us.

The doctor looks skeptical, but must decide not to voice his disbelief. "Danielle was brought in after she passed out. We've run some tests on her and believe we know what happened. Her iron level is very low, she seems to be a little dehydrated and has a low blood sugar level. All of which can cause dizziness and fainting. I feel confident that it's just from the pregnancy, and after the baby is born, everything will go back to normal. But for now, we have her on an IV to hydrate her and I will prescribe some iron tablets. We will also keep an eye on her blood sugar levels, but I think she will be fine."

I'm staring at him in shock. He can't be talking about Dani, can he? "She's pregnant?" I whisper to no one in particular, but it gets the doctor's attention.

"Oh, I'm sorry. I thought you were aware of the pregnancy. Yes, she is indeed pregnant. About ten weeks, to be exact."

I can't believe it; I'm going to be a father.

All my brothers come up to me to slap my back, congratulating me. I smile at them all and then look back to the doctor. "Can I see her?" I need to be with her. I wonder if she knew she was pregnant.

The doctor gives me a smile and nods. "Of course, but only one at a time, please. She needs to rest."

I follow him down the hall to a room that is closed off by a curtain. "Let me know if you need anything," the doctor says before turning around and disappearing.

I take a deep breath before I pull the curtain aside and step into the room. I see Dani lying in a hospital bed looking as white as the sheet covering her. Her eyes are closed, so I quietly walk over to the bedside chair and take a seat. When she doesn't move, I take her hand, bringing it to my lips for a soft kiss. "Thank you, Baby Girl. I promise, I'll be the best father I can be to our child," I whisper against her hand.

She stirs and slowly turns her head to look at me. A weak smile graces her lips, then her tongue peeks out to wet them. "Hey," she croaks.

Grabbing the glass of water from the tray beside the bed, I bring it to her lips so she can have a drink. After taking a couple of swallows, she clears her throat. "What did the doctor say?"

I'm a little surprised that they told us before giving her the news. "You don't know?" I ask, not sure what they told her, if anything.

"No, after I woke up in the ER, they asked me some questions and then hooked me up to an IV. I think I fell asleep after that. Do they know what happened to me yet?" She seems worried and completely in the dark.

I chuckle to myself before looking into her eyes. Before I can say anything, though, she calls me out. "What's so funny?" She is smiling, so I know she isn't pissed that I find anything in this situation funny.

"Well, this usually happens the other way around, but I guess we've never been traditional have we?"

She doesn't respond, still waiting for me to tell her what happened.

"You're pregnant, Baby Girl. You're about ten weeks along."

She looks at me first in disbelief, then shock, then confusion. "I'm pregnant? How is that possible? I've been on the pill for years."

Not knowing how to even begin to answer that, I shake my head. "I don't know, but it happened. You were dehydrated and anemic, which they are pretty sure is because of the pregnancy. They also said your blood sugar was low, so they are going to keep an eye on that." I wait for her to respond, but she says nothing.

She turns her head and stares at the wall in front of her. Does she not want children? Is she upset that I'm the one who told her and not the other way around? I reach over and force her to look at me, my fingers on her chin. "Talk to me, Baby Girl. What's going on inside that beautiful head of yours?"

When she still doesn't say anything, I stand up and carefully move her over so I can lie down beside her. "Are you okay with this?" I really don't know if she even wants kids. We've never talked about it before, not even when we were younger.

I wipe a stray piece of her hair away from her face and hold her. Whatever she needs from me, I will make sure she gets.

Finally, she looks up at me. "I don't know if I want kids, Zane. I mean, what if I'm a horrible mother?" I can see tears building in her eyes and pray that they never fall. It brings me to my knees whenever she cries.

"Baby, you will be an amazing mother. You will love our baby fiercely and you will do anything for him, just like you do for everyone else. So of course you will be an amazing mother." I hope she can see how much I mean what I said. It's a shock to her right now, as it is for me, but hopefully she will get used to the idea. I will spend every second of every day showing her how great she will be with our child and how happy she has made me.

"But I don't even remember my own mother. How can I be any good at this when I have nothing to base anything off of?"

This woman will never understand how amazing she is. "Dani, you may not have grown up with your mother, but you were raised by one of the best women in the world. Your grandmother loved you with all her heart and took such good care of you. Look at the woman you grew up to be. You'll be perfect. It's me we should be worried about corrupting our son." That gets a small laugh out of her, which is what I was hoping for, even though I am a little worried myself.

She leans in and gives me a peck on the lips and smiles. "I love you, Zane."

I wipe the tears from her face and kiss her softly one more time. "I love you too, Baby Girl."

***

Danielle

I was released this morning after they monitored me overnight and did an ultrasound to check on the baby. I still can't believe I'm pregnant and have no idea how it happened, but I guess it doesn't matter.

Zane seems happy about having a baby and even though I'm a little scared, I am happy as well. He thinks it's a boy and honestly, so do I. I can picture a little boy running around the clubhouse, causing trouble just like his father.

I don't know what comes next, but I do know this—whatever destiny throws our way, we will get through it together. Life is good right now and I know it will only get better from here. It goes to show, if you stop letting destiny walk all over you, you will always come out on top. Live your own life and chose your own path—rewriting destiny.

ACKNOWLEDGMENTS

Wow, where do I even start? There are so many people I want to thank, so I'll start at the top and go from there. If I leave anyone out, please know that you are not left out of my heart.

John—Thank you for being amazing to me and standing beside me through everything. I love you for everything you are, but for also allowing me to be who I am and encouraging me to live out my dream. You will never know what your love and support mean to me.

To my parents—You both are the best. I know most children say that about their parents, but you both really are the best there is. You always know what to say to me and your support and love is never-ending. I love you both!

To my dad—You needed your own special line. You are my superhero. You have always been the person I looked up to most and who I was always wanted to be proud of me. I have so many amazing memories of all the things I got to do with you as a child and still continue to do. I've always been Daddy's Little Girl, but I wouldn't want it any other way. So thank you, Daddy, for always being there for me and being the best father a girl could ever ask for or dream of having. I love you!

To my beta readers—Cupcake, Snapshot, and Squirrel. You ladies are amazing. I can honestly say that this story would not be what it is today if it weren't for you three. You pushed me when I needed it, told me how it is, and gave me the encouragement I needed to finish this book. Thank you so much! :)

To Smooth at Smooth Fx in Sauk City, WI—You

are way more than just my tattoo artist, you have been a real support and help while writing this book. Thank you for answering my hundreds of questions about tattooing and the MC lifestyle. I hope you know what it has meant to me and that I truly value your opinion. Thank you for everything! P.S.S. I need to schedule my next tattoo soon.

To all my Facebook followers—thank you all so much for your love and support! You all mean the world to me!

ABOUT THE AUTHOR

I grew up in a small town in Iowa. I have 2 older sisters and amazing parents. Growing up, I was always a daddy's girl, hanging out with him in the garage, fishing, and building stuff. I loved to play softball and swimming, but reading, telling stories, and writing were my passion, even at a young age. I took a break from writing for a while, but you could always find me with a book in my hand.

I have three children–two boys and a girl. They are my whole world. Even when I'm having the worst day ever, they brighten up my day and make me smile.

A few years ago, there was this story that would always play out in my head and no matter how many times I went through it, from beginning to end, it would never fade. So I decided to put it on paper. I didn't plan on publishing it, but when it was almost done, a friend asked to read it. She said it was a story that needed to be shared. And that's what started my writing career.

I love all genres of books, and even though I started with writing MC Romance, I have a whole book of ideas, so you can expect more from me than just MC, though romance is in my blood.

Even though I currently work two jobs, my ultimate dream is to become a full time author. I want to be able to spend my days filling pages with stories. I want to be the reason people find a reason to smile or laugh from lines on a page. Reading a book allows me to live in someone else's shoes, even if only for a few minutes. It's a way to leave my life and troubles behind and I want to be help others do that as well.

Facebook:
https://www.facebook.com/pages/Author-Shelly-Morgan/809266812448318

Twitter:
https://twitter.com/Shelly_Morgan34

Website:
https://www.goodreads.com/author/show/10914599.Shelly_Morgan